"You think wanting me is wrong?" Mia asked softly.

"That's not what I mean at all," he muttered.

He wasn't sure *what* he meant anymore. Wanting her didn't feel wrong. In fact, it had somehow come to feel very right. The problem was that wanting her was also beginning to feel necessary.

It also felt necessary to chase away the demons shadowing her lovely eyes.

For some reason unknown to him, she seemed to take comfort in his touch. She'd said last night that she liked being close to him, too. So, because he couldn't bear to see the shadows, because he ached to hold her against him, he did what he'd been wanting to do all day. He kissed her.

She tasted as sweet as the rain....

Dear Reader,

The holiday season is here, and as our gift to you, we've got an especially wonderful lineup of books. Just look at our American Hero title, another "Conard County" book from Rachel Lee. *Lost Warriors* is the story of a heart that returns from the brink of oblivion and learns to love again. That heart belongs to rugged Billy Joe Yuma, and the saving hand belongs to nurse Wendy Tate. To learn more, you'll just have to read the book. Believe me, you won't regret it.

And here's another special treat: Judith Duncan is back with *Beyond All Reason*, the first of a special new miniseries called "Wide Open Spaces." It's set in the ranch country of Alberta, Canada, and will introduce you to the McCall family, a set of siblings you won't soon forget. More miniseries news: Marie Ferrarella completes her trilogy about the Sinclair family with *Christmas Every Day*, Nik's story. And the month is rounded out with books by Christine Flynn, a bestseller for Special Edition, Alexandra Sellers, and a second book from Julia Quinn called *Birthright*.

So from all of us to all of you, Happy Holidays— and Happy Reading!

Yours,

Leslie Wainger
Senior Editor and Editorial Coordinator

DAUGHTER
OF THE DAWN

Christine
Flynn

Published by Silhouette Books
America's Publisher of Contemporary Romance

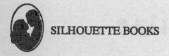 SILHOUETTE BOOKS

ISBN 0-373-07537-5

DAUGHTER OF THE DAWN

This edition published by arrangement with Harlequin Enterprises B. V.

® and TM are trademarks of Harlequin Enterprises B. V., used under
license. Trademarks indicated with ® are registered in the United States
Patent and Trademark Office, the Canadian Trade Marks Office and in
other countries.

Printed in U.S.A.

Books by Christine Flynn

CHRISTINE FLYNN

admits to being interested in just about everything, which is why she considers herself fortunate to have turned her interest in writing into a career. She feels that a writer gets to explore it all and, to her, exploring relationships—especially the intense, bittersweet or even lighthearted relationships between men and women—is fascinating.

She has a grown daughter and lives in the Southwest with her husband and two shamelessly spoiled dogs.

father and never known. The father who had made
lni—half-bred. Outcast.

Prologue

The photograph of the handsome young marine and his pretty girlfriend was faded and cracked. So was the letter, reread so many times that the only thing holding it together was yellowed tape. Years of being carried in a pocket or pressed against bare skin in the waistband of trousers had taken their toll.

The lovely young woman with the haunting gray eyes slid the photo and letter carefully into her purse and leaned her head back as the huge 747 thundered down the runway. The photograph and the letter were all she had left of her mother, and she had guarded, protected and cherished them as much as she had her mother's memory. It had been seventeen years since the awful night her mother died. Seventeen years since she'd become a child of the streets, a nine-year-old lost in a monsoon downpour. But even then she'd never lost those two pieces of paper—her only link to the father she'd never known. The father who had made her *con lai*—half-breed. Outcast.

The label no longer hurt as it once had. She'd learned to lift her jaw to the discrimination and shrug off the hardship. The man was her father. A good person, she remembered her mother saying. *If he knew of you, he would love you as much as I.*

A faint smile touched the young woman's mouth. That was all she wanted. Someone to care about her. Someone she could care about in return. Family. Maybe even a real home. In all her life, she'd never truly belonged anywhere. Even at the orphanage, among so many children like herself, she had been different. Father Marquette, the old French priest who had found her hiding in the bushes beneath his classroom window and who had taught her French and English and how to be a proper lady, had called her inquisitive mind a challenge. The nuns—until they discovered that the easiest way to keep her from running away was to let her help in the nursery—had simply found her impossible.

The jumbo jet roared upward through the clouds. That had all been so long ago. It no longer mattered that her mother's people had ostracized her because of her American father. Nor did it matter that her peers found her confusing because she tended to think in Western, rather than Asian, terms. Father Marquette's influence had been profound. All that mattered now was that she had accomplished what thousands like her only dreamed of—what she had dreamed of and hoped for every day for as long as she could remember.

She had finally found her father. And he was waiting for her in California.

Chapter 1

"Colonel Matlock. You have an urgent call, sir."

"From whom?" came the clipped reply.

Shoulders drawn sharply back, the young corporal kept his eyes straight ahead as the senior officers in the classroom glanced toward him. "The lady refused to give her name, sir."

The two men on either side of the table beneath the wall map in the back of the room—one a captain, one a major, both of them top-flight instructors—glanced toward the tall, leanly muscled officer at the head of the table.

Lieutenant Colonel Caidon Matlock's expression gave them nothing. He merely acknowledged the corporal with a nod, and returned his attention to the matter at hand, his manner remaining unhurried.

"I'll do the electronic-surveillance training myself. Captain Lucas, you can have them for explosives. Phil," he said to the major, his voice low and tinged with the steel in his cool blue eyes, "you and I will finish the last week with deep reconnaissance. Colonel Bidwell wants this team to move like a shadow. I want them moving like air.''

Caid tossed his pencil onto his notes. The unified effort among all branches of the services was creating some interesting training programs. This particular one was for a team of SEALs the navy would send up from San Diego later this month for underwater demolition training. Two months ago, the army had sent over a team for specialized electronic-surveillance work. Some programs were specific to the mission, others more general. But always they held the challenge for Caid to make the teams he shaped the best of the best.

Even creating the best didn't seem like enough, anymore.

With his team leaders scribbling notes of their own, Caid glanced toward the newly assigned unit clerk, who was still standing stiffly at attention. The call holding for him was not of a military nature. Caid was certain of that. If it were, the caller would have identified herself. Since Caid had no living family, a domestic emergency couldn't be the reason for the call, either. Neither could a problem with a woman, since he never allowed himself to get close enough to one to create any ''urgent'' situations—or to give the impression that he would be available should a problem arise. Having eliminated those possibilities, Caid had given first priority to his task. That done, he would now take the call.

As he approached the doorway, the young corporal who had brought the message hastily snapped a salute—and slowly let out his breath in relief when the colonel returned it without finding reason to criticize his demeanor or appearance. Colonel Matlock was regarded as a fair man by the enlisted personnel, but he was also known to be ruthless about procedure and regulations. That penchant for protocol included everything from the proper way to wear the uniform to disseminating information on a strictly need-to-know basis. A rule was a rule. There were no exceptions.

Rumor had it that he was just as hard on himself.

Caid headed into his office, just beyond the clerk's area in the first Marine Division's sprawling instructional facility. On the wall behind his neatly organized gray metal desk, certificates of commission, completion and commendation papered the wood paneling. Those framed documents declared who he was and what he had accomplished during his twenty-four-year tenure with the Corps. For some reason Caid hadn't ever fully considered, he never displayed the certificates awarding him his two Purple Hearts and his Medal of Honor. He supposed the reason lay with the circumstances under which those decorations had been earned, the horrific situations that had necessitated the courage it took to get out of them. Or maybe, unlike some people he'd known, he simply didn't need to prove to anyone else that he was a man.

Turning his back to that wall, he snatched up the phone. "It's line three, sir," he heard the corporal say, and punched the proper button as the young marine closed the door.

His voice deep, his tone decisive, he answered with a clipped "Colonel Matlock."

There was a moment's hesitation. "Is this Caid? Jack Kowalski's friend?"

It was Caid's turn to hestitate.

His brow lowered, his focus sharpening on the unfamiliar voice. "Who is this?"

A roaring noise filtered through the line. To Caid, it sounded like a bus or a truck. The woman, he figured, was either standing near an open window or calling from a phone·booth.

"My name is Mia," came the hurried reply. "I'm a friend of Jack's. I need to talk to you about him. May I, please? As soon as possible?"

"You want to tell me what the problem is first? I'm in the middle—"

"I can barely hear you. I'm sorry," she added, apologizing for either the interruption or the noise. Despite its urgency, the voice held gentleness—and the faintest trace of an accent he couldn't quite place. "Please. I need to see you."

The blare of a horn came through the line, the racket all but drowning out her last few words. Caid had heard her, though, along with the panic in her voice that kept him from insisting she tell him why it was so imperative that she see him. If it involved Jack Kowalski, it could be just about anything.

He glanced at his watch.

"It'll be a while before I can get out of here." The last time he'd heard from Jack, the guy's car had broken down south of Tijuana and he'd needed a tow back to San Diego. That had been almost a year ago. "How about 1930 hours?"

"What?"

"Seven-thirty," he translated into civilian.

"That's fine."

"Where?"

"Will your apartment be all right?" she returned without hesitation. "I know where you live. I'll be there at seven-thirty."

Caid didn't get a chance to say a word, much less to tell her that his apartment wasn't the place he'd had in mind. In the time it took for the training jets roaring overhead to get from one end of the building to the other, he was listening to a dial tone.

Slowly he placed the receiver back in its cradle.

His apartment was not the place he'd have chosen. That was his turf, his private space. His preference would have been his office, or any of a hundred public places in the southern California communities surrounding the huge military base. But it was too late to worry about it now. He had more immediate concerns to deal with.

He headed back toward the classrooms, trying to refocus on the special training operation that would begin in three weeks. This time, though, he wasn't able to filter out distractions as easily as he usually could. That failing had something to do with the desperation he'd heard in the woman's voice on the telephone, the panic in her plea when she'd practically begged to see him.

Caid wasn't a man who rattled easily. In fact, it took a lot to shake his constraint. But for some reason he couldn't have begun to explain, he felt as if he'd just been handed a grenade—and someone had already pulled the pin.

It was exactly 7:30 when Caid walked out onto the wrap-around second-story deck of his apartment, which over-looked the courtyard and the beach across the highway. In one hand he had a cold cola, most of which he'd drained on his way upstairs. With his other hand, he loosened the khaki-colored tie of his uniform. They'd changed from summer to winter uniforms only a week ago, just as the temperatures had taken a hike. Having spent most of the unseasonably warm September day cooped up in meetings of one kind or another, he found the fresh, sea-scented air a welcome relief.

Had Caid not been running late, he would have returned to his bedroom and stripped down to his favorite thread-bare cutoffs. But he didn't have time. Not if he wanted to check out the woman who'd called him before he met her at his door. Tom Bidwell had asked him to the officers' club for a drink just before he went off duty, so Caid had been later getting to his apartment than he'd planned to be. Tom had posed the invitation as a friend. As a full "bird" colo-nel, and Caid's commanding officer, he could have given the request in the form of an order—especially since the topic under discussion had been Caid's career.

"Have you decided to extend your service?" Tom had wanted to know.

Caid had actually hesitated at the question, and that had surprised him as much as it had Tom—who had expected an unequivocal affirmative. Caid hadn't been able to give that affirmative, though. The restlessness he'd felt lately was something new, and, since he'd had no experience with it before, he wasn't at all sure what to do about it. He wasn't at all sure, either, what he'd do if he didn't stay in. The Corps was his life. It had been that way since he was seventeen.

Having no idea why he was wrestling with what should have been a straightforward decision, Caid drained the rest of the can and glanced across the two-lane highway to the shore. A dog of the mongrel variety, as short on pedigree as Caid himself, loped toward the foaming scallops of surf. Crumpling the empty can in his fist, Caid watched the overgrown puppy dart back and forth, its playfulness urging the teenager chasing after it toward the gray-green water. Gulls wheeled overhead, screeching as if to ask what that lumbering canine was doing on their turf. Despite the warm weather, there weren't many people on the beach this evening. Only a dozen or so, and Caid figured most of them to be neighbors from the condominium and apartment complexes lining this particular strip of the California shore. This section of beach was quieter than the area down by the marina.

At the thought, his glance stole in that direction. He couldn't see it from here, but he had a boat moored down there—twenty-two feet of fiberglass and horsepower that could bury anything in its class. He could be on her right now, taking a quick run down to Newport to watch the football game at the dockside sports bar. Or he could be inside, catching what was left of the first quarter on his own set.

She was five minutes late.

The sun still had a ways to go before it descended into the distant fog bank moving in on his view of the Pacific. It hung among the thready clouds, its light the slightly surreal glow the haze helped create. It was in that early-evening light that he saw the girl coming up the walkway.

He noticed her first simply because she was the only person in his frame of vision as he moved to the courtyard side of his deck. As she drew closer, he realized he would have noticed her if she'd been in the middle of a crowd. She had her right hand lifted to her forehead to keep the brisk breeze from snapping the ends of her long and shining dark hair against her face. Because her arm was raised, the waist-length hem of her white cotton top had raised up, too. The six inches of exposed bare midriff was easily as provocative as the gauzy white skirt the wind whipped around her slender legs. That virginal white enveloped her like a mist, and she moved with a mist's silent ease.

Eyes narrowed, he watched her check the numbers on the apartments opposite his own as she hurried past. She didn't know he was watching her. He was sure of that, though it was clear, from the way she kept glancing over her shoulder as she adjusted the weight of the blue knapsack she carried, that she felt someone was.

As analytical as a computer when he needed to be, Caid discerned far more from those moments than her apparent apprehension. She was clearly in a hurry. Yet, even in her haste, there was a vaguely seductive quality to her move-ments. As he saw her glance behind her again, her hand still holding her incredible hair away from her face, he remem-bered hearing that same ephemeral sensuality in her voice— that sweet seduction that had somehow survived the panic in her tone, and that seemed to match the fluid grace with which she moved.

She stopped on the walk in front of his apartment, the ocean droning in the distance and gulls still calling over-head. Hesitating only long enough to be sure she'd found the address she was looking for, she disappeared beneath the deck where he stood.

A moment later, the distinctive creak of the second step of his stairs indicated that she'd reached his door.

A bank shot landed the crumpled can in the wastebasket when he stepped into his bedroom. By the time he'd tossed his tie on his bed and worked another button of his shirt loose on his way downstairs, most of the questions he'd put on hold had resurfaced. The first question that came to mind when he opened the door had nothing to do with why she had called him, though. It had more to do with why he forgot to speak as he watched her eyes widen when she lowered her hand from her forehead.

Up close, she was smaller than she'd appeared from his deck. Boyishly slender and easily ten inches shorter than his own six feet, two inches, she looked impossibly young. Or maybe, just impossibly innocent. She had the face of an exotic angel, a delicacy to her features that was utterly, exquisitely feminine. A hint of the Orient shaped her haunting dark eyes, and her skin had a flawless quality only Botticelli—and some European women—could achieve. She was clearly Eurasian. Or Amerasian. Or some other combination of East and West. Whatever she was, she was stunning.

To be fair, it seemed she found herself a little unprepared for him, too. Her quiet intake of breath preceded a wary "Caidon Matlock?"

"It's just Caid."

A small nod was her only response.

He'd startled her. Caid was sure of that, though, for a moment, he didn't know what it was about him that caused the reaction. He was aware that he had little difficulty attracting the attention of the ladies, but he wasn't vain enough to believe it was his good looks and sex appeal that had this particular woman openly staring. She wasn't even looking at his face. She was staring at what he wore.

There was something about a uniform that demanded attention. Depending on geography and political climate, reactions varied from deference or respect to curiosity or contempt. In an area where military facilities abounded, the attire might be paid little attention at all. Except by some women. Something about a uniform drew a certain type of female. A man in the military learned that soon enough. If that man was smart, he also learned that a woman attracted by the uniform didn't much care what was in it, as long as what was in its pants functioned and the part under the hat could be talked into making her an officer's wife.

Caid didn't believe for a moment that the young woman staring at the mirrorlike shine on his black shoes was the least bit impressed with what she saw. The color actually seemed to drain from her already pale skin when her glance moved up the knife-sharp crease in his olive-green slacks to the rows of service ribbons over the left pocket of his khaki shirt. If he saw anything in her reaction to him at all, it was an inexplicable hint of fear.

As wary as she suddenly seemed, he fully expected her to back away before she made eye contact.

She didn't do what he expected.

Her chin came up, and her gray eyes met his, steady and direct. "Thank you for seeing me . . . Caid," she added, because that was what he'd said to call him.

Her glance flicked down his uniform again.

Increasingly aware of her reticence, he motioned to the redwood chairs on the small patio by the door. "Do you want to sit out here?"

She had her arms crossed over her midsection. Hugging them tighter, she glanced toward the mile-long stretch of sand and sea, then back to him. "Can we go somewhere else? Inside, maybe?"

With a shrug, Caid stepped back for her to enter. It didn't matter to him where they talked. He'd just thought she might be more comfortable with him if they stayed outside—especially considering the skepticism with which she watched him. Yet, whatever the problem that had brought her to his doorstep, she obviously found it more threatening than she found him. That wasn't conceding much, since it was clear from the way she slipped past when he motioned her on in that she seemed to find him more than a little threatening, too.

Caid was neat by training, if not by nature. Therefore, his compact two-story apartment was reasonably clean, though decidedly spare in its furnishings. A tan leather sofa angled across one corner of the white-walled living room, taking advantage of the panoramic window that faced the ocean, as well as a wall containing an entertainment system that rivaled a jet's cockpit for sheer electronic wizardry.

It was near the television on that wall, well back from the window with the telescope with which he sometimes followed passing ships, that she chose to stand.

"I really appreciate your seeing me," she repeated, her voice quiet as she looked from a set of macho-looking free weights near the wet bar to the black lacquered coffee table that supported nothing more personal than boating magazines. "I'm sure this is an imposition, but I didn't know who else to call. You're the only friend Jack has ever mentioned." Cautious, guarded, she turned to face him. "He's told me much about you."

"Whatever he said, I'm sure it was exaggerated." Jack exaggerated just about everything. Good or bad. He had a gift for it. "Do me a favor and don't believe too much of it."

"I'm sorry to hear that. What he said was very kind."

Caid had a way of narrowing his eyes that could make a person feel like a bug on the end of a pin. Raw recruits cowered under that piercing blue gaze; the elite of the special corps he trained did everything possible to avoid it. Caid's own commander sought to imitate it.

Now Caid fixed that keen glance on this woman whose words had sounded so hopelessly naive. Kowalski never said anything kind about anyone. Not unless he wanted something.

"You said on the phone that you wanted to talk to me about Jack. Did he send you here?"

The overhead lights shimmered in her dark hair as she adjusted the weight of her heavy knapsack and crossed her arms over her stomach again. It looked very much as if it took all the courage she had to stand there facing him. Yet she seemed desperate to hide her nervousness. Caid, far more accustomed to seeing such grit in men, couldn't help being impressed by that.

"He doesn't know I'm here. I came because I didn't know where else to go." She swallowed, as if to relieve a sudden dryness in her throat. "Jack said if I ever needed anything and he wasn't around, I could come to you."

Caid's dispassionate expression betrayed nothing. Certainly it didn't lend any credence to his friend's purported claim. Leaning against the open counter dividing living area from utilitarian kitchen, he crossed his arms over his chest. "So what's the problem?"

"I'm not sure." Her voice was a little unsteady now. "And I don't know where he is to ask him. He didn't come home last night."

"You live with him?"

"For nearly three months now," she said dismissively, since that had nothing to do with her immediate concerns. "He hadn't come home by the time I got back from school today, either. And when I called his office, they said he hadn't been in at all."

At her mention of school, Caid's glance moved to her cumbersome knapsack. It occurred to him that the thing probably looked so heavy because it was full of books. What he focused on, though, was her face. He hoped to heaven that she wasn't going to cry. The problem with Jack had a definite domestic ring to it, and the way she swallowed again made tears a distinct possibility.

Caid could easily take responsibility for three thousand men. He'd handled everything from hair-trigger explosives to problems of national security with subtlety and finesse. However, when it came to women and their unreliable emotions, he was an avowed neophyte—and preferred to remain that way. Just the prospect of a weeping female made him nervous.

"Look, I don't know what you want me to do here," he said, as politely as he could. "From what I know of Jack, it's not all that unusual for him to stay out all night." Especially when he'd decided he'd had enough of a particular lady and was wanting to move on. Caid wasn't about to add that little insight, though. "He'll show up." Eventually.

"But he hadn't said he'd be late," she protested. "He would have told me if he'd known he would be."

"If you're all that worried, call the police. They won't do anything until he's been gone for forty-eight hours—"

"No!" Seeming startled by her own reaction—or perhaps alarmed that she hadn't kept that reaction in check—she dropped her gaze to the specks of brown in the beige carpet. Her voice became softer. "I mean . . . I can't."

The fear he'd seen before was back. So was the feeling about the grenade. "Why not?" he asked with utter calm.

Her knapsack had started to slip from her shoulder. Either that, or she wanted the excuse of readjusting it to buy herself some time before she had to answer.

Preferring that she get to the point, Caid reached for the bag himself. He stepped forward, slipping his fingers under the wide strap. A split second later, when she instinctively reached to catch the strap when she felt its weight shift, her hand covered his.

Caid felt her stiffen at the contact, and heard her quiet intake of breath. She seemed to be holding that breath as her startled glance flew to his. Yet she didn't move away from him. For a moment, she didn't move at all. She simply stood there, as if alarmed to find him so close, then slowly drew her slender fingers from where they'd curved above his wrist.

Her hand fell to her side, but she had yet to glance away. As Caid looked into eyes that could have weakened the strongest of men, he felt a faint tremor shudder through her slender body. That reaction could have been nothing more than apprehension. What Caid felt slam into his gut as he breathed in the scent of fresh air and sunshine clinging to her skin was awareness. The quick, unadulterated kind that hit a man in his loins and sabotaged his thinking to the point where his only thought was release.

The muscle in his jaw jerked. Maybe that tremor hadn't been hers, after all. Maybe the trembling he felt was actually in his own hand as he finally lifted the bag away.

"Why don't you go sit down?" he said flatly. He'd been right about the books. The bag weighed an easy twenty pounds. It was himself he wasn't so certain about at the moment.

"Could I have a drink of water, first? Please?"

He told her he'd get it. It seemed easier than showing her where the glasses were, then waiting while she puttered around his kitchen getting water and drinking it. It also seemed like a good idea to get the hell away from her for a minute. He hardly considered himself over the hill. But the kid curling up in the corner of his couch sure looked like jailbait to him, and he found it pretty disconcerting to think that he'd just been turned on by a teenager.

When he remembered that Jack was ten years older than his own forty-one years, he could only shake his head.

Caid had misjudged Mia's nervousness. It wasn't until he returned from the kitchen to find her wedged against the far corner of the couch that he realized how truly unsettled she was. She reached for the glass he held out to her, taking it with both hands as if she didn't trust herself not to drop it.

The only place in the room to sit was on the couch. Angling himself at the other end, thinking she definitely looked more girl than woman, he waited while she drained the glass. He wanted to know why she was so sure Jack would have called her. More important, he wanted to know why she'd reacted as she had at the mention of the police.

"Better?" he asked, his eyebrow raised at the way she'd polished off the contents of the plastic tumbler.

She touched the back of her hand to her mouth, seeming suddenly self-conscious about having so inelegantly indulged her thirst. Her eyes shied away from his. "Much better. Thank you."

"Do you want to tell me what's going on now? From the beginning?"

"The beginning was last night."

"Then start there."

She nodded, her eyes on the blue plastic tumbler in her hands. "I told you that I live with Jack. I'm working with him, too. When I'm not in school or studying, that is. He's training me in his business so he can take on more jobs. He pays me for housework now, but I need more for my tuition, so he'll pay me a salary when I've learned enough." Earning her own way seemed important to her. She smiled. Tried to, anyway. "He says not everyone has the talent for this business, but I'm a natural. He says you know all about what he does," she added, as if to assure him that she wasn't breaking a confidence. "I guess he talked to you about the electronics he uses to get past some security systems."

All Caid had done was confirm that certain types of equipment were available on the open market. Jack had hinted around about some classified stuff, but he knew better than to ask Caid about it. Not that he couldn't have asked. It was just that Caid wouldn't have answered.

Thinking Jack must really be serious about this woman to take her into his confidence about his security operation, Caid asked her to continue. He knew Jack had run into nothing but trouble when he retired from the military ten years ago. He also knew there hadn't been much demand in the private sector for his skills as an infiltrator. To his credit, Jack had tried to make it with straight jobs. But Jack seldom sang out of the same songbook as the rest of the choir, and his drummer definitely had his own beat. He needed the excitement, the adrenaline rush, of covert operations. Nine-to-five bored him silly—which was why he could so easily turn his free time into trouble. The man's biggest problem was his IQ. Jack was a genius—a genius whose intellect had never been properly channeled. He might have accomplished some truly great things had his abilities ever found a legitimate focus.

About a year ago, though, Jack had finally hit on something that looked as if it might work out for him. He'd been employed as an insurance investigator when he hit on a sideline that utilized his unique skills to the fullest. He still investigated claims for an independent adjusting outfit in Newport. But, according to Mia, his new business was growing rapidly. There was apparently a very specialized need among the very rich or the very paranoid—as well as certain technological facilities concerned about their top-secret projects—for a means to test the efficiency of their security systems. As Caid understood Jack's operation, once he had a contract, he would attempt to break into the designated home or facility within a specific time period. The results were simple to determine. If the security systems were indeed secure, somewhere along the line an alarm would be set off or a guard alerted. If Jack succeeded in getting inside, he would move something of value or import to another location within the building to show what could have been taken or copied or destroyed or whatever it was the owner feared could happen, then make recommendations to strengthen the weak area.

It seemed now, as Caid listened to Mia's quiet confirmation of his understanding, that a bit of a problem had developed when she went with him to check out a system at a museum last night.

"It was my first break-in," Mia told him. Her first legal one, anyway, but she didn't want to explain any of that. Not now. Not ever, if she could help it. That had all been a lifetime ago. "Jack said I did a great job."

The pride Mia had felt hearing those words of praise quickly dissolved to the anxiety knotting her stomach. This Caid person wasn't interested in her little accomplishment. Despite his insistence that she continue, she wasn't sure he wanted to listen to her at all. He was a daunting man—big, powerful, and without the slightest hint of compassion about him. Not that she wanted sympathy. She just wanted help. If the brick-hard look on his face was any indication, he wasn't particularly interested in giving her any at all.

Chapter 2

The police were looking for her.

Mia crossed her arms over the knot in her stomach. She couldn't believe what was happening. Not here. Not in this country she'd always thought of as her salvation. Twenty-four hours ago, she had been safe. Twenty-four hours ago, her greatest concern had been keeping up with the second semester of classes she'd begun at UCSD while acclimating herself to the laid-back, anything-goes California life-style. Now, the sensations clawing at the scraps of her composure were the too-familiar feelings she remembered from her childhood—the desperation of not knowing where to turn, and the awful uncertainty of not knowing what would happen next.

She forced herself to meet Caid's intimidating stare. Faced with any situation that seemed bound to get the better of her, she invariably led with her jaw. The tactic had rarely kept her from being knocked down, but she at least had the satisfaction of being defiant.

his fist pressed to his mouth as he listened. She could swear the man never blinked.

"She said that Jack hadn't come in, but that the police had been there looking for him. It seems the crown we moved last night is missing." The breath she drew had a distinctly ragged edge. "The curator and the guard think we took it."

And that meant the police were looking for her, too.

She edged her chin higher, willing herself to ignore the uniform Caid wore. Even as she did, she knew it wasn't just the uniform that made her so uneasy. She'd have felt unnerved around this particular man no matter what he wore.

"The crown was there when we left," she told him, just in case his silence meant he thought she and Jack had actually taken the thing. "Jack even went back to check on it after we'd taken it out of the display case. He'd put it on the head of one of the statues in the main exhibit hall, and he wanted to be sure it was secure. He said he couldn't afford to have it fall off and break. That's why he double-checked."

Caid slowly lowered his hand, his firm mouth twisting as he considered her.

"It was there," she repeated, unable to tell whether or not he believed her. Her insistence didn't seem to faze him. Watching him watch her, she wondered if anything did. "I saw it myself."

His only response was the faint narrowing of his eyes.

"I can't prove a thing without Jack," she went on, wishing Caid would *say* something. "That's why I have to find him. I'm sure he can straighten all this out, but I don't know where to look for him. Do you think something could have happened to him?" she wanted to know, alarmed by the thought. "The only other time he was gone like this, he'd gone down to Tijuana to see some friends. He was back by the next afternoon, though. Do you think he might have gone down there?"

The question finally forced Caid to break his nerve-racking silence.

"With Jack," he said flatly, "anything is possible." Tijuana was only an hour away from Oceanside. Less than that from where Jack lived in San Diego. "Did he mention the names of these friends?"

Mia shook her head, wishing desperately that she had paid more attention at the time. She'd been cooking when he'd come in. Or, more accurately, attempting to cook—a process Jack had quickly learned he was better off not to interrupt. Since he'd had to leave before she finished the soufflé which ultimately resembled the pancakes she'd wound up feeding to some unsuspecting ducks in a park the week before, she hadn't had a chance to talk to him about the people who'd kept him out all night. What she did remember was that he'd said he'd been at a place called La Flor Blanca.

She told Caid that. Then, wondering if he'd actually winced at the name, she told him that she'd called directory assistance for the number, but that she couldn't understand the operator who answered the phone. The woman's accent had been heavy, and the noise from the traffic outside the phone booth she'd used had made comprehension impossible.

"I thought about going down to see if he was there," she went on, setting the tumbler aside before she wore the design off it. "But I didn't know what to expect at the border. Jack said the border check is mainly agricultural, but I didn't think I should go without my passport." Which was at the house, where the police were, she could have added. "I didn't want to risk a problem with the authorities if they wanted to see it when I crossed the border."

Caid didn't bother to point out that she already *had* a problem with the authorities. He also didn't point out that her problem wouldn't have been in getting into Mexico—provided that the police hadn't notified the border patrol to be on the lookout for her. If there was going to be a problem with her not having her passport, it would more than likely be when she tried to get back into California.

None of that mattered at the moment. That she'd mentioned a passport at all was what had his attention.

"You're here on a visa? Where are you from?"

"Ho Chi Minh City," she returned, hesitating a bit at his abruptness. "I think most people here still call it Saigon."

"You're Vietnamese?"

"And American. Not officially American," she had to admit, though she was as much American as anything else. "Not yet. Jack says I will be, though."

At the moment, Caid wasn't interested in what Jack had said. What he was interested in were her answers. "How long ago did you leave Vietnam?"

"A little over a year." Wary, she asked, "Why?"

He ignored the question. "And you're how old? Nineteen? Twenty?"

"Twenty-six."

Caid's skepticism surfaced. If the woman-child trying to disappear into the corner of his sofa was twenty-six, he was a two-thousand-year-old leprechaun. "You want to reconsider that?"

"Reconsider what?"

"Your answer."

It seemed she didn't understand that he was giving her the opportunity to amend her response. She cocked her head to one side and frowned.

The frown faded with her quiet, "Oh, yes," when comprehension dawned. "I forgot that you count age differently here. In Vietnam, when a child is born, he has already been alive a year. So he is one year old when he is born. That is why I think of myself as twenty-six. Here, I am twenty-five."

Caid was not a man to disarm easily. He'd thought her to be much younger, but as she sat there looking incredibly vulnerable and trying desperately not to, he saw what he'd missed before—the sad sort of wisdom in her eyes that went even beyond her years, and spoke of a life far different from anything he could possibly know.

He'd wanted to know why she'd become so fearful at his mention of the police before. The obvious reason was that she was a suspect in a major theft. Being in a foreign country on a visa, it had no doubt occurred to her that, among other unpleasantnesses, she faced the threat of deportation simply for being implicated in an illegal act. Yet there had seemed to be more to her anxiety than that admittedly disconcerting circumstance. Now Caid thought he might understand why.

If she'd left Vietnam only a year ago, that meant she'd been raised in a society of constraints. If she was in her mid-twenties, she was also old enough to have suffered the nightmare of the war. All he had to do was remember the way she'd first looked at his uniform to know that her fear went beyond what was happening to her now. He had no idea what memories had resurrected that fear. He knew only that it would have been easier to tell her he couldn't help her if he hadn't known anything about her.

It had been on the tip of his tongue to say that he didn't have a clue where Jack was. He didn't need Jack's problems right now. He had enough on his mind. But this woman was stuck until Jack showed up to straighten out whatever it was that was going on, and Caid had to admit that his old marine buddy could easily have disappeared on one of his drinking binges and wound up at his favorite house across the border. Caid personally thought the possibility a damn shame, given the appeal of this woman. There was a childlike charm about her that made a man feel he needed to protect her—and she possessed an unconscious sensuality that made protecting her a distant second to the other needs occupying his thoughts.

Suddenly restless, Caid rose, his big frame blocking the sunset slanting through the window and shadowing Mia's much smaller figure. He was a physical man, and he related to situations and surroundings in physical terms. But while the well-honed muscles of his body responded instantly to threat or danger, he maintained absolute control over the sensual side of his nature. His thoughts were another matter. Especially those going through his mind as he watched her small breasts rise with her indrawn breath. Had Jack been able to read his mind just then, he'd have been perfectly justified in decking him.

On the other hand, since Jack had put her in this position, Caid decided, maybe he'd just deck Jack.

He pulled his glance to Mia's face. "I don't think anything's happened to him." Jack not only moved like a cat, which made him very good at what he did, he seemed to have a cat's proverbial nine lives, as well. "But it's possible he's where you think he is."

"I certainly hope so."

"That's very generous of you," he muttered, and started to turn away.

"Why do you say that?"

The faintly sarcastic comment hadn't been meant for her ears. Nor did Caid intend to explain his cynicism. But the innocence of the question, her complete and utter lack of guile, totally amazed him.

"You don't know what La Flor Blanca is, do you?"

"I don't even know what it means."

"It means," he said, his tone dry, "The White Flower."

Thinking he might explain what the place called The White Flower was, Mia watched a muscle in his jaw jerk. He offered nothing else, though. In fact, now he wouldn't even look at her.

"I take it that The White Flower is not a florist's shop."

"It's not a florist's shop," he agreed.

"Is it a restaurant?"

Caid didn't like this. The position he was in felt awkward enough without his having to describe the nature of that particular establishment. He was even less enthusiastic about being the one to inform this woman that her boyfriend had been hanging around a cathouse.

Apparently, his silence was speaking for him.

"Then it must be a bar," came her flat conclusion.

There was a bar downstairs. Part of the operation did, therefore, qualify as a lounge. "I suppose you could say that."

"I know Jack likes them," she said without rancor. "He says he goes to them to relax. I haven't been in one yet, but

I want to go to see what they're like. The ones I've seen on television seem like rather nice places. Except for those where the patrons get involved in fights. I wouldn't want to go to one of those. But something like the ones in the beer commercials would be fun.''

Caid's eyebrow arched ever so slightly, both at what she'd said and at the source of her information. ''You've never been in a bar?''

''No,'' she replied, failing to see what was so remarkable about that. ''Where I came from, ladies don't go into them.''

''Well, this place definitely isn't one you'd want to start with.''

Finding himself growing more curious about her than he wanted to be, Caid moved to the breakfast bar dividing the living area from the kitchen and pulled open the drawer by the telephone. Among the screwdrivers, pens and matchbooks—and the stale pack of cigarettes he kept simply to prove he could avoid the temptation—was his phone book. Jack's home number wasn't written in it. It was on the back of a business card Jack had given him over a year ago which Caid had dutifully shoved in the book and forgotten.

He'd call Jack's house. No sense chasing all over creation if the guy had shown up in the past couple of hours.

After eleven rings, there was still no answer.

''I can think of a couple of places in San Diego he might be.'' Resigned to his task, he dropped the receiver back on its hook. ''I'll check them out on the way and get back to you.''

He turned to see her standing behind him. Her hands were clasped against the gauzy fabric of her skirt, her head raised just enough to expose the long line of her throat as she looked up at him. Relief had washed over her expression at his words, her breath shuddering as she let it out. It occurred to him as his glance focused on the inviting fullness of her parted lips that she'd really doubted he'd be willing to help her at all.

Not until that moment had Caid recognized how truly desperate she was to have come to him. And not until that moment did he recognize how alone she must be to have had no one but a total stranger to turn to.

Irritated with Jack for leaving this woman in such a position, and hoping that the guy hadn't gone and done something truly stupid this time, he started for the stairs. He had to change before he left.

Most of the buttons of his khaki shirt had been undone when he did an about-face. He supposed he should see her out first. "Where will you be?" he asked, seeing that she hadn't budged. She still stood with her hands clasped and her slender shoulders ramrod-straight.

"I want to come with you."

He'd thought before to tell her she had nothing to fear from the police if she was telling the truth. Given the circumstances, however, he wasn't convinced himself that they might not take her into custody. The words *aiding and abetting* came to mind. They might already apply to her. If she was picked up with him, they would apply to him, too.

"No way. I'm not dragging you with me while I check out bars. And I'm certainly not taking you across the border."

"I don't want to *go* across the border. If we haven't found him before we get there, I'll wait for you in your car or something. Jack says it's dumb to take a car into Tijuana, anyway."

"'Jack says,' huh?" How many times had she said that since she'd walked in the door? She quoted the man as if his words were carved in stone. The gospel according to Kowalski.

"I don't care what Jack says. I'm driving across, and I'm not taking you with me. If I do find him, the last thing I want is the two of you fighting it out all the way back home."

She looked puzzled. "I'm not going to fight with him."

"Right," he muttered in abject disbelief. "The guy's been out all night drinking and . . . whatever . . . and you're not going to be upset."

"I'm already upset," she pointed out, trying not to sound that way, "because I don't know what's going on. If he's been out drinking and 'whatever,' that's his business. Mine is to find him."

Caid's eyebrow rose slowly over his scowl. There seemed to be a rather cynical core under all that feminine softness. "I'm sure your boyfriend appreciates your open-mindedness, but I'm still not taking you."

That seemed to stop her. For all of two seconds, anyway. Her chin came up in a way that was becoming almost familiar, and she crossed her arms beneath the gentle swells of her breasts. "I'm not being anywhere near as open-minded as you think. Jack isn't my lover. He's my father. And I don't know where you can reach me if you don't take me with you." Some of the strength slipped from her tone. Still, she held her head high. "I don't have anyplace else to go."

There was no way she was going back to Jack's house until he showed up. Not if there was a chance the police would return. Caid didn't make her point that out, though. Nor did he make her explain that, other than Jack, there wasn't anyone anywhere who would care whether she had anyplace else to go or not. He was too busy frowning at her.

"Your father?" His glance darted from the top of her head to the beige flats on her feet, then shot back to her face. "Did you say Kowalski is your father?"

A moment's hesitation, as if she had let something slip that she perhaps hadn't intended, preceded her quiet "Yes. He is. But please don't tell him I told you."

"Why not?"

"Because he asked me not to tell anyone." She paused, her need to prove her credibility to Caid vying with the need to protect her self-esteem. Her need for Caid's help won out. "He said having a daughter would be 'bad for his image.' If anyone asks, I'm supposed to say I'm his friend."

Caid's scowl softened. Mia had tried to say the words as Jack apparently had, in a way that was teasing—possibly even facetious. But as she repeated what her father had said to her, there was no doubt in Caid's mind that she had been hurt by the request. He also didn't doubt for a minute that Jack would say such a thing. It sounded just like him.

To her credit, Jack's daughter was prepared to defend her father's thoughtlessness. "I don't think it's been easy for him to get used to the idea of having a grown child. Especially one who came from what had to be another lifetime for him. I've known about him for as long as I can remember. I had the stories I remember my mother telling me about him, and his picture, and one of his letters to her. In my mind, he's always existed. But he didn't know about me until about a year ago.

"They told us at the transit center that adjusting can be very difficult for everyone, but he's been very kind to me." Her hurt faded, replaced, it seemed, by thoughts of Jack's more redeeming behavior. Or maybe it was just her own sense of forgiveness. "He even insisted that I leave the transition house where I was staying and live with him while I'm in school," she added, because that had to mean he cared about her, and she needed for the man staring at her to know how much that meant to her. "But none of this changes why I'm here. I still need to find him as soon as I can."

Her little revelation might not change anything about the reason she'd come to him, but the fact that she was Jack's daughter, and not his lover, definitely shifted Caid's perspective on the situation. It didn't do much to keep his body from tightening when she pushed her hair from her face and her shirt rose to reveal a glimpse of her smooth midriff. But he did have a better idea now of what he needed to do.

It had barely occurred to him that it would be interesting to hear Jack's side of this little development when he began to consider his options. He really had none. Caid regarded personal indebtedness as a liability to be avoided at all costs.

If a man owed nothing, nothing could be demanded of him. Yet there was one debt he would forever honor. And that was to Jack.

He owed the man his life. The least he could do was help his daughter lie low for a few hours—even if it would be a little difficult to explain, should the situation arise, why he hadn't turned her in when he learned that the police were looking for her.

The muscle in his jaw jerked, the way it always did when he couldn't let what was going on inside him affect his actions. It jerked again when he found Mia staring at the swirl of chest hair visible between the open sides of his shirt.

"I won't take you with me," he repeated, wondering at the faint spots of color in her cheeks when she lifted her glance to his. It was almost as if she'd never seen a man's bare chest before. "But you can stay here until I get back. It might be a good idea for you to stick by the phone, anyway. Just in case he calls."

A shiver ran through Mia's body, an unfamiliar feeling that had nothing to do with her present fear. There was something quite primitive about the dark mat of hair flaring between the sides of Caid's shirt and narrowing over his flat belly. The muscles exposed by that eight-inch gap looked quite powerful, his body impossibly hard. And for some reason she neither trusted nor cared to consider, looking at it made her feel strangely soft inside.

It also made her more than a little apprehensive.

"Do you think he will?"

"I don't know. It's possible" was all he would say. Seeing her glance venture hesitantly back to his chest, he started for the stairs again. He didn't think she needed to know that the only time he ever heard from Jack was when the guy was in trouble. On the other hand, what she did need to know was how enticing a man found a woman's curiosity about his body—however reluctant or unwanted that curiosity might be.

It didn't take Caid long to change into a pair of worn jeans and a T-shirt. When he came down again, Mia was wedged into her corner with what looked like a textbook in her lap. She wasn't reading. She was staring at the wall, chewing on her lower lip and looking every bit as scared as she deserved to feel. The instant she saw him, she scrambled to her feet, hugging the heavy volume to her and following his movements about the room with definite apprehension.

Caid picked up his keys from where he'd tossed them on the counter when he first came in. He'd thought she might be less apprehensive around him without the uniform. But, watching her watch him as if he were about to pounce at any instant, he thought it was pretty clear that her unease had more to do with him than with his attire. He wasn't sure how he felt about that, or why it even mattered. He did know he wasn't going to waste time worrying about it.

Keys jangling in the moments before he stuffed them in his pocket, he told her to help herself to whatever she could find in the kitchen if she was hungry. He'd be back as soon as he could. It would take him a half an hour to get to the Docksider in San Diego. He'd check there first. Then he'd swing by the Sand Pit. He wrote the names of both bars on a pad by the phone and told her that if Jack should call within the next hour she should track him down so that he didn't have to go running around Tijuana on a wild-goose chase.

Mia promised she would—and was still hugging her book when, moments later, he locked the door behind him.

Knees weak, she sank down on the edge of the couch. There was nothing for her to do now but wait—and hope that this Caid person would find Jack so that he could clear up the confusion. It was all just a terrible coincidence that he had chosen last night to stay out. She had to believe that. Just as she had to believe that nothing had happened to him.

Yet he'd been in such an awful hurry to be rid of her when they left the museum. And he hadn't shown up at work today.

She still didn't know what to make of either fact.

Leaning against the back of the sofa, she let out a long and ragged sigh. The one thing she knew for certain was that they hadn't taken the crown. Someone apparently had, but it hadn't been her father, and it hadn't been her. For all she knew, it could have been the little weasel of a security guard, who'd kept staring at her chest the entire time she was speaking with him. Jack had said she was never to leave a job without making sure the building had been resecured. While she'd gone down to reconnect the backup power for the peripheral system, the guard could have moved the crown to an unsecured area. Then, after her cab arrived, he could have put it in the lunch bag she'd seen on the lobby desk. Pinning the theft on her and Jack would have been easy for him to do. After all, it did seem awfully suspicious that something should turn up missing the very night they were in to check out the building's security.

It was no wonder the police were looking for them.

Every thought she had seemed to lead back to that one. Yet, no matter how she tried to tell herself that everything would be all right, she simply couldn't make herself believe that it would. She knew she'd done nothing wrong. She also knew that in this country a person was supposed to be innocent until proven guilty. But the study of a society's culture and customs couldn't erase years of memories. And nothing, she'd discovered, could erase the experiences she'd thought she'd finally put to rest. She was still afraid of thunderstorms, and she still forgot to breathe when she unexpectedly encountered a man in a uniform. She couldn't seem to help it, though it had been years since she'd suffered physically at the hands of such authority.

Years since she'd been a child of the streets.

Years since she'd been beaten for stealing crumbs, for salvaging a ragged shirt from a garbage heap, for reasons she could no longer recall. All at the hands of men who wore uniforms and carried guns. Men who wouldn't listen when she tried to explain that she was hungry or cold and that the scraps had already been thrown away by someone else. Men who had no idea what it was like to be penned up like cattle in the state-run orphanages that children like her ran away from at first opportunity because it was easier for the spirit to survive on the streets.

The police, therefore, were to be feared.

Certainly they were never to be trusted.

Mia drew a long, deep breath, her glance moving to the view of the ocean and the fading light beyond. It would be dark in a while, and she suddenly felt very exposed, sitting there with that huge window yawning at her. There were windows on either side of the larger one, too. The kind a person could lower to let in the soft breezes.

She pulled the drapes on all of them.

It was after eleven o'clock when Caid, having exhausted his possibilities, let himself back into his apartment. He hoped Mia's luck had been better than his. All he'd learned about Jack during the past few hours was that no one had seen him around for the past few months. Caid did have a couple of messages he was to give Jack when he saw him, though. One was from a bartender at the Sand Pit, reminding him that his bar tab was past due. The other was from one of the ladies at La Flor Blanca, telling him she missed him.

Working at the kink in his neck that came from driving with his arm propped in the open driver's window, he tossed his keys on the counter on the way into the living room. One look at Mia's face and he knew she hadn't had any luck, either.

She stood in the middle of the room, her face alight with bated anticipation. As he moved toward her, watching her eyes anxiously scan his face, he felt something inside him respond to that eagerness. Or maybe what he felt was more like yearning, as he vaguely wondered what it would be like to have someone who always waited so eagerly for his return.

"I take it he didn't call."

Her anticipation vanished as abruptly as had his errant thought. He knew she wouldn't have looked so anxious if she had any news of her own.

"The phone never rang."

There was such disappointment in her expression that Caid couldn't help but wonder if she'd sat there watching the instrument the entire time he was gone. As gutsy as she'd seemed earlier, he didn't doubt she would have willed the thing to ring had she thought such a feat possible. That chin-up bravado of hers was nowhere in evidence now, though.

She seemed so terribly vulnerable without it.

"Did you try calling the house again?"

"There was no answer."

"How long ago did you try?"

"About ten minutes."

Caid let out a breath of frustration. "Try again."

Without a word, Mia moved to the counter. Caid followed, studying the delicate lines of her profile as she punched the redial button on his telephone, then waited while her knuckles turned white from her death grip on the receiver.

When a full minute had passed, he reached over to pry her fingers loose.

At the feel of his hand closing over hers, she tightened her grip. "Please. Let it go a few more rings."

"If he were there, he'd have answered by now." It was a small house. "Let me hang it up."

Her eyes met his, luminous with pleading.

I need for him to answer.

I know you do.

I'm so scared.

I know that, too.

"Look," Caid said, gently breaking her hold. Her fingers felt like ice. Nerves, he thought, since it was easily seventy-five degrees in the room, and let her fingers slip from his before he could curl them into his palm. "There isn't anything else that can be done tonight." It was already nearly midnight. He had to be up in six hours. "If he hasn't called by morning, I'll run by his house before I go to the base to see if he's shown up. Maybe he's got the phone turned off or something." *Or maybe the police already have him in custody,* he could have added, but he figured she'd probably considered that already.

"Maybe," she agreed, unconsciously clasping her hands as if to trap the heat she'd felt in his touch. She didn't sound any more convinced of the possibility than Caid had. She didn't sound as if she believed in much of anything at that moment.

He took a step back, deliberately shoving his hands into his pockets to keep himself from touching her. She looked so utterly lost, so badly in need of reassurance, that he actually considered reaching for her. Just to let her know she could lean on him. If only for a minute.

"I don't have a spare bed," he told her, wondering what she would do if he were to curve his hand over her shoulder and draw her to him. More to the point, he wondered what he would do. When it came to sex, he knew exactly how to please a woman, the right words, the ways to touch. He knew little about offering comfort, though, and even less about what a woman would think of his unsophisticated attempt. "But you're welcome to the couch, if you want to stay here tonight. It's more comfortable than it looks."

He watched her pull her lower lip between her teeth, her expression finally betraying what she'd so valiantly attempted to mask most of the evening. She was afraid of him. To Caid's way of thinking, she had no reason to be. She was safer with him than she probably would be with anyone else. But the fact remained that, while she'd felt she had no choice but to come to him, she didn't trust him.

It was a fair measure of her desperation—or possibly her fatigue—that she accepted his offer anyway. "You wouldn't mind?"

Hell, yes, I'll mind, he thought. "Not for tonight. I'll get you a blanket."

He turned on his heel, realizing even as he did that he had no reason to feel insulted by her lack of trust. Still, for a man who felt he was nothing without his integrity, the implication stung.

"Caid?"

The solid thud of his footsteps halted.

"Thank you," she said, her voice as quiet as the ever-present roar of the ocean and the traffic filtering through the open windows. The drapes fluttered gently, moving with the soft evening breeze. "I didn't know if you'd be willing to help me or not. But Jack was right about you. You are an honorable man."

Slowly Caid turned to look at her. He didn't know what to say to her frank admission, or to her conclusion, or to the fact that Jack thought him honorable.

Mia didn't leave him any time to worry about it. She had concerns of her own. "I hope he won't be too upset when he finds out I told you that I'm his daughter. I really don't think he wanted anyone to know. He didn't even tell his girlfriend."

"He has a regular girlfriend?"

"Roselyn. She owns a diner near his office. It's okay," Mia hurried on, seeing that Caid was about to ask why she was only now mentioning the woman. "I'd already called her. She said she hadn't seen him in a week and didn't care if she ever did. Then she wanted to know if I was the woman who'd moved in with him." Her voice dropped a note. "I guess they had some kind of an argument."

About her, Caid guessed, from the sounds of it. But that wasn't important right now. At least it didn't seem so to Mia. Her concern was about her father, and what he would think of her having told Caid of their relationship.

"Don't worry about Jack," he said, thinking he understood even less about the man than he'd previously thought. "If he gets upset about it, I'll take care of it. I'll be back in a minute," he concluded and headed off to get her a blanket before he could come up with any other promises he had no business making.

Chapter 3

Mia slept with the lights on. Not that she slept much, or well. Long after the creaks and groans of Caid's movements overhead had fallen silent, she sat with the blanket he'd given her tucked up to her chin and tried to hear the sound of the ocean over the sporadic traffic noise filtering through the windows. If she could hear it, she knew the ebb and flow would create a gentle, hypnotic rhythm, and as long as she concentrated only on its soothing cadence, she wouldn't feel quite so apprehensive.

Unfortunately, her powers of concentration were sabotaged by the very apprehension she sought to escape. Under more favorable circumstances, she could focus on a subject, and sometimes hours would pass before her interest would abate enough to allow a distraction. It was that way with her studies, with the classes she took so that she could teach history and languages, as she had at the orphanage. She could become so totally absorbed in what she was reading that little existed beyond what was going on in her mind. That ability had provided escape for her as a child. It still did as an adult. But tonight everything was a distraction: the sound of a car door slamming somewhere behind the apartment complex; the dripping of the kitchen faucet; the whistle of a train in the distance. Even though she heard no sound from upstairs, the man sleeping above her was the biggest distraction of all.

Jack had called Caid a contradiction. The man was military all the way, he'd said, but he was still a loner. She believed him. As she looked around Caid's nearly empty apartment, she could see nothing that might betray a connection to another person. There were no photographs anywhere. Not one picture of a parent or sibling, or niece or nephew, or friend. Even though it had been all she had, the photograph of Jack and her mother that she'd carried inside her clothes as a child had sat at her bedside at the convent orphanage.

It was possible that Caid kept his pictures at his bedside, too, she thought, though even as she did she had the feeling that his room was every bit as austere as the space she occupied.

Feeling like the intruder she was, she cast another cautious glance around the open apartment. The downstairs area was actually one big room, divided only by the beige-tiled breakfast bar that delineated the spare kitchen. There were no paintings or posters or decorations on his walls. Nothing to betray his taste or preferences. Except for the barbaric-looking weights by the wet bar, which he no doubt used to keep his nicely muscled body as hard as it looked, and the boating magazines on the table, the room revealed little about him.

Or maybe it revealed everything. Maybe his lack of possessions simply indicated a lack of need. Maybe he didn't need things any more than he needed people.

There had been a reserve about him that she recognized; a deliberate distance he'd created the moment they met. She knew all about defense mechanisms, about keeping people out. She'd spent the better part of her life protecting herself. Yet, even though trust didn't come easily for her, she'd never given up hope of someday being close to someone. She doubted that Caid even knew what closeness was. Or what fear was, for that matter. He seemed to be a man so totally in control of himself and everything around him that he feared absolutely nothing. And while she would have given anything to be a part of someone's life, she suspected that Caid went out of his way to avoid any such connection.

With that conclusion competing with her growing fatigue, she finally fell asleep, just as the first rays of daylight crept around the edges of the drapes. Because it was so late when exhaustion finally took over, she didn't hear Caid's feet hit the floor when his alarm went off at 0600 hours, or hear the shower when he stepped into it in his usual morning stupor.

He needed coffee.

He needed breakfast.

He needed a couple more hours of sleep.

Caid's mood was not particularly remarkable. It had nothing to do with having missed dinner last night—or with the reason he'd missed it. He was simply not a morning person. He made no apologies for that fact to anyone who happened to be around, either. Though, more often than not, no one was. The only concession he made this morning was his attempt to be quiet as he descended the stairs. He didn't want to make noise if the woman he'd left clutching his blanket last night was still asleep.

Assuming that she was, since the small lump on his sofa didn't move when he glanced into the living room from the entryway, he opened the front door as quietly as he could, grabbed the morning paper from where it had landed in the bougainvillea bush by the door, then headed into the kitchen. He usually had a cup of coffee while he read the paper out on his deck. When the weather didn't cooperate with that plan, he had his coffee and read the paper at the coffee table. He wasn't interested in routine this morning, however. All he was interested in was coffee and figuring out what was going on with Kowalski.

It looked like his buddy had made the front page.

The headline was small, as front-page headlines went. But there, in the lower left-hand corner—and continued on page A17—was an article about the theft of a crown on loan to a local museum from a royal Austrian collection. It was not the major piece of the exhibit. Nor, according to the article, was it the most valuable, though the term "priceless" did get mentioned once or twice. The missing crown was described as "small and simple," though it apparently sported a rare star ruby as its chief stone, several lesser rubies, and a few dozen diamonds.

What interested Caid, beyond the fact that there were other, more valuable pieces that could have been taken, was that "Jack Kowalski, a private security specialist, and an unidentified female assistant" were being sought for questioning about the crown's disappearance.

Leaving the paper open on the breakfast bar, Caid set a cup of water in the microwave to make instant coffee, then reached for the telephone. As Mia had done last night, he punched Redial, since Jack's had been the last number called, and waited for the call to go through. As he listened to the intermittent ring, he looked across the counter to the couch.

The figure curled beneath the beige blanket had begun to move.

Mia had been sleeping in a little ball, her legs drawn up and her head tucked down nearly to her knees. To Caid, the position looked downright uncomfortable, but then, he tended to sprawl all over his king-size bed—usually at an angle. Now her lithe form began to lengthen, her arms going over her head as she stretched with the grace and pleasure of a contented cat. Part of the blanket pulled away, revealing a long and shapely leg, and a tantalizing glimpse of white lace high on her slender hip. When she turned, the gauzy white fabric of her skirt became visible.

Caught between wondering just how high up the lacy scrap of underwear was cut and reminding himself that the woman he was mentally undressing was his friend's daughter, Caid quickly glanced away. He didn't know if he was disappointed or relieved to discover that, beneath the blanket, she was fully dressed.

Neither Caid's ambivalence nor Mia's contentment lasted long. He knew the very instant she realized that she wasn't waking up in her own bed. In the space of a heartbeat, the lazy sensuality of her movements disappeared. Her body stiffened, her motions becoming minimal and abrupt as she jerked herself upright.

Holding the blanket in front of her white shirt, she sat up and pushed her tousled hair from her eyes. "Still no answer?"

He found her clarity of consciousness enviable. "Still no answer," he returned, pressing the hook to disconnect the call. "Give me the number again."

She did, and he punched it in himself, just in case it had been misdialed earlier.

He didn't expect an answer this time, either. And he got none.

Hanging up, he saw her shoulders slump. "You drink coffee?" he asked when the microwave beeped.

At her quiet "No, thank you," he dumped a spoonful of dark crystals in his mug, then carried it back to the breakfast bar to look down at the paper again.

"It's on the front page." Steam curled over the edge of the mug. Blowing at it, he narrowed his gaze at her slender form. "The police are still looking for him. And you." He nudged the paper toward her. "What are you going to do?"

She made no effort to get up. But this time, when she pushed her hair back, her hand trembled. "I'm not sure."

"I think you are."

She looked puzzled. Or maybe alarmed.

He blew across his mug again, then took a sip of the strong black liquid. "You're going to hide, aren't you?"

It wasn't a question. He spoke the words as if they were fact—and a choice he did not approve.

At least it seemed that way to Mia as she looked at the man in the military fatigues and felt the sudden and urgent need to escape his too-quiet scrutiny. Now that her story had been confirmed by what he'd read in the paper, now that he had seen for himself that the police were looking for her, she had the horrible feeling that he was going to insist she talk with them. Or worse, that as a soldier, a man whose job it was to defend his country's security, he might turn her over to them himself.

A heavy, roiling sensation filled her stomach at the thought. There was some distinction between soldiers and police in America; there were some boundaries of authority of which she wasn't at all certain at the moment. The room felt suddenly warm, increasing the distinctly dangerous sensation in her midsection. Putting her fingers to the dampness on her upper lip, she deliberately drew a long, deep breath. Letting it out, she drew another, willing the wave of nausea to pass. She had to get away. But first she had to stay calm. She couldn't let him see that she was afraid.

Caid saw anyway. Not her fear. Not at first. What he noticed was that the color had drained from her face, leaving her nearly as pale as her shirt. Her eyes, dark as they were, looked huge against her alabaster skin, and more than a little desperate. He had set his cup down the moment her slender hand covered her pale lips. Now, as he watched her shoulders fall as she breathed out, every muscle in his body was braced to move toward her.

"Are you all right?"

Her eyes closed. A moment later, she moved her hand to her stomach. Her tentative nod, he assumed, meant she was okay.

He felt his muscles relax. He was a little surprised that he'd been so ready to pick her up and carry her into the bathroom—or whatever it was he'd thought he was going to do. His frown remained, however, growing deeper when his glance narrowed on her belly. There was something a little disconcerting about a woman who looked as if she were about to lose it only moments after she woke up. He certainly had no personal experience with the phenomenon, but he'd overheard enough expectant fathers over the years to recognize what he hoped to heaven wasn't morning sickness.

"You're not pregnant, are you?"

At the blunt question, Mia's head snapped up, her expression absolutely blank.

"Of course not," she said, sounding as incredulous as she did offended. "Why would you think something like that?"

"Well, it's not like it's impossible," he returned defensively. "Things like that happen, you know. The way you looked just now, I thought maybe you were."

"Well, I'm not. I've never even—"

Abruptly Mia cut herself off.

Ever so slowly, Caid's eyebrow arched. His voice became suddenly, deceptively mild.

"You've never even . . . what?"

Her color was returning. Two faint pink blotches sat high on her cheeks as she studied a piece of fuzz in the vicinity of her knee. She didn't look very pleased with herself. But after a few telling seconds she did abandon her fascination with the weave of the blanket.

"Never been asked such a thing," she concluded.

That was not what she'd started to say. Mia knew from the quick spark of interest in Caid's eyes that he knew it, too.

Gamely she held his glance. So what if he thought her provincial. She couldn't dispute that she lacked the sophistication of other women she'd met in the past few months— most of them at school, and most of them younger than her.

Living in a convent orphanage from the age of eleven did tend to cramp one's social life, no matter what country that convent was in. She was absolutely green when it came to men and women and all the things she saw them doing to each other on television and read about them doing in books. But she'd be darned if she'd prove it by admitting she'd never made love in her entire life.

Her glance moved to his mouth at that thought. Caid had a wonderful mouth. Firm and full, and though its set was hard, it looked as if it might be as soft as velvet.

Admitting she'd never known the feel of a man's mouth on hers wasn't something she wanted to do, either. But looking at Caid just then made her remember reading that it was supposed to be pleasurable to have a man's tongue touch a woman's. It was supposed to be pleasurable to have his tongue touch other places, too.

The fuzz claimed her interest again. Her cheeks felt warm. A few moments ago, she couldn't have imagined that anything could make her forget the panic she'd felt. But he had. And while her stomach didn't feel nearly so queasy, the sensation in it now wasn't particularly comfortable, either.

"I'll do what I have to do," she said in response to the statement he'd made before his audacity sidetracked her. The thought that he might turn her in was fading. Had that been his plan, he could have done it by now. "What I have to do is find Jack."

Caid watched her glance away, the quick flare of spirit she'd exhibited turning to obvious consternation at the mention of her father.

As it was, Caid felt a little perplexity himself.

She'd never been with a man. She hadn't come right out and said so, but she hadn't had to. Caid didn't know why he found that thought so provocative. Or maybe it was the boldness she used to cover her innocence that he found so intriguing. But as he watched the hair cascading over her shoulders fall forward to hide her face, he knew he was far more intrigued than he should be.

Crowding in on the heels of that admission came another equally discomfiting thought. She'd ruled out morning sickness. Considering that they had been talking about the police in the moments before she'd paled, he could imagine only one thing that might have provoked such a profound physical reaction from her. Her fear of the authorities. Heaven only knew what she had experienced to have become physically ill at the thought of them.

Caid looked away, his sense of justice affronted. He had seen strong men reduced to tears by the demons that returned to haunt them years after they'd been in battle. Whether those demons were rational or not didn't matter. They existed. Just as Mia's fear existed. He had no idea what her life had been like in Vietnam, but there was no doubt in his mind that at one time she had suffered, and suffered unfairly. All children of war did. No human being should have to live with the kind of fear that had reasserted itself in her unguarded expression.

"You're free to stay here until we can figure out what's going on," he said, before he could change his mind. He could protect her from her fear for a while. At least until he found Jack and everything could be straightened out.

His glance skimmed her leg, which was still bare and exposed by the fallen blanket. She hadn't seemed to notice. "If you want to shower, you'll have to do it upstairs. There isn't one down here. I think I've got a spare toothbrush." Those were the basics. As far as Caid was concerned, the basics were all that was necessary. "Do you need anything else?"

Mia wouldn't have asked even if she had needed something. His tone was short, as if he were issuing orders, rather than extending an offer. But it was the way his gaze had raked over her that she found so unnerving. Unsure how it was possible to feel as if it was his hand and not simply his glance that had touched her skin, she pulled her leg under the blanket and drew her knees to her chest.

Not wanting to take up any more of his time, she limited her answer to a brief "No." Then, because she couldn't let it go with that, she added, "But thank you."

"Towels are in the lower cabinet in the bathroom."

He took his coffee with him, taking a healthy swallow of it as he rounded the counter. The green-and-brown camouflage fatigues he wore today made his shoulders look broader than she'd remembered from last night, his hips narrower. Or perhaps she'd made herself remember him as less overwhelming than he was because she already had enough to be concerned about without having to worry about how he made her feel, too.

He knew she was wary of him. She hated that, hated having him know that she found him overpowering. The knowledge seemed to give him some sort of advantage, and she felt at enough of a disadvantage as it was. That she was having to rely on his hospitality only increased her agitation.

The moment she heard his heavy boots hit the stairs, she scrambled off the couch. Shoving her hair out of her eyes, she smoothed her clothes as best she could and picked up the blanket.

He truly had no idea how hard it had been for her to ask for his help—and he had been her absolute last resort. Even at that, when she'd called him, she'd thought only that he might be able to tell her where Jack was. She hadn't expected that he would actually *do* anything. Having relied only on herself for so long, she'd learned not to expect anything from anyone. And when someone did do something for her, she tended to be a little suspicious about his motives. She didn't like being that way. But even with Jack—though she had begun to believe in him as much as he would let her—she maintained a certain cautious reserve. The only person who had ever really broken through that reserve was Father Marquette. But he was dead, so she didn't know if trusting him counted anymore.

What she did know was that Caid Matlock was no kindly old French priest.

At the sound of something hitting the breakfast bar, Mia whirled around. Busy with her mental wanderings while she folded the blanket, she hadn't heard him come back down. A man his size had no business moving so quietly. On the other hand, she thought, catching the glint of a silver oak leaf on his collar, moving quietly could very well *be* his business.

He'd set a brown leather briefcase on the counter. Mia glanced from it to Caid as he picked up the newspaper beside it.

"Why are you doing this?" she asked. "Letting me stay here, I mean?"

The paper rattled as he turned the page. "Where else would you go?"

He knew she had nowhere else. She'd told him that last night. Because he already knew, she let the question pass. "Do you always take in strangers?"

The muscle in his jaw jumped. "There's cereal in there." He hitched his thumb toward the cabinet next to the refrigerator, eyes still glued to the paper. "I don't usually eat here, so the cupboards are a little bare."

Ignoring his attempt to ignore her question, she took a step closer. "I'd really like to know."

Caid gave up on the sports section. "I owe your father. Okay?"

"Why?"

"Do you always ask so many questions?"

"Yes." She shrugged. She was a curious person. She always had been. "What do you owe Jack? I thought he owed you."

That statement brought the frown that Caid had so far managed to forestall. "What gave you that idea?"

Seeing his expression, Mia hesitated. "It's just an impression I had. We haven't talked about it a lot, but he told me some of what his life was like when he was in Vietnam."

Mostly he had spoken of the time he had spent with her mother, but those conversations were too precious to her to share. All memories of her mother were. Except the one that used to bring the nightmares.

But that had been long ago.

"When he mentioned you, he said you were what he wished he could be. That you never let people down. That was when he said that if anything ever happened to him and I needed something, I could come to you. Since he'd been talking about you two serving together just before that, it made me think you might have been there for him when he was in some kind of trouble."

The compliment gave Caid pause. And, as when she'd called him honorable last night, it left him feeling a little awkward. He'd never been any more noble or principled than the next guy. He'd just tried to do his best. And there had been plenty of times when even his best wasn't good enough.

"It's the other way around. Your father saved my life," he told her, wanting her to know that her father was a bigger man than he'd led his daughter to believe. "He could have left me for dead, and no one would have blamed him. That's why I'm letting you stay here while I find him."

As Mia watched Caid reach for a notepad and pull his pen from his pocket, she couldn't help but notice the defensive set of his jaw. That defensiveness had been in his voice, too. She didn't know if it was there because he didn't like the idea of owing anyone, or because honoring that obligation was causing his privacy to be invaded. Quite possibly it was both.

He set the notepad aside, telling her as he did that he was giving her another number on the base to call, because he'd be in the field most of the day, and that she should contact him if she heard from Jack. If he didn't hear from her, he'd go by Jack's house to check it out. After asking Mia for the name of the diner owned by the woman she'd mentioned last night, he said he'd stop by there, too, to see if this Roselyn knew anything.

"I'll be back around seven," he told her on his way to the door. Reaching for the knob he hesitated, looking as if he weren't at all sure how he felt about leaving his apartment with a stranger in it. But "Lock it" was all he said before he walked out.

With a feeling of relief, Mia slipped the latch into place and leaned against the door's smooth wood. As tempting as the thought was, she refused to indulge any notion that Caid's willingness to help had anything to do with her. She didn't need to be told to know he didn't want her here. She was an obligation he had to honor. That was all. Any concern he felt was for Jack.

An obligation. That was all she'd ever been. Something to be dealt with.

Had Mia not been so badly in need of Caid's help, she would gladly have removed herself from his premises just then. The last place she wanted to be was where she wasn't wanted. But where she wasn't wanted was the only place she had for the moment.

"I know I'm repeating myself, Caid, but I need to know if you're going to be around next year. I've got a brigadier general breathing down my neck about this OPLAN, and he's got a major general breathing down his. I've got two weeks to turn in my report and recommendations. If you're extending, I'm keeping you for my joint forces training. If not, I've got to wade through 201s and find someone equally qualified. I'm not relying on the luck of the draw. You with me on this?"

Caid's hand tightened ever so slightly on the cellular phone as he tracked the flight of two cranes rising from a swamp used for amphibious training.

"Yes, sir," he replied to Colonel Tom Bidwell's not-so-subtle stab at laying on the guilt. Caid wasn't buying. No way did Tom have to "wade" through personnel files to find someone to replace him. Word of mouth was how officers with Caid's training and experience landed assignments like the one he had. "I understand perfectly. But my stint isn't up for seven months. I don't have to make a definite decision until I'm six months out."

The voice on the other end of the line held exasperation. "Come on, Caid," Tom said, easing over the line between friend and commanding officer. "I know the damn technicalities. I also know that with all the cutbacks, there are damn few of us being asked to stay on when we could be retired. You've got expertise we need. Come by before you leave today. I'll buy you a beer, and we'll talk about this."

It was over a beer with Tom last night that Caid had first realized that staying in might not be what he wanted to do. His hesitancy still surprised him. Since he hadn't given it much more thought since then, though, there was little more to talk about.

"Tonight's not good, Tom. I've already got plans."

A series of short popping sounds came from the gunnery range over the ridge behind them. From the sounds, Caid guessed them to be M16s. Tom, who knew he spent most of his free time on his boat, ventured a guess of his own.

"Going fishing?"

"Something like that," Caid muttered, then added that he appreciated the offer of the beer and that he'd get back to him in time for his report.

Tom was sure he would. Or so Caid heard him say as he motioned to one of his team members studying the map spread over the hood of one of the three jeeps lined up on the rutted road. Ending the call, he leaned over the seat of the vehicle he stood beside to slide the phone onto its base and turned his attention to the soldier.

"You want to start on the next quadrant, Colonel?" the man asked, thinking that was what Caid wanted.

Caid and his team were in the field today, trying to integrate probable scenarios with the improbable to test the ingenuity of their latest batch of trainees. Field exercises were

where theory and practice were put to use. It was the part of
the program Caid enjoyed the most: the game of wits.

Today the challenge just wasn't there. Fortunately, the
day was about over.

Telling the major to continue without him, Caid signaled
a driver and swung himself onto the black plastic seat of the
open vehicle. The rains of fall hadn't yet arrived to replen-
ish the summer-parched hills around the rolling stretches of
land where maneuvers were conducted. But Caid paid little
attention to the dusty landscape. Tom's call nagged at him,
right along with the other thoughts his mind had continu-
ally turned to most of the day—thoughts about the conversation he'd had with Mia just before he left her at his
apartment this morning.

It had been a long time since he'd thought about what
Jack Kowalski had done for him. Longer still since he'd deliberately considered what he'd seen and done in Vietnam.
There was a lot Caid's mind simply refused to recall about
the two tours he'd spent in that part of the world—though
he had the feeling that, were he to try hard enough, the
details could be recalled. He didn't want to remember the
details, though. Nor did he need to. Like the troubled years
of his youth, some things were best left buried. He didn't
need details to remember Jack's unselfishness, anyway.

It was because of that selflessness that, despite their differences, Caid would go to the wall for the man if he was in
trouble. Most people who knew Jack Kowalski thought he
had no morals, no sense of honor. But most people hadn't
seen the man as Caid had—as a soldier who refused to give
up in the face of seemingly insurmountable odds, and who
refused to let a soldier in his charge give up, either. When a
punji stake had penetrated Caid's leg and the resulting in-
fection had made it impossible for him to walk, Jack had all
but carried Caid for the two weeks it took them to work
their way through the swamps and the rain and the muck of
an area they weren't officially supposed to be in to begin
with. An area no rescue party or plane could possibly enter

without sabotaging an entire operation and jeopardizing hundreds of other lives.

Jack had carried him, cared for him and cursed him, when he could have left him for dead and exposed himself to a lot less danger than he had been in by refusing to leave him behind to be captured. A man didn't forget someone like that. At least a man like Caid didn't.

The problem, however, was that Caid had begun to wonder if Jack might not finally have stepped over the line. The circumstances surrounding the missing crown did seem a little strange.

The circumstances seemed even stranger when, an hour later, Caid pulled his black Bronco up in front of a nondescript ranch-style house at the end of a quiet, palm-lined street in north San Diego.

The neighborhood Jack lived in was old and a little rundown. It looked better to Caid than it had when he was here, over a year ago, though. There were signs of renewal in the fresh coats of paint on a few of the houses, and the junk had been hauled away from the house across the street. Even Jack's place looked as though he'd recently put an hour or two into the yard. The once-empty window boxes held some sort of bright red flower, and a pot of carnations—the only flower Caid could identify, other than a rose—sat on the porch.

Thinking that Mia was more likely than Jack to be responsible for those touches, Caid approached the front door.

There was no car in the carport, and this morning's newspaper was still on the stoop, so he was pretty sure Jack wasn't there. He knocked on the frame of the screen door, anyway. When there was no answer, he followed the cracked walkway past the shrubs beneath the curtained windows along the side of the house and into the tiny backyard. At one time Jack had kept a key to the house under the frame of an old Cobra he'd intended for years to restore.

The Cobra was still there, shrouded by a weathered green tarp.

The key wasn't.

As it turned out, Caid didn't need the key. When he cupped his hands against the glass to look through the lace curtains on the door's window—another of Mia's touches, he concluded—the door swung inward with a faint squeak.

For a moment, Caid hesitated. He wasn't at all sure what he'd hoped to find by coming here, but he was quite certain he didn't like the feeling he had when he gingerly pushed the door all the way open. Something wasn't right.

The feeling didn't improve when he stepped inside.

The door he'd entered opened onto a laundry room, which led to the kitchen and on into the rest of the three-bedroom house. With the curtains all drawn, the only illumination was what leaked in around the edges of the windows. But even in the dim early-evening light, Caid could see well enough.

Either Mia was being overpaid for her housekeeping services or the place had been ransacked. Quite thoroughly. Not a drawer, cabinet, cupboard or closet had been spared.

Not wanting to touch anything, Caid nudged the light switch with his elbow. The overhead light added a new perspective. The place hadn't just been ransacked. It had been searched. Completely. And whoever had searched it had also lifted fingerprints. As Caid moved down the hall, he noticed that graphite dust darkened several surfaces—the receiver of the white telephone, a glass in Jack's bathroom, the edges of a dresser in what he assumed from its decidedly feminine look to be Mia's bedroom.

The handiwork had to be that of the police.

Five minutes later, Caid was back in his Bronco and headed down the hill, turning that thought over in his mind. If the police had obtained a search warrant, then Jack and Mia had to be wanted for more than just questioning. At least one of them was.

As much as Caid hated the thought, it was looking like more of a possibility that Jack had botched the one good opportunity that had come his way. Caid had thought that Jack kept his business dealings strictly legitimate, that he'd given up on the scamming and the scheming years ago. But maybe the temptation had been too great this time. Maybe, when he'd gone back to check on the crown, as Mia had said he had, he hadn't just been making sure it was secure. Maybe he'd taken the crown then, without Mia knowing it—which would explain why he'd left her as he had.

It wasn't as if Jack Kowalski were incapable of theft. After all, he'd once nearly been court-martialed for "borrowing" a truckload of whiskey some enterprising army personnel had managed to reroute from a bar in Saigon. But Caid didn't think even Jack, irredeemable as he sometimes seemed, would have left his own daughter stranded in such a way.

There were others who weren't quite so willing to give Kowalski the benefit of the doubt. One of them was the outgoing, forty-something Roselyn, the proprietress of the Nickelodeon Diner, an unremarkable place that had somehow escaped the renovations of the surrounding office buildings in downtown San Diego. "Chief cook and bottle-washer" was what she called herself when Caid asked if she was the owner. And tonight, since both her waitresses were out with colds "or their boyfriends," she was the counter help, too.

"What can I get you?" she wanted to know, eyeing the silver oak leaves on Caid's collar and the service ribbons over the pocket of his uniform as he slid onto a stool at the cracked green Formica counter. A carefully penciled eyebrow arched engagingly. "General, is it?"

"Right," he drawled. "In about twenty years." Or never. "It's Caid Matlock. How about just Caid."

"Suits me," she returned, with a smile—and a menu.

"Just coffee." Smiling, too, he handed the menu back. "And some information, if you wouldn't mind. I understand you know Jack Kowalski."

At the mention of Jack's name, her smile evaporated, her expression turning about as warm as the milkshake the guy at the end of the counter was nursing with his burger.

"I know a lot of people . . . Lieutenant Colonel."

Caid ignored the deliberate, and quite pointed, formality. "I understand you know this particular person rather well. He works not too far from here."

"He works right around the corner, at Independent Insurance Adjustments. Most of that office comes here for lunch. Try there."

Maybe he would. "You've seen the newspaper?"

A beige cup and saucer were produced from a basket under the counter. She set them noisily in front of him. "Of course I've seen the newspaper," she replied, grabbing a pot of coffee from the two-pot unit by the pie case. "Who hasn't? You're not the only person who's been in here asking about him, you know. Why are you interested, anyway?" She eyed his uniform, with suspicion now, rather than open friendliness. "He stolen a tank or something, too?"

Caid glanced down at the coffee she was pouring, then back up to meet her glacial glare. She didn't seem at all worried about the less-than-hospitable impression she might be making on her customers. There were only two others in the place, anyway. The guy with the burger, and an old man in a back booth, warily eyeing the blue-plate special. "I'm just a friend trying to figure out what's going on," Caid told her. "I'd heard you were a friend of his, too, and thought you might know where he is."

"If I had a clue, I'd have turned him over myself when the police came asking for him. You want pie or anything with that?" she asked, pointing her pencil toward the steaming coffee.

He didn't even want the coffee. He'd only ordered it so that he could talk to her. "Why would you have turned him in? Do you think he did it?"

"No," she returned flatly and stuck her pencil into her short, frosted hair. "I don't. But then, I didn't think he was two-timing me, either, so what do I know? You want to know where Jack is? Find that little concubine he's got living with him." The faint lines around her mouth deepened. "I can't believe she had the nerve to call here looking for him."

With that, she laid his check on the counter, adding a quiet "Excuse me" before she headed through the double doors of the kitchen.

Strike two, Caid thought, and he tossed a dollar bill on top of the check as the old man fired up the jukebox in the corner. Roselyn's disposition would no doubt improve if she knew the true relationship between Mia and Jack. But that information wasn't Caid's to relay, and he didn't want his friend upset with him for talking out of turn. Caid's concern was only with what Roselyn knew, anyway. Which was nothing, apparently. As angry as she'd been, Caid didn't think she was holding anything back. Except, possibly, how much she cared. Beneath her hostility, she had looked truly hurt, and more than a little worried. Rather the way Mia had looked when she told him that Jack hadn't wanted Roselyn to know who she was.

It seemed to Caid that the two of them ought to get together and string the guy up by his...ears.

As it was, he just might do it himself. Once he showed up. All day long, Caid had been trying not to think of the woman he'd left in his apartment. It was bad enough that he didn't know what to *do* with her. Now he had to go home and tell her what had happened to her house.

Chapter 4

For the past hour, Mia had watched for Caid. Every few minutes she would abandon the project she'd undertaken in his kitchen to look out the window over the sink to see if he was coming. And every few minutes she would say a silent prayer that he had found Jack. Now, seeing Caid move past the kids playing soccer in the building's courtyard, she felt her heart jerk anxiously in her chest—and felt the sensation of warmth gathering low in her stomach. The anxiety, she was sure, was strictly because of her father. But she couldn't so easily account for the warmth. The disconcerting sensation seemed to have something to do with Caid himself, with the way he moved, with the sense of purpose and strength in his long-legged strides. Or maybe the strange, liquid feeling was caused by the aura of absolute masculinity surrounding him, the primitive element that had been tamed in most other men, but refused to be contained in a man like Caid.

Before he could slide his key into the lock, Mia had deserted her post at the kitchen window and jerked open the door. What she saw in the grim set of his mouth immediately quashed the hope she'd so foolishly allowed herself to feel.

He hadn't found her father.

"Did you find out anything?" she had to ask, just in case.

"Nothing that will do us any good." The shouts of the kids chasing the soccer ball followed Caid inside. A moment later, the exuberant sounds were shut out with the bang of the door. "I guess you didn't hear from him, either."

Frustrated, hungry, and uneasy with the way the hope had so quickly vanished from her eyes, he pushed his fingers through his hair. He'd heard on the radio that the police were still looking for Kowalski and his "unidentified assistant." The story had been a tag at the end of the broadcast, almost an afterthought to the latest scandals, slayings and traffic reports. But the crown's disappearance had been of enough interest to warrant mention, and, unlike the article in the morning paper, the radio item had included a brief description of Mia obtained from the museum guard. "Thin, with long brown hair and dark eyes."

The guard was no poet.

Caid wasn't confusing himself with one, either. But her hair wasn't just brown. It was shades of the deepest sable, shot with gold and hints of fire, and her eyes were the gray of a dark and misty morning. As his glance slid down her body—and came to rest on the thin blue dish towel tied around her waist—he could think of a dozen adjectives to describe her shape, too.

Before he got completely sidetracked, however, the aroma from the kitchen caught his attention. So did the fact that there was very little light in the place.

"Why is it all closed up in here?" he wanted to know as he crossed the carpet. Taking off his baseball-style fatigue hat, he dropped it on the coffee table as he passed, and opened the three sets of drapes. One of the reasons he'd taken this apartment was that it was an end unit and had lots of windows. He hated feeling closed in. "Have you been sitting in the dark all day?"

The ceiling light was on in the kitchen, and she had the lamp on the end table by the sofa turned low. With the rustle of heavy cream-colored fabric, Caid added the fading light of the early-fall evening to the room. Then, hands on his hips, he turned back to scan the mixing bowls and pans on the counter.

Mia hadn't answered, but he didn't seem to notice.

What Mia noticed, however, was that he did not look pleased. Not, she thought, scooting past the counter to pull her creation from the oven before it dried to leather, that she had any idea how he'd look if he was happy about something. She'd never seen him come anywhere close to a smile. It took precious little imagination, however, to see that what had seemed like such a good idea to her a couple of hours ago did not hold the same appeal for him.

"It's meat loaf," she said, in case his frown meant he didn't recognize the item she set on the tiled counter by the stove. She'd had to do something other than pace and stare at her textbooks for the past twelve hours. Aside from the matter of her sanity, she'd thought he'd be pleased to have dinner waiting for him. Jack usually was, assuming that her experiment du jour proved edible.

"All you had in your freezer was hamburger. Since meat loaf is the one thing I can make that usually comes out like it's supposed to, I thought I should fix it for you. So you didn't have to cook or go out," she explained, when all he did was continue to frown. "You said this morning that you didn't eat here very often. I knew you'd be late because of what you were doing for me, so I wanted to save you the trouble of having to get something somewhere else."

The only sound in the room when Mia fell silent was the clatter of the lid on the green beans as the pot began to boil. Jarred as much by the sudden racket as she was by Caid's silence, she immediately reached over and set the pot off the burner.

"You don't like meat loaf," she finally concluded.

She was trying not to let her disappointment show, but standing there with the corner of her lower lip tucked between her teeth, she looked like a child whose balloon had just popped. Wondering why Jack couldn't have had a son instead of a daughter, Caid had to admit he felt like the bully who'd just stuck the pin in it. He didn't appreciate the feeling any more than he appreciated the position Jack had put him in.

Steam hovered over the brown rectangle of meat by the stove. "I'm not picky," he said, annoyed at having his space so thoroughly invaded. He hadn't meant for her to cook for him.

His scowl changed directions. "Where did you get those?"

Now that she was standing more than an arm's length away, he could see what he hadn't noticed when she'd greeted him at the door. She was wearing white shorts.

"These?" With her index finger, she pulled outward on the hem. "Out of my backpack. I had a tennis class yesterday, so I had my court clothes with me." Looking a little puzzled as to why he'd ask, she glanced back up. "I didn't leave your apartment today, if that's what you were wondering."

Caid's nod was vague, more acknowledgment that she'd spoken than recognition of what she'd said. What struck Mia, though, was that his expression hadn't altered in the slightest. As his scrutiny moved once more to her legs, his jaw remained locked, and his brow pleated in a frown.

"You're taking a class in tennis? Are you majoring in sports or something?"

"I'm taking tennis because it's a game I've wanted to learn since I was fifteen." Turning to the stove, she set the beans on the burner again. "It was mentioned in a book I read. I didn't know what the word was, so Father explained it to me."

The book was *The Great Gatsby*, and the nun who found her struggling to read it had been utterly appalled to learn that Father Marquette had given the novel to her. The good sister had labeled the work "licentious." Father had called it a superb example of post–World War I English literature, and an excellent means for Mia to improve her knowledge of the English language, since quality English texts were so hard to come by. Mia's English had ultimately improved, although she couldn't begin to relate to the lifestyles and affairs portrayed in the story. Still, she'd always wanted to learn to play the game called tennis.

With the beans on low heat, she turned to him. "My major is education."

Caid's eyebrow arched. "You want to teach?"

"Why do you say it like that? It's an honorable profession."

"Of course it is. I was just...surprised."

The conclusion was as lame as it sounded. The truth was, beyond finding her father, he hadn't thought about what she might want, about what she might need, or about anything else connected with aspirations, hopes or dreams. She was simply Jack's daughter. It therefore wasn't necessary that he know anything else about her—which was why he didn't ask who this "Father" was that she'd referred to, or what she'd been doing when she was fifteen.

Unfortunately, the need-to-know principle of military intelligence didn't seem to be working where Mia was concerned. She was not the kind of woman a man could keep in a neatly labeled box. She was deceptively easy to underestimate, too. Maybe it had something to do with her size. Or, he thought, admitting to the chauvinist in him, her gender.

"Have you taught before?"

The overhead lights shimmered along the length of her hair as she nodded.

"In Saigon?" he asked.

"At the small orphanage where I lived before I came here. I taught English and Russian to the older children."

For years, Russian had been the politically correct foreign language to study. And Mia, *ma petite éponge*—my little sponge—as Father Marquette had affectionately called her, had soaked it up along with every other grain of knowledge anyone fed her. She didn't mention that to Caid, but she did tell him that the priest had taught her English, too, along with enough French to keep her from starving should she ever be fortunate enough to see Paris. So, when the Vietnamese government decided a few years ago that it would be economically expedient for its citizens to speak and understand English, her knowledge had enabled her to teach it, as well as to gain her greater access to English tapes and periodicals.

"Here, though," she told him, remembering how she'd devoured every scrap of information she could get her hands on about her father's country, "I hope to teach first grade."

Honest confusion clouded Caid's expression. He clearly didn't see the appeal of her goal. "Why would you want to do that? With your language background, you could probably teach at the university level. Or work for a corporation. Or the military," he threw out, as if she would be wasting her time with anything less. "As important as international communication is right now, you could go just about anywhere."

That was what Jack had said, too. More or less. What he'd actually said was "You're fluent in three languages. Why in the hell do you want to teach kids how to spell?"

The answer to that had been easy—and as basic to her as Jack's response had been to him. She liked children. More important, she missed being around them. At the orphanage and, later, at the transition center, there had always been a child in need of a hug, or a lap to sit on, or a hand to hold. Whenever there had been a minor crisis over a game, or someone had wanted a story read or a nose wiped, they had come to Mia for help. She missed being needed that way.

Because Caid's reaction made her doubt that he would understand her rationale any better than Jack had, she didn't bother to explain her choice. She simply told him, "It's not what I want."

"Why not?" he demanded, then immediately checked himself.

He held up his hand, backing off in the literal, as well as the figurative, sense. "I'm sorry. What you do is your business. Teaching kids is ... good. Yeah, it is. It's good." He shrugged. "Somebody's got to do it."

"Rather like taking out the trash?"

"I didn't mean it like that."

He'd backed toward the breakfast bar. Far enough for her to see that he was scowling at her legs again.

Despite his disclaimer, he'd made it clear enough that he found her goals lacking. To Mia, it seemed equally clear that he found her lacking in the physical sense, too. Compared to many of the curvaceous, buxom and leggy women running around the UCSD campus, Mia felt she was built like a stick of bamboo. Certain from Caid's dispassionate expression that he would have found the bumps on bamboo more appealing, she moved to the sink to avoid his inspection, wondering in spite of herself what kind of woman he *was* attracted to.

Dumping soap in the sink, she started cleaning up the dishes she'd used in preparing the meal he didn't seem to want.

"Did you talk to Roselyn?" she asked, hoping for even the tiniest scrap of information about Jack, and hoping, too, that she wouldn't have to impose on his friend much longer.

Caid leaned against the counter, crossing his arms over his chest and his boots at the ankle. He'd been wrong about her legs. They weren't just good. Though she was slender, there was strength in the long, lean muscles of her thighs and calves, a kind of feminine strength that he found sexy as hell.

"Yeah," he muttered, jaw clenching. "I did. She said she had no idea where Jack was."

"Is that all?"

"Basically. The police were asking her about him, too. Apparently she couldn't tell them any more than she did me."

Caid saw no point in mentioning Roselyn's acerbic comments. He didn't see any point in letting the meal Mia had prepared dry out any more than it already had, either. He was hungry, after all. She might not be, though, after he told her about the mess he'd found at Jack's house.

"How long before that's ready?"

Mia didn't look at him as she set the bowl she'd rinsed in the dishwasher and picked up another. "It's ready now. All I have to do is dish it up."

"Go ahead. I'll go up and change. Then we can figure out where to go from here. Roselyn's a dead end, but there's got to be someone who knows where he is."

He started for the stairs. A twinge of conscience had him turning back.

"Thanks for fixing dinner, Mia," he said to her, because she had done it to repay him, and like it or not, he couldn't ignore the effort. Feeling awkward and not too pleased about that, either, he had to add one more thing. "It's not that I don't appreciate it."

Before she could fill in the *but* that would have told her he wasn't crazy about the idea of her being here, he told her to give him five minutes, and turned to the stairs. He wanted her to go. But not until he knew she'd be all right.

By the time Caid had traded fatigues for his favorite threadbare cutoffs and a faded blue T-shirt, Mia had his plate served and sitting on the breakfast bar. The knot in her stomach allowed room for little else, so while Caid gamely polished off most of the meat loaf, along with a fair amount of catsup, she cleaned up the kitchen and tried to not think about what she would do when she finished.

As she had all day, she concentrated on getting from one moment to the next, and tried not to dwell too much on what might happen beyond that. In a twist of fate so swift it seemed like some awful dream, her world had been reduced from a newfound future full of promise to a nightmare of doubt and uncertainty. Adding to that uncertainty was the man whose eyes were following her every move.

"I think it's clean."

At the sound of Caid's deep voice, the spoon she'd already washed twice clattered into the sink. Grabbing at it to still the nerve-jarring sound, she mumbled a faint "Sorry" and laid the utensil on the counter. "I'm just a little jumpy, I guess."

"That's understandable," he conceded, feeling bad that he'd startled her. He could tell she'd been preoccupied. That was why he'd said what he had when he noticed that she'd spent the past two minutes rewashing the same utensil. But he hadn't thought she'd jump out of her skin at the sound of his voice.

He stabbed at the last forkful of beans. "I think it would help if you told me exactly what happened the night Jack disappeared. Everything. From the beginning."

Mia turned to see the last of the beans disappear from his plate. Caid was obviously a man who ate to refuel, rather than for pleasure. He also appeared to be a man who didn't expect to be waited on. He brought his plate to the sink, rinsed it himself and stuck it in the dishwasher. Then, with a look that she couldn't have begun to decode, he took the dishrag she held and handed her a towel to dry her hands with.

"I was only cleaning up my mess," she said, defending her presence in his kitchen.

"You didn't make that big of one." She'd cleaned the stove and the counters and nearly polished the porcelain off the sink. He had the feeling she'd start in on the cabinets next if he didn't stop her. "Come on. Let's see if we can't get to the bottom of this."

Wanting nothing more, Mia followed Caid into the living room. The drapes were still open, but the sun had set, leaving nothing visible but their own reflections in the blackened glass. In that mirrorlike surface, she could see Caid's reflection towering over hers. The top of her head didn't even reach his chin, and his shoulders were so wide that, were he to step in front of her, he would block her reflection completely.

Mia went still at the thought. As intimidating as she found his size, she found it rather reassuring to know that he could so easily conceal her.

That reassurance faltered. She couldn't allow such thoughts. As tempting as it was, she couldn't let herself be lulled into relying on him any more than she absolutely had to. Relying on someone meant counting on him to be there, and Mia had accepted long ago that she really couldn't count on anyone.

Still, the reflection in the window held a certain security.

She turned away, but not soon enough. Caid caught her quick frown and glanced toward the window himself. Something there had bothered her. Since there was nothing to be seen, he couldn't imagine what it could be—until he remembered how dim it had been in the apartment when he came home. Vaguely he recalled asking why she hadn't opened the drapes as he'd drawn them back himself. In his impatience, he hadn't waited for her response.

"Did you keep the drapes drawn all day?"

She said she had, and when she did, he wanted to know why.

"Just because," she told him, not wanting it to be important.

"Does it bother you having them open now?"

It seemed she was about to say that it did when a quizzical look touched her face. She glanced back at him, the delicate line of her eyebrows drawn together, as if she couldn't quite believe whatever it was she'd just realized.

"Not with you here," she told him, because, amazingly, it was true. Since he'd come home, she hadn't experienced any of the awful panic she'd suffered off and on all day. "I don't really like being inside all that much. I get kind of claustrophobic sometimes, so it was nice when you opened everything. Before it got dark, anyway."

"If you get claustrophobic, why did you have the place all closed up?"

Her words were barely audible, a mere whisper in the quiet room. "It felt safer."

The light from the lamp caught the shades of deep umber and gold in her hair as she lowered her head. Thick and shining, the tresses fell forward, curtaining her face. Still considering her words, he felt his hand lift toward her cheek.

He made her feel safe.

Incredible.

Realizing what he was about to do, not at all sure what she'd do if he did it, he stuck his hand in his pocket before she caught the motion.

"Nothing's going to happen to you here, Mia. No one knows where you are."

"I told myself that all day." Her smile was soft as she looked up, a mere shadow of what it could be. "It didn't work."

For the first time since he'd walked in the door, Caid allowed himself to acknowledge the tension that suffused her entire body. Her arms were crossed, her fingers digging into her upper arms. There was something vaguely threatening about being that sensitive to someone. But, threatening or not, he'd be willing to bet his boat she'd be pacing the nap off the carpet right now had she been alone.

Feeling like a louse for having earlier begrudged her the time she'd spent in his kitchen trying to make the best of her confinement, he pulled the drapes on their reflections and headed for the entryway.

The closet door groaned when he pulled it open.

"Do you have a sweater or anything in that bag of yours?" he asked.

"No." A puzzled look crossed her face. "Why?"

"It'll be cool down by the water. We're getting out of here for a while. It'll be okay," he assured her when she hesitated. "It's almost dark."

No one would see her, if that was what she was worried about, and he needed to get out of the apartment as badly as she did. Not because he was feeling the nerve-stretching restlessness he'd experienced so often lately, but because a walk on the beach sounded infinitely safer than standing there wondering if her mouth would feel as soft as it looked.

An olive-green sweatshirt hung on a hook inside the closet. Grabbing it, he handed it to her. The thing would probably hang nearly to her knees. He hoped she didn't mind.

She didn't seem to mind at all. In fact, as with everything else he'd done for her, she appeared most grateful for the loan. With a tentative smile when her head popped out the neck, she rolled up the dangling sleeves, her smile increasing when she saw him shaking his head at the fit.

The warmth of that unexpected and unrestrained smile made him feel as if he were standing in the sunshine of a bright spring day. Generous, natural, uncomplicated, it seemed to reveal her very essence. Its impact hit him like a fist.

For some reason he didn't begin to understand, he didn't want her gratitude just then. He didn't want to hear her say the "Thank you" poised on her lips, or hear her tell him he was kind, or offer whatever phrase she felt obligated to utter. He just wanted them out of here. So he robbed her of the opportunity by cutting her off with a curt "Here," and shoved the baseball cap he'd pulled from the shelf at her.

"What's this for?"

"Your head."

Her glance was tolerant, her tone droll. "I assumed that much, but it's not going to be that cool on the beach, is it?"

"It's not for warmth. They have your description, Mia."
Without thinking, seeing only that she wasn't putting the hat
on, he reached over her shoulder to pull her hair around.

Her voice faltered. "My description?"

"It was on the radio," he heard himself say as his fingers
closed around a fistful of the waist-length silk. "Long dark
hair, dark eyes," he repeated. "They made you sound like
half the women in southern California. But there's no sense
waving any red flags. This," he added, gathering her hair at
her nape, "would definitely be one."

Her hair was one of the first things he'd noticed about
her. Circling the bulk of it between his thumb and forefin-
ger, he lifted it over her shoulder. "Tuck it under the hat."

Looking a little numb, she watched him bring the make-
shift ponytail forward. His knuckles brushed the side of her
neck, startling her with the contact. But she was more aware
of the weight of his hand where it settled on her collarbone.

Mia didn't know which was more disconcerting—the heat
she could feel through her shirt, radiating toward her breast,
or the way her stomach tightened when she breathed in and
his scent filled her nostrils. He smelled of the soap she recognized from his shower because she'd used it herself, and
of a hint of male sweat. The combination threatened to tie
her already ragged nerves in knots. Especially when, a moment later, she saw the hard edges of his expression fade.

He lifted her hair again, seeming drawn by its weight. Or
perhaps, from the way he tentatively tested the strands, by
its softness. A certain fascination entered his eyes, and a
kind of longing he probably didn't even know was there. He
wasn't accustomed to softness in any form. Or to gentleness. Yet it was gentleness she felt when, as if holding
something that his big hand might easily break, he settled
her hair back on her shoulder.

As if he suddenly realized what he'd been doing, Caid's
glance jerked to hers.

Amazement swept through him. Mia hadn't moved. He
could see uncertainty in the quiet way she watched him, but

he could see anticipation, too. It was there in the shallow breath she drew, the quickened beat of her heart beneath his hand.

She wants *me to touch her,* he thought, and let his glance fall to the gentle part of her mouth.

Suddenly his chest felt tight, his pants even tighter, and he knew that if he didn't get his hands off her he was going to spend the rest of the evening in real pain. The woman staring at him with those sultry gray eyes and those full, pouting lips was an innocent. In the physical sense, anyway. She didn't know the feel of a man, didn't know the madness a man and a woman could bring each other.

With great reluctance, he let the thick gossamer strands slip through his fingers. "I think you'd better do it."

His voice was gruff, contradicting the heat in his eyes. Not at all sure what she'd done, what she should have done, Mia took the hat he held toward her and, with a couple of expert twists, made a neat knot of her hair and plopped the hat over it. If she looked a little shaken as she preceded him out the door, she hoped Caid would think it was only because of what he'd told her about her description having been on the radio.

The first week of fall had been warm, but the sun took the warmth of the day with it when it set, and the evening air felt considerably cooler. With Caid's sweatshirt warding off the chill of the ocean breeze, Mia hugged her arms around her waist and followed Caid across the road to the strip of scrub grass and onto the beach beyond. The fog hadn't come in tonight, and a crescent moon hung bright in an inky sky. In that moonlit darkness Caid loomed next to her, his footsteps silent in the sand as they skirted the driftwood scattered over the deserted shore.

He'd wanted her to tell him what had happened at the museum. He reminded her of that again as they came within a few yards of the surf and headed parallel to the water. The moon reflected off the wet sand as the water rushed in and then flowed back to the sea. But Mia didn't comment on the play of light on water and waves, as she might have under other circumstances. Caid's manner didn't allow it. He was less than an arm's length away, yet his manner was as distant as the horizon.

Wondering if he kept that same distance between himself and the men under his command—and everyone else he came in contact with—she told him that she and Jack had arrived at the museum about nine o'clock.

"Jack wanted it to be dark," she explained, her voice hushed against the drone of the waves. "But he didn't want to go in too late, because he knew I wanted to get back to study. After he disabled the backup batteries and main power to the exterior systems, he had me use the scope to detect the lasers on the interior systems once we were inside." It was hard for her to believe it had only been the day before yesterday. The past thirty-six hours felt more like a week.

"How did you get in?"

"I don't think I'm supposed to say. Jack said the details of a job were con—"

"Mia," Caid interrupted, his voice flat. "I don't give a damn right now what Jack said about confidentiality. We're trying to figure out what went wrong here. Now, how did you get in?"

"Through an air-conditioning intake." Under the circumstances, she supposed, Caid did have a right to certain details. "I went in through a vent on the roof."

"He had *you* do that?"

"It's not like I haven't crawled through tight spaces before. It's been years, but I used to crawl into vents like that all the time. To sleep in," she explained when she felt his eyes narrow on her.

"How did you know where the vents led?" he asked, because he didn't want to think about why she'd had to sleep in the cramped metal spaces of a building vent. He had the feeling he knew anyway.

It felt safer.

As Jack had explained it to her, since a copy of a public or commercial building's blueprints were filed with the city for fire-department access, any thief worth his weight in stolen goods would pilfer, borrow or steal a copy to study when preparing to hit a target. These weren't small-time clients he was dealing with, and the crooks who targeted the types of buildings and facilities Jack was paid to check out weren't small-time, either. They were the cats, the silent, sophisticated burglars who possessed the patience and the sophisticated minds necessary to conquer the latest electronic technology.

As Caid listened to Mia explain that the reason it had taken longer once they were in was that she'd had some trouble judging distances with the scope, he began to suspect that she possessed that same patience and sophistication. He also couldn't help but notice the edge of excitement that had crept into her voice. She didn't have to say so for him to know she'd been fascinated the first time she looked through the high-tech instrument and seen the infrared laser beams forming a network of crisscrossing lines in the exhibit room. To get to the crown they'd decided to move, they'd had to step over the beams as if they were strings. Breaking a beam would trigger an alarm, usually a silent one that the intruder wouldn't realize he'd tripped until he found himself facing a welcoming committee in blue uniforms.

Jack and Mia hadn't set off any alarms, though. Everything had gone perfectly.

"We took the crown out of the case and moved it to a room full of modern sculptures. Jack saw one that looked like a figure holding a pole and put the crown on its head. Then we went straight to the security guard in the lobby to tell him who we were."

"You said Jack went back to check the crown."

"That was while I was talking to the guard. He was gone only for a minute."

That was all it would have taken for him to take the crown himself. Caid didn't mention that, though. From the way Mia paused, he was pretty sure she'd already considered the possibility.

"It was when he came back," she went on, "that he seemed in such a hurry to leave."

"Did he have a bag with him? Anything he could have put the crown in?" Frustration added to his insistence. "How big is this thing, anyway?"

In the moonlight, Mia formed a circle the size of a tea saucer with her hands. "About like so," she said. "But he couldn't have had it on him. He was wearing a long-sleeved T-shirt and pants. The tools he carried were in his pants pockets, and I had the bag with the scope and the decoding device. There wasn't any place on him to put it."

Caid wasn't convinced. "You said he was in a hurry. What was he acting like?"

"I don't know." She lifted her hand, then let it fall. "Like Jack, I guess."

"Mia. That's not going to do us any good. You've got to remember exactly what he was doing."

Remembering would be a lot easier if he'd stop talking to her as if she were three. "I noticed him looking out the windows a couple of times. Like he was anxious to get to the car, maybe?"

"What windows?"

"The lobby windows. The front of the museum is mostly glass."

"You could see the car from there?"

"We'd parked in the back."

"What was he looking at out the window, then? If he kept looking out it, he must have been looking at something. Come on, Mia. Think."

"I am thinking. If he was looking at something, I didn't see it. I know you're only trying to help, but there's no need to get so impatient."

"I'm not getting impatient," he snapped, but he knew he was. He also knew that badgering her wasn't going to help. She wasn't some raw recruit who hadn't paid attention on a training exercise. "I just want to know what the setup was. What you might have seen or heard. Were there any other people around?"

He might not have thought he was being particularly abrupt, but she could feel his frustration with her. Since it was easier talking with him when she couldn't see him studying her, she kept her eyes straight ahead as she told him that the only person they'd seen was the guard. Since Caid wanted all the details, she also told him about the brown paper sack she'd noticed on the guard's desk—and that there had been plenty of time for the guard to take the crown himself when she went back to reset the alarm system.

She hadn't noticed whether or not the lunch bag had been moved when she returned to the lobby. Nor, she realized when Caid asked, whether there had been any appreciable difference in the guard's manner. The overweight little man, who'd gone from being scared out of his wits when they caught him sleeping to parading around with his chest puffed out to show his authority, had seemed exactly the same to her. Officious.

Still, she had to agree with Caid when he said it seemed awfully strange that the guard hadn't been arrested and that it was Jack the police were looking for.

Turning into the breeze so that it could blow the hair from her face, she watched the surf's rhythmic ebb and flow. Arcs of black surf, tipped silver by the moon, scalloped the shore beside them. "Do you think he took it?"

She looked up at Caid, her eyes luminous in the surreal light.

Do you think my father left me?

Aw, Mia. Don't ask me that.

You think he did, don't you?

Caid looked away.

"They've got a warrant out for him now. That means they'll probably have one out for you. Once they figure out who you are."

Mia jerked around, her hand on his arm to make him look at her. "How do you know that?"

"I went by your house before I went to see Roselyn. Somebody'd done a pretty thorough job of going through it." He let out his breath, hating the fear he'd caused her to feel. "I'm sure it was the police. It looked like they'd been lifting prints for identification."

"They went through my room, too?"

It wasn't guilt or fear of discovery that robbed her voice of its strength. It sounded more like disbelief, and a sense of violation.

"If yours was the one at the end of the hall with the drawings of the little kids, then yes. They did."

Caid remembered the drawings well. She'd apparently done them herself, and, to his inexperienced eye they'd looked good. One in particular had struck him: the one showing a young girl holding the hand of an even younger boy as they faced a raging sea. It had hung at a forty-five-degree angle over her bed. Mia obviously liked kids. Only a while ago, she'd made it quite clear to him that her desire to teach children held more appeal than what he'd have thought she might want to do with her education. At the moment, though, seeing the distress in her face, Caid didn't know which had the bigger impact on him where she was concerned: the realization that he knew absolutely nothing about children, or the fact that he felt angry himself at the way her possessions had been violated.

Not liking the track his thoughts had taken, he waited for Mia's reaction to what he'd told her.

Despite the bright light of the moon, it was impossible for him to read her expression. Anyone who'd had her privacy violated as she had would be perfectly justified being upset. But she said nothing, seeming to pull into herself as the ocean droned on behind them.

He supposed he should be grateful that she was taking it so well, that she wasn't getting angry or hysterical or whatever it was he'd been afraid of. Instead, he found himself wondering just how much she could take before it all caved in on her. Or if she'd just numbed herself to the point where she couldn't feel anything at all.

"When I was at the house," he said, "I noticed a couple of prescription bottles with Jack's name on them in the bathroom. Has he been sick?"

She started to shake her head. Then her forehead pleated with a frown. "A couple of bottles? More than one?"

"Yeah. There were two. Both the same."

"You're sure?"

"Yes," he repeated. "I'm sure. The medicine cabinet was open, and they were sitting together on the middle shelf. The only reason I paid any attention to them was because they were the only things in the cabinet, other than some shaving stuff and a tube of toothpaste."

"Then he didn't plan to be gone. Don't you see? If he'd planned on being gone overnight, he'd have taken those things with him." She paused, her mind racing. "Especially those pills. He needs them, Caid. He's got a problem with his heart, and the doctor told him he absolutely has to take them on schedule. If he stops too abruptly, he could have a heart attack."

Jack had a bad heart? "Maybe he had some with him."

She shook her head. "I just picked up a new prescription two days ago. He only had a couple of pills left in the other bottle." Without thinking, she curled her fingers over his forearm. "Do you think he's okay?"

It wasn't her fear for Jack's health that caught Caid so unprepared. It was the way she'd reached for him, and the unexpected need he felt to assure her that everything would be all right. He had no business wanting to tell her any such thing. The feeling might not have troubled him quite so much had he not experienced it with her before. But she was looking to him for the reassurance she needed, and he couldn't honestly offer it. That bothered him, too.

"I don't know what to think." *Except,* he thought, *that I can't turn you out until I come up with some answers.*

That circumstance didn't disturb him quite as much as it had just a short while ago. He didn't question why that was. He simply acknowledged that Mia was an interesting woman—clever, he'd bet, and probably stubborn as hell under normal circumstances. But these weren't normal circumstances. And before he forgot why he was standing there with her in the moonlight, he figured, it was best to think of her only as the frightened daughter of a friend, who'd come to him because she had nowhere else to go. As restless as he was beginning to feel, had he been alone, he'd have gone down to his boat and polished brass or tinkered with the navigation system. He didn't want to leave her alone, though. After all, she felt safer when he was around.

Chapter 5

Caid didn't believe in dead ends. It wasn't his nature. To his way of thinking, there was always a way over, under, around or through an obstacle. So it followed that there had to be someone, somewhere, who had seen Jack since he'd left his daughter at the museum. A man didn't just vanish into thin air. Everyone left a trail.

That was why, as he and Mia headed back up the beach to his apartment, he had her go over, yet again, the details of the evening when Jack had last been seen. It was also why, later, pacing like a panther in his living room while she sat deceptively still in the corner of his sofa, he tried to make her recall as much as she could about what Jack had said and done the previous week. He wanted to know if his routine had varied, who he'd talked with and seen, his attitude toward his new business venture in general, and the museum job in particular.

Mia quietly abided behavior others would have found intimidating. She spoke with utter calm, exhibiting a kind of patience with his questions that told him she didn't blame him for his frustration when she couldn't come up with anything, because she shared that frustration herself. She was only beginning to know the man who was her father, she explained. And even though Jack had her living with him until she graduated and could support herself, their relationship was pretty tentative.

In the time she'd been with Jack, she'd met few of the people he knew. Her world revolved around her full load of classes and trips to the beach, where she sometimes spent hours with her pad, sketching the children she would see playing in the ocean. Jack's world seemed occupied with promoting his new business, his job adjusting claims, and, until last week, his friend Roselyn. Jack never had anyone to the house, and she'd only met the people in his office once—when Jack had had her meet him there the afternoon he took her to her first horse race. That had been right after she moved in. He'd introduced her then as the daughter of an old friend who would be staying with him for a while.

Mia had, both in wisdom and in charity, once conceded that it couldn't be easy for a man to suddenly discover he had an adult child. What Caid had begun to notice this evening, though, was the hesitant way Mia regarded Jack herself. She spoke of him as if he were only one step below the Holy Trinity. Yet Caid had the feeling she was afraid to believe Jack really cared about her.

He didn't expect that she would ever say as much. It wasn't the kind of thing a person ever wanted to consciously admit about a parent. Especially a parent she wanted very much to please. Caid understood the hollow ache of not being wanted, understood it better than she could possibly know. It had been a long time since he'd thought about his own mother or father. Longer still since he'd acknowledged any influence they'd had over him. Watching Mia pull protectively into herself as he continued to probe for some scrap of information that might help them find Jack, he didn't particularly appreciate that she'd made him recall the memory of them, either—even though he had the distinct feeling that she might be the one person in the world who would know exactly how it felt to be so completely alone.

Caid's feelings weren't quite so certain where Jack was concerned, however. Mia's absolute insistence that Jack wouldn't have gone anywhere overnight without his medication had thrown a kink in Caid's thinking. He wasn't prepared to absolve Jack of involvement in the theft, but that new bit of information made him concede that something else might be amiss.

That was why, having left the base in civilian attire on his lunch break the next day, Caid found himself at the offices of Independent Insurance Adjustments, hoping to get a look at Jack's calendar. The only lead Mia had come up with was the possibility that Jack had scheduled an appointment after he left the museum that he hadn't mentioned to her. It was a long shot, but it was all they had to go on.

"Isn't it just too awful?" the strawberry-blond receptionist whispered, leaning over her crossed arms to bat her baby blues up at Caid. "I mean, who could ever suspect someone as sweet as Jack? We just can't believe it. Well," she added, lowering her voice, "most of us can't, anyway. The police were actually here to arrest him, you know what I mean?"

"I think I do," Caid replied, seeing that his buddy could still charm the barely-out-of-high-school set. *Make the young ones feel wise and the old ones feel young,* Jack had once pronounced when a sergeant of lesser experience insisted on learning the secret of his legendary success with the ladies. "You haven't heard whether they've found him yet, have you?"

Bright curls danced around her face as she gave her head a negative shake. "We'd have all heard if they had. Some of the guys in back have a pool going to see who gets closest to the time they pick him up. You know, kinda like a Super Bowl thing? Anyway, Al, he kinda sets up all the office

pools, you know? Like, he's been keeping his radio on all
the time, so the whole office'll hear when they do.'' Her expression grew serious. Relatively speaking. ''What did you
say you wanted?''

''Tickets for a Chargers game. Jack told me if he wasn't
here, he'd leave them in his desk.'' His shrug was deceptively casual, like the blithely delivered excuse he hoped
would get him into Jack's office. ''I was supposed to have
picked them up a few days ago, but I got busy.''

The girl's gregariousness was probably what had gotten
her this job. She immediately flashed him a smile in the
hundred-watt range. ''Oh, I know what you mean. I get
sidetracked all the time, you know? Like, there's always so
much to remember to do. Most everybody here's been pretty
nice about it, though.''

Not sure what ''it'' was, certain only that he wasn't about
to ask, Caid offered her a smile. ''May I see if the tickets are
there?''

''Don't see why not. Everybody else has been though his
office. It's the last door on the right. Around there.''

She pointed over her left shoulder, then frowned at the
typewriter in front of her as if she knew she was supposed
to be doing something with it but had forgotten what it was.
Evidently giving up, she answered the ringing phone.

Except on one large, glassed-in office, there weren't actually any doors anywhere. The large space behind the re-
ception wall was divided into cubicles by six-foot-high
partitions. The occupants of the first two workstations were
ladies; the next two were men. He passed one cubicle that
seemed to be a storage area, nodded to the bespectacled man
who looked up from his ledgers in the next, then stopped by
the nameplate that read Jack Kowalski. Caid didn't know
why he noted the layout. He just did. Much as he noted ter-
rain on a mission.

The quick survey he took of Jack's office as he entered
was a little more detailed.

The room was pretty standard, as such work areas went. It held the usual desk, and a couple of client chairs. It also contained a small credenza that served as a combination file cabinet and bookshelf. It was the credenza that seemed to hold the most clues about the office's occupant.

Unlike the items many people used to personalize their space, Jack displayed no pictures of family. Like Caid, he had none. At least Caid had never heard him speak of any. But Jack's need to constantly occupy his amazingly quick mind could be seen in the small collection of brain-teasing puzzles scattered at one end of the wood surface. At the other sat an empty coffee cup with the triangular logo of SecuriTech—the only evidence in the room of the business Jack had started for himself—and two books of matches. One of the matchbooks was from a lounge Caid had never heard of. The other was from the diner around the corner where Roselyn worked.

Pocketing the matches from the lounge, Caid turned to the desk and the large appointment calendar by the telephone. It was open to Tuesday, the day Jack and Mia had been at the museum. Other than a small *x* by 9:00 p.m.—the time Mia had indicated she and Jack had arrived at the museum—there were no notations after three in the afternoon.

"Can I help you?"

Not by so much as a muscle was it apparent that the vaguely condescending request startled Caid. As if he had all the time in the world, he calmly looked up to see the burly character he'd noticed scratching his stomach in the third cubicle blocking the doorway. Despite the slacks and tie, he had the beefy look of a bouncer, and a definite air of temporary authority—that self-important attitude that spoke of someone left in charge when the boss was out.

"No thanks" was Caid's easy, and purposely pleasant, reply. "I'm just looking for some tickets. Jack said he'd left them here for me. The receptionist told me to come on back."

"I heard you tell her he'd left them in his desk. That's not where you were looking."

The sounds of a local news station drifted over the partition. The receptionist had said some guy named Al was monitoring his radio for the office pool. Since the volume had gone down within seconds of the big guy's arrival, Caid bet the office bookie had been more interested in monitoring their conversation over the sound of typewriters and ringing telephones than in waiting for a news flash.

The bulldog in the doorway stepped inside. Smelling vaguely of the beer he'd had with his lunch, he sauntered over to the credenza, checking it as if to see that nothing had been disturbed.

The move was obviously for show. He didn't notice the missing matches.

"Who are you?" he wanted to know.

"A friend of Jack's." The response was a cop-out. Caid didn't care. Not liking that he was getting awfully close to having to identify himself, he kept the conversation on his search. "I told you, I'm just looking for tickets. I've already paid for them, and I don't want to have to do it again."

Amazingly, the guy's annoying smirk softened. "Resign yourself to it. I always knew Kowalski was a crook. Wouldn't be surprised if he'd taken your money and never bought the tickets in the first place." With his beefy hand, he gave Caid a companionable slap on the back. "Let's say we give old Jack the benefit of the doubt on this one, though. Hey Al," he called out, his voice booming over the partition. "You were here when the cops came in the other morning. You know if they came across any football tickets in here?"

From the other side of the partition, Caid heard the squeak of chair springs. A moment later, a tall, wiry-looking fellow with sandy hair and a pocket protector in the pocket of his white shirt appeared in the doorway. His glance darted to Caid, then quickly to the man who'd just made himself comfortable in Jack's chair. From the way his jaw clenched, it didn't appear he was terribly happy with the way he'd been summoned.

"I don't know that they did, Keith," he replied, his low and disgruntled tone designed to let his co-worker know he found his volume inappropriate. "To the best of my knowledge, nothing has been removed from this area. If the tickets were supposed to be in his desk, I would imagine they still are."

"Nothing gets past Al," Keith obligingly explained, tipping back the chair. "He's the first one in in the morning and the last one out at night."

The man in the doorway had a pencil in his hand. He kept twirling it between his index finger and his thumb, the motion increasing at the hint that he'd been brownnosing. To his credit, he ignored the dig. "As I said, I don't know about any tickets. What I do know is that it isn't necessary to tell everyone you meet that Jack Kowalski is a crook."

"Damn." The snap of Keith's fingers was exaggerated; the sympathy in his voice totally insincere. "I keep forgetting he was your idol."

"I won't deny that I respected Jack." Al spoke to Caid, seeming either nervous or angry. The pencil in his hand picked up speed. "I very much admired the initiative he showed by starting up his own business. It takes a lot to make a new venture work, and he was getting more and more referrals all the time. Enough so that he'd planned to quit here by the end of this month. The only initiative some people have ever shown," he added, pointedly glancing back to the man lounging in Jack's chair, "was to marry the owner's daughter."

The chair sprang forward, protesting the weight of its occupant with a groan. Keith's skin mottled with fury, but not a word passed his tightly compressed lips—either because of an outsider's presence, or because he couldn't argue the point.

The look of impotence about the man made Caid decide it was the latter. The man Al had called Keith was all hot air.

It was as evident as the mustard on the windbag's purple paisley tie that there was no love lost between these two particular men. Caid, who was not at all impressed with him himself, suspected there was probably little love lost between Keith and anyone in the whole office. A position obtained by marriage usually demanded little real respect from anyone. Resentment was far easier to cultivate.

As if sensing that their visitor might realize just how powerless he was, yet refusing to be bested by a geek, the owner's son-in-law rose to his full six feet. Hands clenched into fists, he elbowed past his co-worker and all but stomped down the hall.

The man named Al remained. His glance darted to Caid, then to Jack's desk. A moment later, absently scratching at a pink patch of psoriasis near his receding hairline, he stepped toward the desk. "I'll help you," he offered, and pulled open one of the drawers.

"No need." Caid waved him off. "I've already looked through there."

The lie seemed harmless enough, given that he'd already found what he wanted—which was nothing, really. No sense taking up the guy's time. Just to make it look good, though, he quickly flipped through the calendar. "They're not here, either." With a philosophical shrug, he muttered, "Guess I'll have to buy another set after all."

The man called Al had stopped the seemingly perpetual motion with his pencil. Now he fidgeted with a paper clip. He seemed agitated, nervous. Judging from the tips of the chewed-up red pencils protruding from his pocket protector, Caid figured he was just the nervous type.

No doubt the little face-off with the office bully had left him more anxious than usual.

"If you'd like, you can leave your name with our receptionist, and she'll call you if they turn it up." His smile was hesitant, almost apologetic. "Or," he suggested, apparently thinking of their receptionist's tendency to get side-tracked, "give me your address, and I can have them delivered by our courier. I'd be happy to do it. Since you're a friend of Jack's," he added. "When is the game?"

Caid didn't have a clue when the Chargers were playing next. He was a Braves fan. He did know he didn't want to leave his name, though. Not even with this man who, apparently as a friend himself, had come to Jack's defense. It wasn't uncommon for police to question friends and acquaintances of a suspect. The last thing he wanted was the police knocking on his door, should they return to this office inquiring as to who had been asking after Jack.

"I appreciate the offer, buddy," Caid told him, because the man was only trying to be helpful. "But don't worry about it. I've taken enough of your time."

Offering a quick "Thanks," he left the cubicle. He said the same thing to Keith, when the man sent him a scorching glare on his way out of the office.

Caid dismissed the bigger man's animosity. It was Al he was interested in. Whether the man knew it or not, he'd provided Caid with more information than he could possibly have hoped to gain when he first arrived. Buried in the little disagreement between him and Keith had been a remark about Jack leaving his regular job at the end of the month. Mia had said that, according to Jack, his new business was doing well. But she hadn't said a word about him quitting so soon.

The reason Mia hadn't said anything was simple. She hadn't known about Jack's plans. She told Caid that, too, surprised by the news herself when he called while she was in his bathroom using his scissors on her hair. She'd been considering cutting her hair for weeks, thinking a shorter style might make her look more her age. Since the police were looking for a woman with long hair, there seemed no better time than the present to make the change.

"Did you know Jack was leaving his job?" he asked the instant she answered the phone by Caid's bed.

She hesitated, both at his brusqueness and his question. "Jack said he wanted the security business to be full-time," she replied, pushing her fingers through her newly cropped coif as she hurriedly tried to recall just what Jack had said. "He never said anything about leaving his regular job so soon, though. Where did you hear that he was?"

Caid's tone was as unenlightening as his response. "From someone in his office. Look, I've got to get back to work. We can talk when I get there tonight." He paused. "I'll bring dinner."

He had begun the conversation without any preamble, and he ended it without saying goodbye. He'd had a question he wanted answered, and once he had what he wanted, he was gone. The tactic was not unlike a military strike. In and out before the enemy even knew you were there.

In those thirty seconds, he'd even managed to convey a rather blunt message: Don't cook.

Mia was too realistic to be insulted. She was lousy in the kitchen, and she freely admitted it. Not that she even cared at the moment. As she hung up the telephone, she was more concerned with the fact that Caid had called at all. He wouldn't have done that had he not thought what he'd learned was important.

From his silence after she'd told him about Jack's medication last night, it seemed he believed Jack might actually be in more trouble than he'd first thought. He wouldn't say what kind of trouble, though. That annoyed her a little. Even if he was only guessing, she wanted to know what he thought might be happening. She wasn't a child, and she didn't want to be treated like one. In any respect.

Grabbing a fistful of Caid's pillow, she jerked the case off and added it to the sheets she'd also stripped from the bed. At the moment, annoyance—fueled by fatigue—was a lot easier to deal with than the other emotions she could have faced.

She hadn't slept at all last night. Very little the night before. Yet, even as tired as she was, her mind would leap from one awful possibility to the next the moment she tried to rest. What was worse were the brief flashes of claustrophobia she'd so suddenly feel just as she started to drift off—an awful sensation that seemed to bear down on her from out of nowhere, making it hard to breathe and jerking her awake with her heart racing. So instead of lying down after Caid left this morning, she had kept herself as busy as possible. By late afternoon, she'd worked her way through his entire apartment, polishing floors and the bathroom until they shone, and tackling the small mountain of laundry growing in the corner of his bedroom closet.

It wasn't as if she'd been snooping around his bedroom. She'd merely gone in to vacuum, and had opened the closet to hang up a jacket he'd tossed over a chair. Even without poking her nose in places it didn't belong, she'd discovered some rather interesting revelations about the man who occupied the decidedly Spartan space.

If the collection of books in the tall bookcase and the picture of the breaching whales above his bed were any indication, Caid was fascinated with the sea. Subjects ranged from marine life to the topography of the ocean floor. He was interested in boats, too. All manner of them. Ornately carved vessels created by the warlike Vikings, nineteenth-century windjammers, modern battleships. Even his bedspread was a swirl of the sea's deep blues and greens.

As compelling as she found his interests—and she had always been drawn by the power of the sea herself—it was his laundry that ultimately claimed her attention.

Specifically, his underwear.

Mia did Jack's laundry all the time, but he wore something he called boxers. Caid wore what magazine ads she'd seen called briefs, the white cotton kind. But it was what she came across atop a pair of running shorts that was definitely more . . . interesting.

It was white, too, but consisted of nothing more than a wide elastic band, two small straps, and a pouch. A rather sizable pouch, too, considering the skimpiness of the rest of the garment.

Holding it by one of the thin straps, she turned it around, not quite sure what it was, much less how it might be worn. Or even if the thing was meant to be worn at all.

With a shrug, she tossed the garment on the pile of whites and kept sorting through the jeans, socks, T-shirts and uniforms. The faint dizziness of fatigue made itself felt every once in a while, but it wasn't until she had his laundry folded in neat stacks on the coffee table, and his uniform shirts pressed to match the creases of the shirts in his closet, and she had sat down on the sofa to fold the last load of towels, that she gave in to her body's demand for the sleep it had been denied.

The room was dim, the towels were warm, and mercifully, when she curled up with the towels in the corner of the couch, the odd feeling of suffocation didn't make itself felt.

She'd left the drapes closed again. That was the first thing Caid noticed when he opened the door. The second, from the way she jerked upright when he stepped inside and set the two white bags on the breakfast bar, was that she must have been sound asleep. Her quiet "Hi" had a distinctly startled sound to it, and when he crossed the beige carpet to open the drapes and let in some light, she squinted to accustom her eyes to the brightness.

Caid suspected that she hadn't been sleeping well at night. Early this morning, well before dawn, he'd heard her get a drink of water. A while later, she'd turned the television on low. As quiet as she was being, he probably wouldn't have noticed the sounds at all, except that he'd been listening for her. He'd had a little trouble sleeping himself.

At the moment, he wasn't considering how difficult it had been to know she was down there, probably feeling alone and uncertain. Or how he'd made himself stay where he was rather than go down to keep her company because he remembered how tempting she'd been in the moonlight. He wasn't even wondering what his clothes were doing all folded and stacked on the coffee table—or why, when he opened the door, he'd inhaled the fresh scents of pine cleaner and lemon oil. As Mia rose, picking up a towel that fell from the pile on the sofa as she did, the sole focus of his attention was her hair. What was left of it, anyway.

Three strides had him squarely in front of her, dwarfing her with his large frame. "What have you done?"

His hand shot out to touch the ends of the dark, shining hair curving below her jaw. The beautiful length was no longer there.

Caid wasn't thinking when he reached toward her. He had no idea how the disappointment he felt shadowed his face, or how that dark, forbidding expression might be interpreted. He wanted only to touch her hair, as if to confirm for himself that so much of it was actually gone.

But Mia couldn't read his mind. Ever since she'd seen the police in front of Jack's house, old instincts had unconsciously resurrected themselves. In the awful insecurity of the past few days, years of living in relative peace were slowly being erased by old patterns of survival. That was why, the instant Caid's hand came up, she saw only its quickness, its direction and his displeasure. Her heart leaping to her throat, she flinched, her own hands coming up to ward off the blow as she jerked her head away.

But the blow didn't come.

Slowly her hands fell.

It was Caid who looked as though he'd been struck.

"My God," he breathed, realizing what she'd thought he was about to do.

His incredulous glance swept her pale face. "I wasn't going to hit you." He started to reach for her. Thinking better of it, he let his hands fall to his sides. "Honest, Mia. I wasn't. What made you think I could?"

For a moment, all Mia could do was look at Caid, the breath she couldn't yet release making her lungs feel as if they were about to explode. His expression was so stark, as if he could no more believe what she'd done than what she'd thought he was about to do.

Her breath shuddered out. Mortified, her head still clouded from lack of sleep, she couldn't begin to explain why she'd reacted as she had. All she knew at the moment was that her reaction had been an insult to his integrity, and that she couldn't stand the way he was looking at her.

Heart still racing, knees weak, she sank to the edge of the sofa. "I wasn't thinking. I'm sorry. I just didn't know what you were doing."

She still wasn't sure.

"Your hair." He nodded toward her, looking far more cautious than she'd ever seen him. "I was just surprised to see what you'd done."

She touched her nape, her hand still shaking. "I cut it."

Obviously he could see that. Still totally discomposed by her overreaction, it didn't occur to her to wonder why he would care one way or the other what she'd done to it. He didn't like the new style, though. There was no doubt in her mind about that.

"I've been meaning to cut it for a long time. It'll be easier to take care of this way."

"A long time meaning since yesterday?"

"No. I mean for a long time. Weeks."

The caution began to ease from his expression. His next question was spoken in a gently chiding tone. "The matter of your description being on the news didn't have anything to do with it?"

Her chin came up. "Maybe. A little. But," she added, because that truly wasn't the whole reason, "I've wanted it shorter."

"It is that."

"What's wrong with it?"

Caid shrugged, more relieved than he'd have thought possible to see the flash of spirit enter her eyes. He couldn't have begun to describe how he'd felt when he saw her shrink from him. "There isn't a thing wrong with it. If you want to look like a boy."

If he hadn't turned just then, she would have caught the full brunt of his smile. As it was, she caught a hint of it anyway, the unexpected softening in his expression effectively silencing the protest she'd been about to make. Her hair wasn't that short. But she wasn't about to defend how she looked to him. Especially if he thought she looked like a boy. She was going to be grateful to him, though. He wasn't going to hold her reaction against her.

More relieved by that than he could imagine, she stood up. Crossing her arms loosely, so as not to draw attention to her lack of endowment and thus enhance the image he apparently had of her, she watched him glance at the clothing on the coffee table.

"What's all this?" he wanted to know.

"Your laundry." She pushed her shoulders back, standing straighter. "I had to do something today, so I cleaned your apartment. Don't worry," she added hurriedly. "I didn't move anything from where you had it. And I didn't touch your desk."

"I appreciate that."

From her quick frown, he had the feeling she couldn't tell if he meant he appreciated the cleaning or the fact that she hadn't invaded his privacy any more than she had. Whether she knew it or not, despite her obviously conscientious efforts, she was getting into places she didn't belong.

Cleaning his apartment was one thing. He was willing to concede her need to keep occupied, and he wasn't quite so ready to begrudge her the activity as he had yesterday when he'd found her in his kitchen. He just wasn't at all sure how he felt about her having taken care of his clothes.

An empty basket sat at the end of the couch. Picking it up, he piled in his neatly folded colored T-shirts, his undershirts and his briefs. Since he was going upstairs anyway, he might as well take them with him.

"It'll all be finished as soon as I fold the towels," he heard her say as the item she'd wadded atop his cutoffs fell when he added his shorts to the basket.

Seeing what had fallen, she frowned. "I wasn't sure how to fold that. Or which stack it went with."

"This?"

He scooped the article under discussion up from the carpet, letting it dangle from his index finger by its wide strap.

Caid didn't know how the rest of the world folded them, but every buck private in boot camp—of the male variety anyway—learned the exact way a jock was to be folded and stowed in his locker. He wasn't sure it was necessary to show Mia the procedure, though. He doubted she came across very many.

Or any, for that matter. From the way she was looking at it now, he doubted she realized what it was.

"I didn't know if it would shrink, either. I didn't think it would, because of all the elastic, but I washed it in cold water just to be sure."

"You did, did you?"

Nodding, she gave the towel she picked up a snap and began to fold it.

"Hot probably would have been better. I get pretty sweaty when I run."

"You wear that when you run?"

He knew she was curious. It was her nature. That was why he could have sworn she was about to ask how the object was worn. Or where. Or some such thing.

That was exactly what Mia wanted to do. But she didn't trust the glint in Caid's eye at all. His mouth looked as hard as ever, but there was a smile lighting his blue eyes that turned them to the color of a summer sky. He was laughing at her. She was sure of it.

He was waiting for her to say something, too, but she wasn't about to ask what the contraption had to do with running. The thing obviously wasn't a sweatband. Nor was it intended to hold identification and house keys. Having figured out that much, she realized there was only one place something like that would fit under sweats or running shorts. She'd changed enough diapers at the orphanage to have a basic idea of male anatomy. And heaven knew some of the swim trunks men wore on the beach hid precious little. It was just the way Caid was watching her—and perhaps the size of the pouch swinging from the end of his finger—that she found a little disconcerting.

Feeling her cheeks heat, pragmatically telling herself it was only logical that, since he was such a big man everywhere else, he was probably big there, too, she watched him fold the strips of elastic into the pouch and load the rest of his clothes into the basket.

He was still smiling to himself when, picking up the basket, he headed toward the stairs. That smile was still there—inside him, anyway—when he came back down to find her frowning into the sacks on the counter, trying to figure out what he'd brought for dinner.

Chapter 6

"You went to Jack's office?"

At Mia's question, Caid nodded. He wasn't looking at her, though. He sat on the sofa, a cushion away from her, his elbows propped on his knees as he eyed the tortilla-wrapped concoction he was preparing to attack.

"That's where I heard about him quitting. What do you know about the people he works with? Jack ever talk about any of them?"

The last question was barely out of his mouth when, with more gusto than grace, he went for the burrito. Mia watched, fascinated. The man's stomach had to be made of cast iron. Before he'd added jalapeño peppers, he'd emptied two packets of fiery hot sauce into the tortilla.

Her tongue still tingling from the microscopic bit of jalapeño he'd coaxed her to try, Mia broke off a piece of taco. Her taste buds were the only thing about her that hadn't easily adapted to the Western world. She missed sticky rice steamed in coconut milk, and the noodle soup called *pho*.

And what she would give for a great big *buoi*. Grapefruit came close, but they weren't nearly so juicy or sweet.

"He'd mention Jessica every so often," she said, pushing Caid's beer closer to him in case he needed it when the jalapeños hit. "When he would, it was because one of the people in the office had gotten upset with her that day for taking so long to make copies or something. I guess this is her first job and he thinks they should give her a break."

"I'm sure she appreciates the thought," she heard Caid mutter. "What about a guy named Keith? The one that's married to the owner's daughter?" He raised his burrito again, tilting it to catch the strands of shredded cheese and heaven-only-knew-what-else oozing from the end. "Jack ever mention him?"

A quarter of the messy culinary creation disappeared.

"All the time. He said he's a real pain in the butt."

A strange choking sound escaped his throat when Caid swallowed.

Concerned, Mia glanced toward him. Seeing the light of a smile in his eyes, wondering if he was laughing at her, she turned back to her taco. "Well, that's what he called him," she said defensively. "He said Keith never did anything other than make life miserable for a couple of people in the office. Jessica was one of them."

"Was the other a guy named Al?"

Jack hadn't said. However, as she watched Caid devour his burrito with considerably more enthusiasm than he had her meat loaf, she did say that Al often went to the races with Jack. He'd gone with them the day Jack took her to Del Mar. He'd seemed very nice.

"Do you think any of those people know anything?" she wanted to know.

Caid doubted it. He wasn't really sure why he was asking about these people, anyway—unless it was just to hear Mia talk. There was something about her voice that he found soothing. Its gentleness, maybe. Or perhaps it was the intriguing inflections of her accent that drew him. Whatever it was, the dulcet sounds affected him like the sounds of the sea—subtly calming, yet always mysterious.

A man could drown in the sea.

Not liking the track of his thoughts, not wanting to be drawn to her at all, he decided he kept her talking only so that he wouldn't have to answer the question he knew she wanted to ask. Mia had already confirmed that none of the people Jack worked with were involved in his security business. And it seemed from the comments Jessica and Al had made today that none of them, other than Keith, believed Jack was guilty of theft.

Caid wished he felt the same way.

"If you don't think anyone in his office knows what he's doing, tell me what you think has happened."

Caid stopped in midbite. There it was. The question he'd hoped to avoid.

Given the circumstances, the conclusions taking shape in his brain would do little for her peace of mind. Mia wasn't anywhere near as calm about all this as she tried to appear. She had only picked at her dinner. And when he'd turned on the television a few minutes ago, inadvertently hitting the volume button as he had, the unexpected blast of sound had sent her a good six inches off the couch.

He'd turned the volume down low. Now, as she waited for him to respond, that droning murmur was the only sound in the quiet room.

"I don't know that conjuring up scenarios is all that wise, Mia." Not in this case, anyway. "Let's just see what happens tomorrow."

"I want to know what you think," she persisted, reaching for one of the white paper bags the Mexican food had come in. "Even if it's just a guess, you must have some opinion about what he's doing."

"I do. But you wouldn't like what I've come up with." Paper crinkled as he wadded up yellow wrappers. Handing them to her to add to the bag, he muttered, "I'm not all that crazy about it myself."

The warning stilled her movements. Or maybe it was the fact that he'd admitted to having reached some sort of conclusion that brought her eyes to his face. "I don't have to like any of what's going on, Caid. I can't say that I really *like* having to hole up in a stranger's apartment, waiting for something to happen. Or that I'm having to rely on someone I don't even know to dig around for information because I can't leave his apartment. I have no idea what's going on outside these walls. If you have an idea, I need to know what it is.

"Please don't misunderstand," she added, her voice quiet despite the agitation she couldn't quite hide. "I'll never be able to thank you enough for helping me. But Jack is my father, and I need to know anything you've come up with about what has happened . . . whether you think I can handle it or not. Just because you've been kind enough to let me stay under your roof, that doesn't give you the right to make decisions about what I should or shouldn't know."

I'm not making decisions for you, Caid started to say. But he knew as he held her level gaze that neither of them would have believed it. He was accustomed to being in charge, to deciding how much he needed to pass on. He did it every day.

Since he was just being who he was, he wasn't about to apologize. "Fine," he conceded. "If you want something else to worry about, then I'll tell you how it looks to me right now. I think it's awfully coincidental that Jack planned to leave his job in a couple of weeks. It's even more coincidental that he planned to leave his job just before he was scheduled to test the security system of a museum exhibiting a major collection of jewels."

"But his medicine—"

"Isn't that big a deal, if you think about it," he said interrupting her. "All he had to do was get another prescription before word of the theft hit the street the next morning. Was his prescription refillable?"

Mia hesitated. "Yes."

"Then he could easily tell the pharmacist he'd lost the one you just picked up for him. After a call to his doctor, he'd be back in business. He could even have left his other prescription at the house to throw you off."

There didn't seem to be a way for her to counter his last statement. So, looking uncertain, she didn't try. "He never said anything about quitting, though. Not to me."

"There's a lot he's never said about a lot of things, Mia. Not to you and not to anyone else. Like that fact that you're his daughter. Did he ever act all that accountable to you?" he went on, neither expecting nor getting an answer. "You said yourself you were just beginning to know him. Isn't it possible that you haven't gotten to know him at all?"

She hadn't wanted to be spared the possibilities, so he'd given it to her point-blank. Both barrels. The scenario he'd drawn was only a possibility. After all, everything he had to go on so far was strictly circumstantial. But she'd wanted to know what he thought. So he'd told her.

He hadn't meant the words to sound as harsh as they had, however. And he certainly hadn't intended to cause the flash of pain she tried to hide as she turned away. There was no time to do anything about it, though. As Mia stood, the white bag in her hand, her glance fell on the television.

Her quiet gasp as she sat back down had him looking toward the television, too.

The picture on the screen was of her passport photo.

Caid grabbed the remote-control unit. An instant later, the anchorwoman's polished voice filled the room.

" . . . for questioning in the recent theft of a sixteenth-century crown from Pacific Museum. According to neighbors, Mia Tu had only recently arrived in the United States. She has lived with Kowalski for the past three months, and is believed to be his girlfriend. Neither she nor Kowalski has been seen since Tuesday night.

"On the national front, the recent decrease in unemployment rates has resulted in lower—"

The sound level dropped at the push of a button.

"How did they get my passport?"

Mia's voice was an incredulous whisper. Her eyes were huge.

The bag she'd held had fallen to the floor.

Caid picked it up. "I imagine the police took it when they searched Jack's house." He paused. "You said the guard at the museum was the only person you saw or talked to that night?"

Her nod was almost imperceptible.

"Since he was the one who gave the police your description earlier, he must have confirmed your ID."

Mia sat unnaturally still as she continued to stare at the talking head on the television. Not by so much as a blink did she betray the fear in her eyes. It was as if, by keeping it inside, she could deal with it, could keep the anxiety from taking over.

"What am I going to do?"

The question wasn't intended for Caid. For all practical purposes, he might not have been there. She had simply spoken the thought aloud.

Caid answered anyway.

"Just what you've been doing. Jack had to leave a trail, Mia. Sooner or later, it'll turn up. What you've got going in your favor right now is that you're still wanted only for questioning. That's a lot different than having an arrest warrant out on you." Given the fact that she was purposely making herself scarce, however, that circumstance could very well change.

"I can't go back, Caid."

She turned to him then, outwardly composed, inwardly terrified. "I've spent my life dreaming about America. About my father and his country. My mother's land doesn't want people like me. There is nothing more important to the Vietnamese than lineage. It's the source of each person's identity. Family is everything. From the living, to the ancestors whose spirits are revered, and to those yet to be born. There is no way to break that bond or the loyalty family demands. Except to disgrace it. That was what my mother did when she became pregnant by an American. Her family disowned her when they learned of my father. They did it publicly. In the newspaper.

"She had nothing after that. Except me," Mia continued quietly. "And she was all I had before she died. I never knew the security of an extended family. I only knew I didn't belong. That I never really had. Jack is my father. My family. I refuse to believe he has abandoned me."

For several seconds, Caid said nothing. He had just been told, quite eloquently, that he could shove his theory about Jack. But that wasn't what turned his eyes hard, or his words deceptively soft.

"I understand loyalty, Mia." He lived his own life, after all, by a code that demanded absolute fidelity to his corps and his country. "But there's a difference between loyalty and blind faith. Or loyalty and a dream. I prefer to deal in realities. If you want to hold on to a fistful of nothing, that's your business. Just prepare yourself for a few falls. I'm not saying Jack has set you up. Hell, for all I know, the reason he was in such a hurry that night was because he had a hot date with a poker game in Reno and doesn't even know he's in trouble. But family will dump on you just as fast as the next guy. You can count on it."

"That doesn't have to be true."

"Oh, yeah?" His eyes were hard, his voice was flat. "Just look at what they did to your mother."

The muscles in his neck were taut as he wadded the sack in his hands and carried it in to put it in the trash. That same tension fairly rippled through his body when, discovering it was full, he took the bag from beneath the sink and carried it out the door to the Dumpster in the parking lot.

Hugging her arms to herself, Mia watched him march past the kitchen window, his stride filled with a kind of anger she didn't understand. What she did understand, though, was that she'd touched a nerve. A rather raw one, from the looks of it.

Instead of considering how very precarious her own existence was at the moment, Mia could think only of how thankful she was to believe in the dreams and ideals Caid's cynicism denied him. He might think her a fool—and she might very well be one for wanting to believe in a man she'd only started to know. But she had something Caid apparently didn't: the ability to dream, to hope. She thought it sad that his own bitterness had robbed him of something so precious. And she thought it quite unfair that he should have taken all she had—that ability to hope—and shaken it so badly with his remark about her mother.

Caid didn't say much when he returned. He had some paperwork to do before Monday, so he took it upstairs to finish while Mia tried to study for a psychology quiz she might, or might not, be taking next week. Tomorrow he would drive down to Pacific Museum and see if the guard Mia had encountered was on duty. Caid was fairly sure there wouldn't be an arrest warrant out for Jack if the police had anything on the other man. But the guard might have seen something Mia had missed. It was entirely possible, of course, that the police had instructed him to keep his mouth shut and the trip would prove a waste of time. On the other hand, being interviewed by the police and the press could be the most exciting thing to have happened to the guy in months. He could be more than happy to retell his story to a curious museum visitor.

It was worth a shot.

Caid figured it would also be worth his time to track down someone who would know where a person in Mia's position stood as far as the Immigration and Naturalization Service was concerned. He'd ask—hypothetically, of course—what her risk of deportation was, since, next to the police themselves, that seemed to be her biggest fear. Aliens weren't usually deported unless they had entered the country illegally, were criminals or were considered undesirable for some other reason. Though he didn't know for sure, suspicion of criminal activity, or even association with a criminal—if Jack had actually taken the crown—might well qualify as "some other reason." But who knew what a bureaucracy would decide?

In Caid's estimation, fearing the unknown was a monumental waste of time. If what he learned tomorrow wasn't good, Mia would at least know what she faced and could plan accordingly. If what he discovered wasn't all that bad, she could stop worrying about it.

Theoretically, the philosophy was sound. When Caid told Mia what he would do, and why, she could even appreciate his logic. But Caid was a man who had a pretty good idea of what his day would involve when he woke up every morning, so he wasn't facing many unknowns at the moment. Mia took nothing for granted. Ever. Until the very second she raised her hand to take her oath and become a citizen of her father's land, she would worry that the day might never come. Five years had to pass from the time of her arrival in the States before she could become a citizen. An awful lot had happened to her already—and she still had four years to go.

Thinking about what had happened to her was exactly what Mia was trying not to do when, hours later, she tossed her pillow to the other end of the couch to see if her chances of falling asleep would improve in a different position. The lamp on the end table was on low, but the dim glow had been in her eyes. She wouldn't turn it off, though. The dark had become too threatening. Almost as threatening as the doubts Caid had planted in her head about her father. She could almost have hated him for putting them there.

Punching her pillow, resigned to the thoughts that plagued her, she curled up on her side and wondered if Caid was asleep. Since she hadn't heard a single sound from overhead for well over two hours, she assumed he must be. No doubt he would be quite annoyed if she woke him just because she could use some company. She seemed to annoy him a lot—especially when they inadvertently touched while moving about the apartment.

Whenever that happened, Caid's jaw would lock and he would ease away, as if he found her touch offensive. Yet she was constantly aware of his watching her, of his glance moving over her body. The look was a bold one, disturbing, provocative. As intriguing to her as the man himself. He'd said she looked like a boy, yet the way his eyes darkened when he watched her mouth as she spoke made her feel very much like a woman. Even tonight, when he'd come down the last time to give her one of his T-shirts to sleep in, his glance had moved from her mouth to her breasts and back again as she'd asked if there was anything she could do for him.

She'd never known a man who could make her skin feel hot just by looking at her. Or a man who made her wonder how it would feel to have his hard body cover hers. But she was certain any heat she'd seen in Caid's eyes was mostly the heat of annoyance with her presence. His offer to get what information he could about her position with the immigration service had no doubt been prompted as much by his desire to be rid of her as by his need to help her because of her father.

It was as she considered what an imposition she must be—and wished she had somewhere else to go—that her eyes closed and her thoughts finally became random enough for her to notice the sounds beyond the apartment's walls. A train whistle moaned in the distance, announcing the approach of an Amtrak on its way north. Water ran in the pipes next door. From somewhere along the highway came the honk of a horn. The sounds had a peaceful, lulling effect, and as the blasts of the train's whistle grew louder, she imagined herself on that train, headed away from all the doubts and insecurities she'd once thought she'd left half a world away.

The sound of the train began to ebb. As it did, a barely audible scratching noise drifted toward her. A few moments later, it came again; then, after a while, what sounded like the faint clink of glass. On the edge of sleep, not sure she'd really heard anything at all, Mia opened her eyes to glance around the room. In the dim pool of light cast by the lamp, she looked to the darkened television and the wall of drapes opposite where she lay. But there was nothing to be seen, and the sound had stopped. Certain it was just the stress of the past few days making her hypersensitive, she began to drift off again.

She had no idea how long she'd lain there when the lamp on the end table snapped off.

At the small click, Mia shot bolt upright. Had she not, the knife slicing past her face would have been buried in her neck. As it was, the suddenness of her movement, and her impact with a very solid arm, must have knocked the weapon away. Something heavy hit the coffee table as, her scream clotting in her throat, she started to her feet.

She didn't quite make it. As she raised up, she met a pair of large, gloved hands. One went over her mouth, so hard that her lip jammed against her teeth. The other clamped around the back of her neck and squeezed.

The indistinguishable black shadow didn't speak. By its size and strength, she didn't doubt that it was a man pulling her mercilessly by her head as he looked for where the knife might have landed. The coppery taste of fear sat on her tongue. It mixed with the taste of sheer terror as he jerked her around in the darkness. Her leg hit the coffee table painfully as he turned her toward the apartment's door. It sat ajar, a pale thread of light from the courtyard leaking through the six-inch gap. Mia had no idea what was happening. She had no idea who this man was, or why he was doing this to her. Her heart pounding, shaking so hard inside that her knees felt as stable as damp grass, she knew only that she wasn't going anywhere with him, if that was what he now had in mind. Not willingly, anyway. If she'd learned anything on the streets, it was when to give in and when to fight back. She remembered those lessons as clearly as if she'd learned them yesterday.

Without another thought, she made herself go limp. At worst, the tactic would earn her a blow. At best, her attacker might think she'd fainted and bend down to reach for her.

The Fates were with her. As she sank toward the floor, the leather-covered hand left her mouth to grab her under the arms. Keeping her arms pressed to her sides so that he couldn't get a grip, she screamed for Caid at the top of her lungs. Before the shadow could jerk her up again, she'd screamed again, then bit his arm through his shirtsleeve when he reached down to cover her mouth.

His yelp of pain was cut off by a low, succinct curse, and the sound of something heavy hitting the floor overhead. Had there been rafters, they would have fairly shaken with the footsteps stomping toward the stairs.

Those footsteps were still too far away when Mia felt herself being pulled up by her hair, her aggressor's considerable anger at her ploy making itself plainly felt. As much as his hold stung, she refused to set her feet. He could drag her if he wanted. No way would she make it easy. She'd just thought to grab his legs to try to trip him when he must have decided he wouldn't be able to get away from whoever was coming fast enough with her fighting him. In the space of a frantic heartbeat, he vaulted for the door just as Caid hit the top of the stairs and came barreling down.

Light from the security lamps in the courtyard streamed through the entry. Without even seeming to pause, Caid took one look at Mia scooting backward on the floor, turned to the gaping door and dived out it himself.

"He had a knife" was all Mia managed before it registered on some obscure plane of her benumbed consciousness that Caid was already gone—and that he'd just run outside in his underwear.

Not even aware of what she was doing, Mia kept scooting away from that door. She didn't feel the sting of her scalp, or the raw scrape on her leg. Nor did she notice the blood at the corner of her mouth. She just kept moving back in the faint gray light, as if to put as much distance as possible between herself and the door—and the shape of the wicked-looking carving knife on the carpet a few feet from the coffee table.

She had herself flattened to the wall, her knees drawn to her chest, when, a seeming eternity later, Caid came back. He said nothing as he closed the door and turned on the overhead light. But it occurred to her, as she watched him cautiously come toward her, that she'd never seen anyone look as dangerous as he did at that moment. His eyes were cold; his expression as hard as stone.

That was how his near-naked body appeared to her, too. He wore nothing but a pair of skimpy white briefs and a set of dog tags on a silver chain—and every beautifully developed muscle in his chest and legs and arms looked as if it were carved of granite. Hard. Unyielding. When he saw the knife and bent to pick it up with a corner of the blanket that had fallen off the sofa, only the pulse hammering in his neck betrayed him as mere human flesh.

It was impossible to tell what he was thinking as he turned over the sharply honed instrument. But as Mia watched the play of muscles in his back when he set the knife on the table, she couldn't help thinking that whoever it was that had just escaped should bless his good fortune. From the sheer power contained in Caid's body, she didn't doubt he could have snapped the man in half.

As oblivious of his state of undress as Mia was aware of it, Caid came down on his haunches in front of her. His eyes searching her face, he slowly reached out his hand.

Fury and gentleness warred within him. The fury was in his eyes and the clench of his jaw at the sight of the blood on her lip. The gentleness was in his touch as he moved his index finger to the swelling corner of her mouth.

"Did he cut you anywhere else?"

"No. I . . . no," she concluded, because she didn't know what else she wanted to say.

"Let's get you over to the couch."

"I'm all right."

Caid doubted that. She looked as if she were about to break. "You don't look all right. Humor me. Okay?"

She made no move to cooperate. Except to hug her knees tighter, she didn't move at all. A picture flashed in Caid's mind just then. Of her. Huddled very much as she was now. Only younger. Much younger.

"Did you see him?" she asked.

To Caid, her voice sounded stronger than it had any right to be. "I'm afraid I didn't. I checked in the shrubs and under the cars, but he could have gone anywhere." When it came to tracking, Caid was good. Better than good. But he also knew his priorities. He hadn't been about to play cat and mouse with Mia inside, alone and unprotected. Nor had he thought it a good idea to hang around outside in his skivvies and have some neighbor call the police on him. "Did you?"

She shook her head, pushing her trembling fingers through her hair. As she did, she winced. "All I can tell you is that he had gloves on. He just came at me with that knife. I never even heard him come in."

As she'd spoken, Caid had locked his fingers around her wrist to draw her hand from where she rubbed her scalp. Her assailant had used a glass cutter and a suction cup on the window by the door. Caid had noticed the neat ten-inch hole, dead even with his doorknob, when he came back in. All the guy had to do was reach through the hole, lift the security chain and turn the dead bolt. Piece of cake.

"I doubt he made much noise," he said, far more concerned with her unnatural calm than with the ease with which his domain had been breached.

His eyes steady on hers, he took her face between his hands. Gently, because he had no idea how bad off she was. "Tell me where you're hurt, Mia."

"I'm okay."

"I need to know. I think it might be a good idea to get you away from here. But I'm not taking you anywhere if you shouldn't be moved."

She didn't think to ask him where he would take her. For that moment, she thought of nothing other than the way his fingers slipped upward through her hair as he angled her head to see what had caused her to flinch. When she told him her head was sore only because her hair had been pulled and not because it had been knocked against anything, he seemed satisfied—though the tension she could feel radiating from his body did increase perceptibly.

He wanted to know what else her attacker had done. His hands never left her as she told him as best she could everything she remembered from the moment she'd heard the faint click of the lamp being turned off. By now she was accustomed to the way he took seemingly insignificant things and asked questions about them until she reached some point she'd forgotten. He'd done it with her before. About Jack. But there was a difference this time.

His tone, while matter-of-fact, as always, was quieter than usual. His expression, except for the darkly dangerous glint in his eyes, seemed different, too. More concerned. Or maybe he was just preoccupied. In a very abstract sort of way, she found the hard lines of his face incredibly compelling. It was like viewing a sculpture close up. She'd never seen Caid quite so close before, so close that she could count the individual black lashes surrounding his eyes, and the weathered creases fanning from their corners.

He was a beautiful man. She doubted very much that he would like to hear that, though. He was surprisingly tender, too. And that she was sure he wouldn't want to hear. It amazed her a little that a man as callused as he could possess a touch so gentle. But that was exactly what he was with her as he drew his hands from her neck, across her shoulders and down her arms to unwrap them from around her knees.

He touched her surely, as if her body were as familiar to him as his own and he was determined to find any change in it. Carefully he drew his hands down her legs and felt the small knot where she'd banged into the coffee table. Then he carried that touch back up her calves and on to her waist, asking again if she hurt anywhere. There was something almost mystical about his touch. To Mia, as she told him again that she was all right, it seemed to change the very quality of the trembling inside her.

"I'm not hurt, Caid. Honest."

His reply was an utterly ambiguous "Okay."

Having assured himself that she wasn't badly hurt, Caid drew himself to his feet. She needed ice on her lip, and he wanted to get her over to the breakfast bar, where the light was better. It hadn't taken him but a few seconds to realize the reason Mia hadn't moved before. The surge of adrenaline that had allowed her to fight off her assailant had long since dissipated. All the strength had drained out of her.

So Caid, being Caid, didn't listen when she said she'd be okay if he'd give her a minute. He saw only that she needed to get from point A to point B and that she couldn't do it under her own steam. Sliding one arm under her knees, the other across her back, he lifted her as easily as he would have a child.

The moment he had her in his arms, he realized that picking her up had been a mistake. As he had checked her over, he'd tried not to think about the silkiness of her skin, or the strength he could feel in her slender muscles. He'd also quite deliberately avoided imagining her shape beneath the loose cotton T-shirt she wore. Having his hands on her had been difficult enough. Now, holding her, he could feel her trembling.

Something inside him was trembling, too.

He didn't want to acknowledge whatever it was, but as he carried her to the breakfast bar, it felt as if a lock had just broken on something deep inside him.

Caid didn't have any stools, so when he reached the bar, he sat her on the waist-high counter. He'd thought he would let her go—so that he could get the ice. He'd even started to when, with a tremulous smile, he saw her hug her arms around herself in anticipation of his pulling away.

He couldn't do it. He didn't know a hell of a lot about offering comfort, but he knew that leaving her just then—if only to go across the room—wasn't what he should do. She really looked as if she could use a pair of arms. For whatever it was worth, she was welcome to his.

Hating the desolation in her eyes, he reached for her.

"It's okay," he whispered when he felt her stiffen. "I'm just going to hold you."

The words were spoken even as Caid gathered her to him. She heard them, but she didn't quite believe what seemed to be happening. He wanted to hold her. He *was* holding her—and as she drew her small fists between them, huddling into herself and into him, she had never felt so uncertain in her life.

Mia had never needed anything as desperately as she did the solid strength she felt wrapping itself around her just then. Caid's body felt warm, his chest and arms impossibly hard. Impossibly secure. But in those scattered seconds, when she didn't know how to react or what she was supposed to do, the very core of her own strength had never felt more threatened. He was, if only for that moment, taking the burden of being so completely alone from her—and that knowledge threatened to break the tenuous hold of her already questionable composure.

It was easier to hang on when she had no one but herself to rely on, when she had no choice. He was making holding on that much harder.

"Relax, honey." Caid's hand skimmed up her back, his touch as reassuring as his voice. "It's okay. Just lean on me for a while."

Part of her wanted very badly to believe him, to believe it was okay for her to lean on him. But the part of her that had survived alone for so long didn't know how to make that happen.

Caid showed her. At least he showed her what to do other than sit so stiffly in his arms. He must have felt the tension in her muscles. Covering the back of her head with his hand, he gently pressed her cheek to his chest.

A tiny sound escaped her throat. A moan or a sob, she couldn't tell which. It didn't matter. As Caid pulled her closer, pressing his cheek to the top of her head, she realized that she'd never known how badly she yearned for that simple human contact. She was being held. She couldn't remember the last time that had happened. It had to have been when she was a child, for surely no one had held her as a teenager. It definitely hadn't happened to her as an adult.

And never had she been held by a man.

But this wasn't just any man. This was Caid, and because of that, she let her weight sink forward and her arms slip tentatively around his waist.

Caid knew the moment she gave up the struggle. She felt so small, so fragile, her heart beating like a bird's against his naked chest. He could feel the smooth skin of her cheek where it pressed below his shoulder, and the firmness of her small breasts where they flattened against him. It was only the thin fabric of the T-shirt she wore that kept him from feeling those tight buds against his skin.

He wished he hadn't thought of that.

The breath he took was deliberately deep, intended to remind him that he was offering comfort. And while he'd had little experience with it, he was damn sure that his body's reaction to the way she felt and smelled and melted against him was not what offering comfort was all about.

He spoke her name against the top of her head—and he felt her stiffen again, much as she had when he'd first reached for her. He ignored the reaction. Much as he tried to ignore the bulge in his shorts.

What he couldn't ignore was the look in her eyes when she raised her head. The plea there tore through him like strafing fire.

He'd meant to get ice for the small cut inside her lip. Instead, he found himself cupping her face. A moment later, his lips touched the corner of her mouth. Once. Twice.

Her mouth parted with her indrawn breath.

He'd thought he only meant to kiss where she'd been hurt. If he'd thought at all. But that had been before the sweet scent of her breath filled his lungs.

"Caid?" she whispered.

"Kiss me back, Mia."

She leaned into him. Without a moment's hesitation. But when his mouth covered hers, she only drew a deeper breath.

She wanted to kiss him back, but she wasn't sure how. His lips were warm on hers, soft, mobile. She pressed back, wanting him to kiss her harder. But what she felt, instead, was his thumb moving below her mouth. When it was just below her lower lip, she felt him pull down ever so slightly. Her heart slammed into her ribs. Opening to him, she knew she understood what he wanted her to do.

His mouth had looked so hard. But, as she'd thought they might be, his lips were amazingly soft. It was the warm, velvety feel of his tongue she hadn't been prepared for. Or the shocking intimacy of what he did with it as he traced the shape of her lips, then began to stroke gently inside her mouth. She touched him back that same way. Tentatively at first, then more boldly, when his breathing seemed to alter.

He pulled back. "Put your arms around my neck," he told her, a strange light in his eyes as they swept her face.

"Like this?" she asked, trembling as she lifted them.

The light turned fierce.

That must have been what he wanted. His mouth came down on hers, and one hand slid between her thighs, pushing them apart so that her legs were on either side of his hips. He didn't pull her completely against him. But that was what Mia wanted. She wanted to get as close as she possibly could. He was warm and solid and strong, and as his hands worked over her back, his heat seemed to seep into the corners of her soul. She had felt cold inside for so long, and he was taking that chill away. Replacing it with something that made her feel wonderfully alive—something that felt as vital to her as her next breath.

She moved closer, discovering as she did that the outside of his thighs, roughened with coarse male hair, felt deliciously abrasive against the smoother skin inside her legs. The friction felt good. So did the tingling in her nipples when his hands skimmed up her sides. The sensations seemed to pile on top of each other, each new and different and maybe even a little frightening. But never so frightening as what she'd felt in those awful moments before he came crashing down the stairs.

The thought made her cling all the harder.

God, honey. Slow down.

Caid only thought the warning. Or maybe he actually said it. He wasn't sure. He was sure only that if she moved one inch closer, he would pick her up and carry her to his bed. He had an erection that was going to embarrass the hell out of her when she saw it, but if she pushed against him with her legs spread as they were, she'd be a lot more than embarrassed.

With a groan that was as much lust as frustration, Caid pulled her head to his chest. He didn't believe for a second that she was crawling all over him because she was as hot for him as he was her. More than anything, he had the feeling she was reacting to what had just happened, that she was clinging to him because of an understandable need to affirm that everything was all right. He had to believe that. If he thought for a moment that she knew what she was doing to him, he'd forget all about who she was and why he couldn't bury himself inside her, forget the bed and haul her to the floor. As it was, he'd started it, so it was up to him to bring it to an end.

"Mia," he breathed, his voice husky with long-denied need, "are you okay?"

Beneath his hands he felt the tension slowly return to her muscles. She lifted her head, the desire she was only beginning to discover clearly evident in her darkened eyes. The hunger there was real enough. But so was her trepidation.

Her glance shied away as she lowered her head. An instant later, she went completely still.

Caid was right. Now that she'd seen how she'd affected him, she was indeed embarrassed. There was no time to worry about having offended sensibilities, though. Or to worry about how she felt about what had just happened. Aside from its being a little late for proprieties, they had more pressing matters to consider.

He angled her legs to one side to get them out of the provocative position, and tipped her chin upward. "I've got to get you out of here," he said flatly. "Tonight."

Beneath the flush of passion lay the pallor of apprehension.

"You think he'll come back?"

"I'd be willing to bet on it."

"But he knows you're here. He heard you. That's why he ran."

I'm safe with you.

The implied message was indeed heady. Unfortunately, as good as her confidence was for his male ego, Caid didn't share her conclusion as to any deterrent effect his presence might have.

Caid hadn't been in the door ten seconds before he concluded that the intruder hadn't had a simple burglary in mind. His wallet and keys lay right where he'd left them on the breakfast bar, and his television and his expensive tape equipment hadn't been touched. When he added that conclusion to what Mia had said about the attacker coming at her with the knife, the motive seemed much more threatening.

Her attacker had turned off the lamp. That meant he'd seen her as she slept. So, at that moment, the attacker had known his intended victim. With all the weirdos on the loose these days, he could have been after her just because she was female, or a brunette, or simply because she was there. Or the reason could have been more specific. Something more to do with Jack.

Since Caid's apartment hadn't been broken into once in all the time he'd lived there, the fact that it had been to-night made it seem much less coincidental.

"He probably already knew I was here, Mia." He touched the corner of her lip again, hoping he hadn't hurt her when he kissed her. "How big a guy was he?"

As if to hold on to his touch, she touched the corner of her mouth herself. "What makes you think he knew you were here?"

"How big, Mia? My size? Taller? Shorter? Stockier? Thinner? Come on."

"Shorter. By a couple of inches." Her glance moved to his chest. "And smaller. I think. It was so dark, Caid. And it all happened so fast."

"About six foot, then?"

"I guess."

That wasn't good enough. "Shorter? About Jack's size? Five-ten or five-eleven?"

"No. He was bigger than Jack."

"You're sure?"

She hesitated. "Not really."

It wasn't Jack, was it?

Caid pushed his fingers through his hair. Rather than voice that awful question, he latched on to the other possi-bility that had occurred to him. Right now it didn't matter who was after her. All that mattered was that apparently someone was.

"You think something might have happened to Jack," he began. "If that's true, then it's possible that whoever's re-sponsible for whatever has happened to him is now after you. And whoever that is, he's desperate to keep you quiet about something. If he knew you were here, he had to know I was here, too. Desperate men do desperate things, Mia, and nothing's going to stop him from trying to get to you again."

His hands slid from her arms. "It would just be nice to know why someone wants you dead."

Mia shuddered at the thought. "It would definitely be helpful," she agreed, trying for the bravado that had always seen her through before. "But it's not like I'm worth anything dead, and I'm certainly not a threat to anyone."

She was still trembling when Caid spanned her waist to set her on her feet on the floor. Reaching for his shoulders to balance herself, she caught the dark furrowing of his brow.

"Get your stuff together," he told her, letting her go as soon as he was sure she was steady on her feet. "I'm going upstairs to grab a couple of things. Then we're leaving."

His frown troubled Mia.

"Caid?" Her fingers curled over his forearm, stopping him before he could walk away. "You thought of something just now. What is it?"

The furrow deepened. But there was too much on Caid's mind just then to wonder at how easily she'd read him.

"Is there any chance that you saw something the night Jack disappeared? Or someone? Someone who might have looked as if he belonged there, like a maintenance person, or an employee working late?"

Wishing desperately that she could remember something that would help, Mia could only shake her head. "Only the guard."

Caid let out a long, frustrated breath. "It's okay," he muttered, seeing her frustration. *Only the guard.* The man who'd given her description to the police. "Let's just get out of here."

Chapter 7

It didn't take Mia but minutes to change into the white cotton shirt and shorts she'd washed with Caid's laundry that afternoon and to pull on her tennis shoes. She left the T-shirt he'd lent her folded on the sofa, and stuffed her books and the white skirt she'd left to drip dry in the downstairs bathroom into her knapsack. She had no idea where Caid was taking her, or how long she would be there. But she was waiting by the door with her knapsack when Caid, now wearing jeans, a heavy sweater and sneakers, did double time down the stairs with a small duffel bag over his shoulder.

"Put this on," was all he said when he saw her. He held out a dark blue zip-front jacket with a hood on it and a drawstring hem. "It'll be cool on the water. We're going out on my boat."

Mia couldn't zip the jacket. When she didn't catch the zipper after the second try—she was shakier than she'd realized—Caid dropped his bag beside hers and did it for her. She thought he looked a little awkward doing it, too. Probably because he'd never dressed anyone before. But she was too busy trying to quell her trembling to really appreciate his gesture. All she could really appreciate was that he wasn't being impatient with her as he handed her back her knapsack and turned her toward the door.

A moment later, he stepped out the door ahead of her to make sure no one was around. Seeing nothing out of the ordinary, he took her hand and led her through the courtyard to the parking lot at the back of the building. A minute after that, they were in his Bronco, heading up the old highway through the wispy pockets of ocean fog.

The fog wasn't all that heavy, but the traffic was. It was Friday night, and with the bars closing and the late shows at the cinemas letting out, it seemed to Caid as if half the personnel from the base and most of the civilians in the area were on the streets—along with every police cruiser the city owned. But Caid was more aware of what was going on behind him than of what was in front. He was especially interested in any vehicle that came into his rearview mirror, his glance darting to it constantly to be sure they weren't being followed. He didn't think anyone had followed them out of the apartment complex. At least he hadn't seen anyone. Still, he watched. Even as he did, he was acutely aware of the woman crouched low and silent in the seat beside him.

Mia remained silent, too. Even when he'd parked the Bronco and they were heading toward the marina, she said nothing. Not once did she ask about their destination. Or even if he had one.

Her unspoken trust humbled him. But Caid didn't question her trust just then, any more than he questioned his own actions. He was doing what had to be done—keeping her safe. Because of Jack. Once that decision had been made, his energy would be used only to carry it out. The time for questions was past. Maybe that was how Mia looked at what she was doing, too.

The air was cool and damp, the breeze not nearly as stiff as it would be out past the breakwater. Still, there was a definite bite to it, and already Mia was cold. She wasn't the type to complain about it. In fact, she didn't say a word about the dampness or the chill. It was her occasional shiver that gave her away.

A middle-aged couple headed toward them. Nodding amiably, Caid slowed to slip his arm around Mia's shoulder. The gesture was partly to offer warmth—and partly because it afforded him the opportunity for a surreptitious glance to see if anyone was behind them.

The marina wasn't nearly as big as some, but it was large enough to moor a couple hundred boats. Shaped in a half-moon, its docks and walkways jutted out into dark water that smelled of fish and gasoline and engine oil. Tonight it wasn't the smells or the sound of lapping water or the anticipation of leaving the masses behind that had Caid's attention. It was the woman at his side—and the man who had just stepped onto the dock several yards behind them.

The marina was well-lit, but the fog was heavier on the water. It swirled up around the security lamps, diffusing the light, weakening it, so that any object—or any person—more than a few yards away was somewhat blurred in the pale gray vapor. From where they were, midway down the pier, the man appeared tall, and thin as a blade, and seemed to be wearing dark clothes. He stopped the moment Caid turned. For several moments, he stood there, still and silent, before he looked away. It was almost as if he were waiting for them to gain more distance before he moved again. Or, Caid allowed, even as adrenaline surged, maybe he was only trying to get his bearings as he looked for a particular boat.

Assuming that a situation was harmless was a mistake some soldiers didn't get the opportunity to make twice.

Pilings creaked as he and Mia continued on, the sound giving way to the noise of laughter and the beat of rock music coming from a sloop moored a few slips down. A whoop met with more laughter and the murmur of conversation drifting toward the shore.

Caid carried his duffel bag in his left hand. Wanting his hand free, just in case, he slipped the bag over his shoulder by its straps and urged Mia on. Pressed to his side, she had immediately sensed the quick tension in his body, and she started to look around herself.

"Slow down, but keep going," Caid told her as the man began to move behind them. "There's a guy behind us. Let's let him pass."

"Who is it?"

"I haven't a clue. But I'm not taking any chances. You just be ready to dive into the nearest boat when I say 'Move.'"

They slowed their steps, taking their time reaching the walkway that led to the sloop with the giggling women and the now-booming music. Caid didn't think anything would happen if there were other people around. Especially lots of people. The one thing he didn't want to do was head to the deserted end of the dock, where his own boat was moored.

He slowed their pace further, letting his arm fall from her shoulders as he prepared to shove her behind him if the guy tried to grab her. The man was coming forward now. Slowly, still seeming to hang back.

"Caid?" Mia whispered. "What's he doing?"

She turned then, her cheek brushing Caid's arm. Their shadow had begun to sprint forward, his footsteps muffled eerily by the fog.

Caid's expression never changed. In one deft motion, he'd blocked Mia, setting himself between her and the man who, to the greetings of his friends on board, took a sharp left to join the party he'd apparently been looking for.

Caid let out a long, deep breath. Not caring that Mia wasn't finished drawing in a stabilizing breath of her own, he grabbed her hand and hurried her past the rows of cruisers and catamarans and sailboats with their skeletal masts disappearing in the fog. In a few minutes, they would be away from the dock and the land, and they could both breathe easier. Until then, he wasn't trusting anyone he saw.

Destiny rocked lightly in her slip.

"This is it," Caid said as they reached the blue-and-white powerboat and he moved alongside to unloop the stern rope. The twenty-two-foot day cruiser certainly wasn't the biggest or classiest craft on the water. In fact, it could still use a lot more of the TLC Caid had already lavished on her. But she was in a lot better shape than when he'd bought her last year, and the two hundred and fifty horses in her inboard engine could make her bury just about anything she came up against.

He hopped on board, legs spread for balance. "Give me your hand."

Again Mia didn't hesitate. Giving him her bag first, she then took his hand and stepped lightly over the side. As soon as she was balanced herself, she reached for the bags and nodded toward the door between the first mate's and captain's chairs. "Do you want these in there?"

She moved quietly, efficiently, stowing their bags in the small cabin when he unlatched the door, then returned to pull life jackets from under the seats as he asked her to do, while he started the engine and checked the running lights. They spoke little, working quickly to shove off. Yet, even as occupied as Caid was, he couldn't help but notice something in her shuttered expression that told him she had done this before. Run in the middle of the night. He didn't like knowing that. Yet, like it or not, he was finding it harder all the time to tell himself that whatever had happened to her in the past shouldn't matter to him. She would be in his life only until the question of her father's whereabouts could be resolved. And that was exactly how he wanted it. He had decisions to make that were tough enough without his having to worry about somebody else.

As they left the marina, slowly, so as not to rock the other boats with their wake, Caid had to admit that things didn't always go the way he wanted. Already he was coming to know her. How else would he have known that behind the carefully composed expression of the woman in the seat next to him was one very frightened lady? It was almost as if, whenever things threatened to become more than she could handle, she instinctively shut herself down, conserving her energy for whatever happened next. He'd seen her do it before. And because he was compelled, however unwillingly, by what little he knew, he wanted to know more.

The thought seemed like a bad joke to him. As hard as he found it to open up, he hadn't the faintest idea how to get someone else to do it.

He kept his focus straight ahead, his attention on the fog-fuzzed glow of the beacon lights lining the breakwater.

He hated fog. It made navigation trickier and speed impossible.

"The ride might be a little choppy going past the breakwater. It should smooth out once we're in the channel." He glanced behind them. No one was following them out. No one with running lights on his craft, anyway. "Once we're through it, you might as well go below and get some sleep. There's only one bed."

It was impossible for Mia to tell from Caid's cryptic tone if his last statement was a warning of some sort, or if he was saying they would sleep in turns. In the glow of the console lights, all she could conclude from his hard expression was that he didn't want her up here with him.

Already on emotional overload, she simply acknowledged his suggestion with a quiet "Okay" and tucked her freezing legs up under the wide bottom of the jacket. The wind whipped her hair, stinging her face, and the cold leaked down the collar of her jacket. In a way, the discomfort was a blessing. So was the distraction of having to hang on for balance as the boat left the protected water to pound its way over the waves racing through the opening in the breakwater toward the shore. Focusing on the immediate kept her from marveling at the absolute control Caid exerted over himself and the powerful craft, and, after the waves gentled and the running became smoother, it kept her from wondering at the reason for his implacable manner when he told her that it was now all right for her to go below.

She left him with a quiet "Good night," and when he didn't answer, she told herself it didn't matter that he seemed relieved to have her out of his sight. She wouldn't think about anything. Not now. She could think later. When she'd rested. When the terror of waking to see that knife flash past her face had finally gone away. When her fears of the past three days didn't seem as if they'd just grown so much larger. When she didn't feel so desperate for the sensations of strength and security she'd felt in Caid's arms. His holding her, his kissing her, had been an aberration. Something he'd done because of the circumstances. It had meant nothing to him. She would see that in the morning. Everything was always so much clearer, so much easier to face, in the morning.

It was the differences she noted first. Subtle, strange differences that, in her waking consciousness, could have been as much dream as reality. She had fallen asleep to the hum of a powerful engine and the steady, sometimes pounding motion of the boat speeding ahead. It had been dark, too, the only illumination a tiny yellow light above one of the windows that ran along both sides of the cabin. When she'd come in, she immediately crawled under the covers of the double-size bed fitted under the bow and curled into a tight little ball. Now, turning over to stretch out, she realized that darkness had given way to daylight, and that the only sounds to be heard were the gentle lapping of water, the cries of sea gulls and a raucous barking noise unlike anything she'd ever heard before.

"Watch your head."

Mia had started to sit up. At Caid's warning, she immediately ducked. All but the outermost two feet of mattress were under the bow of the boat. Had she straightened, she'd have met that bow head-on.

She scooted to the edge, dragging the thick blue blanket with her, and blinked at Caid's bare feet.

He stood in the middle of the cabin, wearing only the jeans he'd had on last night. Her glance moved up his flat stomach, following the arrow of hair to where it flared over his nicely molded chest. Giving herself a mental jerk, she raised her eyes to his face. Dark stubble shadowed his jaw, making him look quite rakish and very—terribly—sexy.

He looked as if he'd just wakened himself.

"I told you there's only one bed," he said, as if he knew exactly what had just crossed her mind. "But it worked all right. You didn't take up too much room."

His comment about her sleeping habits barely registered. What did was that she hadn't awakened when he came in. Or when he lay down. The rocking of the boat must have masked his motions.

"I was just going to make some coffee," he said, apparently thinking she could use some. "The head's in there, if you need it."

"The head?"

"The bathroom."

"Oh," she mumbled, then went still when she ran her fingers through her hair. She'd forgotten that she'd cut it.

Caid hadn't. Shaking his head as if to say I-still-can't-believe-you-did-that, he turned away. The cabinet above the tiny stove and sink opened with the click of the latch. Out came coffee and a can of peaches. From another cabinet came a coffeepot.

From the looks of it, the cabinets on his boat were better stocked than his apartment. Certainly the small cabin contained more creature comforts than did the larger space. A built-in tape deck held storage for a sizable collection of tapes; the blue cushions on the short side benches exactly matched the blue curtains on the windows; and the warm wood of the small table and the interior walls positively glowed with polish.

The strange, deep-throated sounds she'd wakened to grew more intense.

"What is that?"

Without so much as a glance toward her, Caid said, "Seals," and turned on the gas stove.

Seals? "Where are we?"

Caid started to tell her. Then, for some reason he didn't care to define, he reached over and pushed open the cabin's door.

"Go see for yourself."

The air spilling through the doorway was cool. Not nearly so cool as it had been on the water last night, but the chill definitely required shoes. Slipping them on, she pulled Caid's jacket more tightly around her and stepped up onto the deck.

Mia caught her breath.

They were anchored in a cove, the bow of the boat less than twenty feet from a sandy beach that ran straight into a fog-tipped and mountainous ridge of striated rock and wind-bent grasses and trees. Ahead of her, facing out into the morning-gray ocean, was a sight that turned her gasp of pleasure to a delighted laugh.

Seals. Brown, shiny, slippery-looking seals, with stubby flippers and whiskers that jutted out from their dark noses like the fingers of splayed hands, were tumbling and twisting and having an altogether great time about fifty feet out in the gently rolling surf. The water positively churned with their antics, and the air was filled with their incessant barking.

Mindless of how unsophisticated Caid might think her, she ducked her head back in the cabin, grinning.

"What is this place? It's incredible! There must be a dozen of them out here!"

Caid pulled his shirt over his head. He'd wanted to know what she thought of his cove. Her radiant smile gave him his answer. It actually told him more than that she liked it. It told him that what she thought mattered to him—and that bothered him a lot more than the stupid way his heart jerked at seeing her so completely enthralled.

He should stay where he was, he told himself. He should finish getting dressed, and once he'd done a slam dunk with a cup of coffee, he should haul himself over to Miller's Marina and Market and call Tom Bidwell. That was exactly what he'd planned to do when he anchored a few hours ago. It had still been the only thought he allowed himself when he awakened with Mia sleeping a scant foot away.

Figuring two more minutes wouldn't hurt anything—and not sure he wanted to interrupt Tom's family routine so early on a Saturday, anyway—he followed Mia back out and watched her turn to the craggy rocks beyond the shore.

"Are we on a peninsula? I didn't think southern California had a coast so deserted."

"This isn't the mainland. We're on an island about twenty-two miles from shore." They were near the north end of Santa Catalina, off the California coast. "There's a resort at the other end. About thirty miles away. But that's about it." With a few exceptions for locals, cars were prohibited. Access was strictly by boat or by air, and travel on land by foot or on horseback. "There's a place called Land's End not too far from here. We can get supplies there. And use the phone. We'll head over in a while."

She had her hands stuffed in the pockets of the jacket, her shoulders hunched against the ocean breeze. "You're making a call?"

"To the base," he said, wondering if he should tell her what he wanted to do. He decided it could wait. Tom might not go for it, anyway. "It's not about what happened last night, Mia." Not directly, anyway. "I'm just calling my commander."

"Then we'll come back here?"

The tension had already fallen from her shoulders. She raised her face to him, her eyes alight at the prospect of returning to this place.

Caid felt himself go still. She was close enough to touch. Close enough that he could see the fine grain of her skin and the flecks of silver in her gray eyes. Daylight could be merciless on a woman's face. It hid nothing. Especially on the face of a woman who'd just awakened and hadn't had time for creams and lotions or whatever all it was they used. It hid nothing on Mia's, either.

There were traces of laugh lines at the corners of her eyes. They were at the corners of her mouth, too, where it tipped up when she smiled. Those lines would deepen over the years, adding even more character to a face that would always be hauntingly beautiful. She had the elegance and grace of a woman who might have come from rank or privilege. But she had certainly never known privilege. And Caid seriously doubted she'd ever been coddled or cosseted or pampered in her entire life. Last night, as he held her, he'd even wondered if she'd ever had anyone offer her the simple comfort of a pair of arms. Yet there was nothing about her appearance to betray any harshness or hardship in her life.

The pragmatic side of Caid told him she'd just been blessed with good genes. Or maybe it was just that impossible sense of hope of hers that kept her from realizing the gravity of her situation. There was nothing really all that special about her.

The part of him that had responded to her trembling when he held her in his arms last night didn't believe that for a minute. Yet, as he stood watching the breeze toy with her hair, all he was prepared to consider was that it had been a mistake to think about last night at all. Certainly he shouldn't be thinking about it when she was so close that her scent came to him with every breath he drew. He could recall exactly how she'd tasted when she opened to him, how tentatively she'd first touched his tongue. She had seemed shocked at first by the sensations of moisture and texture and warmth. Or maybe she'd just been surprised. Whatever her reaction had been, it hadn't taken her very long to figure out that they both liked the smooth feel of his tongue sliding over hers, and that when both people liked something, the turn-on was even better.

The memory was dangerous, standing there staring at her mouth while he recalled it, even more so. The quality of the anticipation in her eyes had changed, and he could tell from the quickened rise and fall of her chest that her memories of last night were as vivid as his. She might be inexperienced, but she wasn't timid.

With his knuckles, he brushed her cheek. "We'll come back later." His hand fell. He had no excuses now. If he responded to the quick heat darting through his body, it wouldn't have anything to do with needing to offer comfort. She had no excuses, either.

That thought didn't help in the least. "The marina at Land's End ought to be open by now," he added, and turned away from what he could have sworn was disappointment in her eyes. "While I'm making my call, you might want to see if they've got anything that fits you. I'm sure Marta won't mind helping you out."

Mia blinked at his back as he headed into the cabin. Refusing to acknowledge how badly she'd wanted him to touch her, she turned her energy to tempering the quick jolt of alarm she'd felt at Caid's suggestion. Not the part about the clothes. Though she was certainly grateful for the clothes she had, having something with a bit more warmth would be awfully nice. It was the part about being seen by other people that gave her pause.

With Caid occupied in the cabin, she sat down on one of the thickly cushioned outer benches and glanced toward the magnificent rocky face looming behind them.

"You have friends here?" she asked over the sound of water lapping at the side of the boat.

"The Millers. Hank and Marta," came the muffled reply. "I've known them for a couple of years."

Mia hesitated. "Do you think it's a good idea for me to go with you? Maybe I should just stay here."

"Where? You're on a boat, and I need the boat to get there," came the dry reply. "It's five miles overland. I'm not walking."

"I meant here. On the beach. There's a beautiful spot right over there by that waterfall. I wouldn't mind."

She liked his waterfall. Caid didn't care. He wasn't leaving her alone. "You're coming with me. I doubt that the Millers have any idea what's going on anywhere beyond this island, so they aren't going to recognize you. Even if by some chance they do, we can trust them."

Business appeared to be slow at Land's End this morning. Only one boat bobbed by the pier that jutted into the small inlet housing Miller's Marina and Market. From the *Marta II* arching over the stern, that boat appeared to belong to the Millers themselves. Its white and gray paint matched the pristine Cape Cod house set back on a deep lawn, and the paint of the tiny market at the shore end of the pier.

There was no one in the market, though. On the door hung a sign that read Please Ring Bell for Service. So Caid did, but not until after he'd cupped his hands to the paned and rain-stained windows to look inside, and checked out the bait in the barrel by the weathered door. Having assured himself that his friend wasn't there and that the bait was fresh, he leaned against the rusting gas pump at the edge of the pier and glanced toward the house.

A few moments later, the front door opened and a woman with hair as gray as her shutters and wearing a print apron over a flannel skirt and sweater came scurrying across the stepping stones set in the lawn.

"Good morning," she said when she was only halfway there. "Do hope you haven't been waiting too— Why, Caid! It's you!"

To Mia, the transformation was remarkable. One moment Caid's features were defined by their usual hard edge. The next, an easy, relaxed grin spread over his face as he pushed himself away from the pump and moved forward to accept the hug promised by the woman's outstretched arms.

Almost immediately the woman pulled back, keeping her hands on his forearms.

"Hank will be so upset to know he missed you. He's just left to pick up our grandchildren from the airport. Susie—she's our youngest daughter...." she offered, in case he didn't remember. "She and her husband are going to a seminar for their business, and we're taking the children for the weekend. He didn't leave but five minutes ago."

She glanced around Caid, all but setting him aside to see who was with him. Speculation danced in her eyes, bright as the sun trying to peek through the overhead haze. "You've brought a friend with you?"

Caid could see the wheels turning in Marta's head. The woman had a heart of gold, and she was as transparent as cellophane. She could hide nothing.

At the moment, neither could Mia. She hung back by the old red gas pump, not appearing at all convinced that her coming here was a good idea. She looked as hesitant as Marta did curious.

"Mia's father is a friend of mine. An ex-marine," he added, snagging Mia's hand to pull her forward.

"Ah," Mia heard the woman say, as if being an ex-marine were of some significance. "Then, I am most happy to meet her.

"Your name's Mia?" she asked, extending her hand with a pleasant smile. "Well, I'm Marta. You're always welcome here."

Her glance swung back to Caid. "Have you two time to come up to the house? I'm in the middle of making a birthday cake for Lisa. She's the older of the two coming today," she explained. "She'll be six on Monday, but we wanted to celebrate while she's here. Anyway, if you don't mind my finishing up, I'd love to have you both to the house. I just put an apple strudel in the oven, and there's fresh coffee."

"I hate passing up an offer like that," Caid said, since he'd tasted her strudel once before. "But I'm afraid we can't. I need to use your phone and to gas up. And Mia'd like to take a look in the store." He glanced at her legs. "She didn't quite know how to dress for the trip out here."

At Caid's comment, Marta glanced at Mia's legs, too. Except for a layer of goose bumps, they were quite bare from above her knees where Caid's jacket ended, to the tops of her tennis shoes.

Marta, having seen every imaginable sort of attire on members of the boating set, simply smiled. A woman draped in a man's jacket was hardly an uncommon sight. But the moment the older woman's back was turned to unlock the door, Mia didn't bother tempering the frown she aimed at Caid.

Caid, having come up with the best explanation he could, simply shrugged.

The inside of the store smelled of the wood stove used to heat it. "You know where the phone is, Caid," Marta said, and stopped between a row of canned goods and fishing supplies to turn her smile on Mia. "It's past the end of the season, so I don't know if there's anything left in ladies' sizes to fit you. You don't look too big under that thing."

Caid didn't use the pay phone at the front of the store. The phone Marta had referred to was in back. That was where he headed as he heard Marta say that maybe the boys' sweat suits she had in stock might fit Mia. He was pretty certain Mia wouldn't be too flattered by the kindly woman's remark, but he didn't catch the rest of the conversation as he picked up the handset of the black rotary-dial phone as soon as he reached the cluttered desk. His only concern was contacting his commander.

He was in luck. Tom Bidwell was home, though he was in the middle of replacing a window one of his teenagers had knocked out with a soccer ball. As soon as he heard Caid's voice, Tom offered him a beer in return for his help putting in the new one.

Tom must have sensed something wasn't quite right. Normally Caid would have made a comment about being easy but not cheap, to which Tom would have responded with an equally flip reply. All Caid said was that he was sorry he couldn't help right now, that he needed to talk to Tom, and that what he wanted would require some paper- work.

Tom caught on within seconds. "You asking me for leave, Caid?"

"Yeah. I am." Lord, how he hated doing this. "Is it go- ing to be a problem?"

"Come on in and we'll talk."

A few moments later, having agreed on a specific time, Caid hung up the phone. As he did, his glance fell on the jumble of papers and ledgers and catalogs on the desk—and a small, twenty-year-old black-and-white photograph of a young marine. Hank Miller had said his son had been about Caid's age.

Mia was standing in front of Marta wearing a pair of sweats when he came out of the tiny office. They'd obvi- ously found something in a woman's size that fit. The sweats were pale pink, with a white-and-silver anchor on the sweatshirt, and little sparkly silver things around the neck. Walking toward her, Caid decided he liked her in pink. He kind of liked her in the sweats, too. She looked cute in them. Comfortable. Chic.

What he wasn't so sure about was the floppy pink hat she'd plopped on her head. Or the pair of huge gold-colored sunglasses. Between the glasses and the hat, her face had all but disappeared.

Which, he was sure, was exactly what she had in mind.

Seeing Caid's raised eyebrows, Mia took off the hat and glasses and set them on the counter, along with a few other items she intended to purchase.

"I need to pay for these." Her money was in her knap- sack. "Let me run to the boat for my wallet, and then I'm ready. You're all finished with your call?"

"I'll get your bag. I need to talk to you for a minute first."

Busy with the purchases, Marta reached across the counter to lay her hand on Mia's arm. "It's all right, dear. You talk to Caid. I'm going to go in back and get the scissors to cut these tags off for you."

Mia's voice dropped, her expression showing concern as soon as Marta disappeared around the corner. "Is something wrong?"

"No. It's nothing like that," he said, meaning to assure her that what he wanted to talk about had nothing to do with her father. "I've just got to go to the base for a while. Come here."

He drew her back from the counter, putting more distance between them and the woman in the other room. "It'll take five, maybe six hours." They both knew he couldn't take her with him. They both also knew that, at the moment, it would be best to leave that fact unmentioned. "I'll ask Marta if you can stay with her."

Mia's expression was cautious, but the look in her eyes was quite certain. "That isn't necessary. I'm not going to impose on Mrs. Miller. Just take me back to the cove."

"I'm not going to leave you alone."

"Honestly, Caid. I don't need a baby-sitter. I'll be fine there. I'm buying a couple of blank pads. I can do some sketching while you're gone."

Caid's voice was already quiet. It now grew quieter still. "I'm not leaving you alone. Understand?"

"And I'm not imposing on that lady. Just take me back to the cove."

"Are you always this damn stubborn?"

"Yes," she answered without hesitation. "Are you?"

Caid's eyes narrowed. The woman was part imp, part spitfire, and God help him, part of him was beginning to not give a damn about who her father was. When her eyes challenged him, as they were now, all he wanted to do was kiss her senseless.

He stepped closer, not wanting Marta, who was already back at the counter, to hear. "Look, Mia, you're not in any position—"

Marta cleared her throat.

"Excuse me. I'm sorry." Scissors in hand, expression concerned, she joined them in the aisle of camping gear. "I really wasn't trying to listen. Truly. It's just rather difficult not to overhear conversations in here. It wouldn't be an imposition at all for you to stay, Mia. Hank won't be back for a couple of hours, and when he does return, he'll have chores to do. It will just be me and the girls. I really wouldn't mind the company."

The woman was truly as kind as she appeared. She almost made it sound as if Mia would be doing her a favor by staying.

Since she would have seemed unpardonably rude to not accept, Mia quietly thanked Marta for the offer. Her appreciation of the woman's generosity was most genuine. So was her irritation with Caid. She would have been just fine back at the cove by herself. But creating a scene could easily have raised questions in Marta's mind about what was going on, and Mia wasn't willing to risk that. Still, the look she sent Caid made it clear that she wasn't at all pleased with the prospect of imposing on yet another virtual stranger.

Marta didn't catch the glare. Being the kind of person who took everything and everyone at face value, she seemed to notice only that Caid needed to go back to his base for a while, and that it didn't make sense for the daughter of his friend to spend her trip to the island alone, waiting for him to come back.

"Don't you worry about her, Caid," Mia heard her say. "She'll be right here waiting for you when you get back."

Marta was true to her word. Relatively speaking. Mia was still there, but she wasn't exactly pacing at her post, waiting for his return. At least Caid didn't think her overly anxious for him to get back when he tied *Destiny* to the pier and crossed the dock toward the house six hours later. In fact, she looked pretty contented to him.

She was sprawled on a colorful patchwork quilt on the front lawn with two towheaded little girls, each in an identical sprawl on either side of her. They were all on their stomachs, and she seemed to be reading to them, or looking at pictures, or doing something that had them focusing on a single spot at the edge of the quilt. He couldn't really tell what they were doing. He also couldn't tell why he should find the sight of her with those two little heads bent next to hers so disturbing.

They were watching a worm.

All three of them looked up from the night crawler burrowing through the grass and dirt as he approached.

"Hi," Mia said, tucking her legs in Indian-style as she sat up. "You're back."

Her laconic greeting would actually have fooled him if she hadn't so quickly looked away from his eyes. He might actually have believed she couldn't have cared less if he'd shown up on time or five hours from now. But he caught the relief in her expression before she glanced away. Even now, as she looked back up at him, he could sense the anxiety draining from her.

It hadn't occurred to him until that moment that she might have been afraid he wouldn't return for her at all.

Two sets of blue eyes blinked at him, drawing his attention from the woman between them. Both girls had curly blond hair, and both, seeing the unsmiling mountain of a man looming over them, sat up as Mia had. Warily they scooted closer to her.

Not sure why the kids were looking at him as if he were about to stuff them in a sack and carry them off, Caid chose to ignore them. "I'm back," he agreed, not sure, either, why he felt disappointed that Mia had doubted him. "Are you ready?"

"Anytime you are. You're going to say hello to Hank before we go, though, aren't you? He'll be disappointed if he doesn't get to show you his model. It's all finished now."

Caid's brow lowered. "How do you know about his models?"

"He showed them to me. He showed them to all of us, didn't he?" she asked the kids, who immediately agreed with her, but still didn't look overly trusting of the stranger frowning at their new friend.

As if sensing the children's hesitation about the man she was speaking with, or perhaps sensing his own hesitation about them, she put her arms over the girls' shoulders.

"Lisa, Danielle, Colonel Matlock is a friend of your grandma and grandpa. Why don't you run and get them and tell them he's back? I have to go with him now."

"Do you hafta?" the girl she'd called Danielle, the younger one in the red overalls, asked.

Clearly disappointed, the one in blue—Lisa—piped in with "Now?"

"Now," Mia repeated, and with a smile as warm as the sunshine peeking through the cottony clouds, she rose to pull both girls to their feet. Drawing them to her, she whispered something to them that made them giggle, then sent them racing toward the house and the woman smiling at them from the doorway.

"Hank's on his way," Marta called out to Caid as the girls raced on inside. "But instead of running off, why don't the both of you stay to supper? Unless you've got plans, of course."

The kids were back. They didn't leave the porch, though. They just stood on the step and stared at Caid. Beside him, Mia quietly folded the quilt, her own preference impossible to determine.

Had it just been the elder Millers, and had Caid been alone, he might have considered staying. But the idea of him and Mia at a cozy family dinner was not a scenario with which he was at all comfortable. Add the children staring at him from the porch, and the idea wasn't even worth considering.

"Thanks, Marta. But I'd planned to take Mia deep-sea fishing. She's been dying to try it.'' Taking the quilt from her, he handed it to the older woman. "Haven't you, Mia?"

Caid hadn't had any idea what Mia might have been doing while he was gone. Truthfully, he hadn't thought about it at all. All the way back from the base, he'd considered only that by securing the leave he'd asked for, he'd just created what could be a very awkward position for himself. What he hadn't been considering was that, while he was away, Mia had been charming the socks off his friends.

To her credit, Mia went along rather well with the excuse about deep-sea fishing—even though Caid seriously doubted that she had the slightest idea what the sport entailed. As Hank, his white beard neatly trimmed and his pants held up by red suspenders, came out to see how Caid's boat was running, Mia said goodbye to the little girls and to Marta—who, in turn, told Mia and Caid that they were welcome to come back tomorrow for birthday cake if they were still in the neighborhood. The two little girls seemed to think that was a heck of an idea. Where Mia was concerned, anyway. The way they kept staring at Caid from behind their grandma's skirt made him pretty sure they'd be just as happy never to see him again.

Anxious to get back to the peace of his cove, and still brooding about the conversation he'd had with Tom, he didn't think anyone else had even noticed the girls' behavior. Until Mia brought it up.

Chapter 8

"**D**on't you like children, Caid?"

Mia voiced her observation as she leaned back in the first mate's chair and propped her knees against the hull. Sunglasses perched on her nose, one hand holding her floppy pink hat on her head, she watched Caid as he idled the boat past the rope-lashed pilings at the end of the Millers' pier. It didn't matter to her whether he liked children or not. Or so she told herself. She just wanted to understand the man who'd become so hard that even a small child couldn't break through his wall.

Dark sunglasses hid his eyes. "Why do you ask that?"

"Because of the way you were with the girls."

"What way? I never said a word to either one of them."

Looking perplexed, not sure why they were even having this discussion, Caid frowned at Mia when he caught her knowing glance. "What was I supposed to say? They kept staring at me like I was Jack the Ripper."

It was his expression that gave him away. Seeing it, hearing his defense, Mia felt a smile touch her heart. "That's probably how you looked to them, too," she told him, intrigued by the possibility that this big, burly marine might actually be intimidated by little ones. "It would have helped if you'd smiled a little."

When he said that he had, Mia lowered her glasses to peer over the rims at Caid. His expression was as stony as the section of shoreline they were leaving behind.

She pushed the glasses back in place with the roll of her eyes. "You did not. You're a very formidable-looking man, Caid. Especially when you frown like you're doing now. The girls looked at you the way they did because you're a stranger and they were frightened of you."

Formidable? Him? "Do I scare you?"

She hesitated only for a moment. But that moment was long enough to cast a definite shadow of doubt over her very even "No."

Despite the anxiety that had been eating at his gut ever since he left the base, Caid felt a smile threaten. The woman had a stubborn streak as wide as the Pacific. He doubted she'd ever backed down from anyone without at least a token show of resistance.

He doubted, too, that she had any idea how appealing she looked in that damn hat—like a little girl playing dress-up in her mother's clothes.

"The Millers' granddaughters are very sweet," he heard her say, as if she felt he should give them another chance. "I'm sure that Marta would like it if you got to know them." Still holding on to her hat, she glanced over at him. "She said she and Hank have known you for a couple of years. But they'd like it if you'd visit more often. And longer."

Caid already had that feeling. Every time he saw the Millers, they extended the invitation for him to stay. And almost every time, he politely declined. To say hello and visit for a while was enough. "They're nice people," he mumbled.

"They really appreciate what you did for them, too."

Caid had his head turned from her as he piloted the boat around a kelp bed. But Mia didn't miss the displeasure that swept his face. "They told you about that?" he asked, his question deceptively mild.

With the distinct feeling that he'd have preferred the basis of his friendship with the Millers to remain his business, she cautiously confirmed what Marta had said. While Mia had sat at the table in Marta's cozy kitchen, the older woman had told her how Caid had started coming to their end of the island a couple of years ago. He always came alone, and would always gas up at their pump shortly after he arrived at the island and buy bait at their store for his weekend of fishing. After a few weeks, he and Hank had gotten to talking and when Hank had found out Caid was a marine, he'd told him about the son he and Marta had lost in an embassy skirmish years ago. They'd never really learned what had happened.

"She said you found out for them."

Caid said nothing to confirm or dispute what he had done. He simply kept his glance straight ahead, his jaw working, as if he really wished Marta had just kept her mouth shut. Because of that, Mia didn't comment on how much his help must have meant to the Millers, or how grateful they must have been to him for finally putting their minds at rest. Their son had died in the line of duty, not in the brawl the military had invented to cover a sniper incident that would have had international implications. Caid would be the last to admit it, but he was a generous man. Quick to give his help when it came to a matter of honor, morality or loyalty—as he had done with her.

Mia glanced away. She couldn't let herself confuse her situation with that of the Millers. Nor could she hope that, as he seemed to do with the Millers, he would think of her as a friend. At best, they were allies. More realistically—and though she hated being dependent on him—he was simply her protector. It was just that there were times when it was deceptively easy to forget that what he was doing for her really had nothing to do *with* her. His willingness to help was because of his friendship with her father. That was all.

Even now, by his silence, he was reminding her of that. His silence put a certain distance between them. Realizing that, and realizing, too, that he kept a safe distance from the Millers—people he regarded as friends—she sought to emulate his attitude. Distance was safe. Yet, as she noted the concentration in his profile, she began to think it wasn't just his bent for privacy that was keeping him so reticent. Caid clearly had other things on his mind.

She turned back to him, watching the breeze blowing his dark hair. "Was everything all right at your base?" she asked, needing very much to avoid thinking how obligated she was becoming to Caid. "Your meeting went well?"

Waves pounded against the bow of the boat. The water was rough this close in, so Caid headed them out to sea and calmer waters for the trip back to the cove. The sky was swathed in wisps of white on pale blue, the grayer clouds mere puffs on the horizon. Gulls screeched overhead, wheeling and diving for fish below the foaming surface.

Caid scarcely noticed.

"As well as could be expected. I'm taking leave. Some time off," he added, in case she wasn't familiar with the term.

Her knees slid down, her tennis shoes hitting the deck. "Why?"

Caid said nothing.

"You're not taking time from your job because of me, are you? To keep me out here and away from whatever's going on?"

Sliding off her seat, needing to be closer because the engine was so much louder now that he'd opened the throttle, she grabbed on to the back of his chair to stand next to him. The power of the boat tilted the bow up, making footing precarious. "Is that what you're doing?"

Wind rushed over the top of the windshield. From the corner of his eye, Caid saw Mia pull her hat off so that it wouldn't blow away. He'd opened the throttle deliberately, hoping the distraction of noise and speed would make her think he couldn't hear her.

He should have known better.

"Sit back down before you fall," he shouted over the noise of the waves and engine and wind.

"Not until you answer me."

"If we hit a wave the wrong way at this speed, you'll wind up overboard."

"Then slow down," she shouted back, refusing to let the matter go. "You've done enough for me without taking time away from your work. I don't know exactly what you do, but I can't imagine that someone in your position can just take a vacation any time he wants." The boat jerked, causing her to grab his arm for balance. "I don't want to cause any problems for you, Caid. Especially not with your job."

It was her concern that did it. It was in her voice, and in the touch of her hand as he eased off the throttle. The bow of the boat came down as he decelerated, leveling the deck and alleviating her need to hold on to him for balance. She didn't let go, though. Even when he looked down at the fingers curled over his forearm, she stayed right where she was, waiting.

When he glanced up at her, the concern in her voice was also in her eyes.

"I know your job is important to you."

Clearly skeptical, he cocked his head. "How do you know that?"

Because you don't have anything else. "Jack said it was."

For once, Caid actually didn't mind his friend's big mouth. Mia was actually concerned about his job. No one had ever been so unselfishly concerned about him before.

"It's all right," he heard himself say, liking the way her concern made him feel. "Taking leave right now wasn't a problem. The project I was working on is ready to go, and I'll be back before it's time to implement it." He glanced toward the shoreline, watching for the outcropping of rocks that led to his cove. "My commanding officer was all in favor of my taking some time off now, anyway. I'm trying to decide whether or not to stay in. He thinks I can use the time to make up my mind."

"Stay in?"

"The Marines."

What Tom had actually said was "I'll expect your answer when you get back." Since Tom was also a friend, he'd said he thought taking a couple of weeks in the meantime to fish and camp out might be exactly what Caid needed to do to set his priorities. Personally, Tom thought Caid would be making a huge mistake if he left the Corps. The decision had to be Caid's, though, and Caid's alone.

Since that was the only way Caid had ever made any decision concerning himself, he wasn't at all sure why he'd mentioned his little problem to the woman quietly watching him. Maybe it was only because it was on his mind. Or maybe he'd only wanted to let her know that she wasn't the only reason he'd done what he had. Whatever his rationale, now that he'd said it, the concern in Mia's expression underwent a subtle shift.

"What would you do if you left?"

Caid blinked back at her. Her question, so simply asked, pierced right to the crux of his problem.

The muscle in his jaw jerked. "I haven't the faintest idea."

"Don't you like what you do?" she asked, her innocent inquiry pulling him up short again. "Is that why you're thinking of leaving?"

That wasn't it. Not exactly. Caid didn't dislike what he did. He told her that, too. There was a definite challenge to training elite troops, and a definite standard to maintain. Standards were important to Caid. So was the reason for training those special units in the first place. As a soldier, he truly believed that a prepared military was the strongest deterrent to war. And Caid strongly believed in the causes of peace. But there was more to the decision he faced. To be effective at what he did, he had to be willing to give one hundred and fifty percent. That was what he demanded of his men. And he could demand no less of himself. The problem was that the adrenaline rush of a covert operation had long ago lost its edge, and the idea of eventually being assigned to a desk instead of doing hands-on training in the field held as much appeal for him as an assignment in a jungle swamp.

Still, he had no idea what he'd do if he didn't stay in. As restless as the thought of a couple of weeks' leave made him feel, the prospect of retirement was enough to make him climb walls.

That was what he told Mia, too, wondering even as he did if the awful ambivalence he felt was anything like what Jack had suffered when he floundered all those years after he got out. The last thing he wanted to do was wind up like Kowalski.

He didn't say that to Mia, though, as they cruised on to their destination. That much he kept to himself, a little surprised as it was that he'd said as much as he had. He hadn't thought he'd want to talk about it at all, but Mia seemed to understand how very important all this was to him. And how unsettling. But because Mia didn't expect him to have an immediate answer, as everyone else did when a situation was put to him, he found himself admitting that he'd never made the kind of plans many men did about their futures. He was, always had been, and had thought he always would be, a marine. Therefore, staying in the service was probably the only logical course for him to take. After all, he'd joined when he was seventeen, and he hadn't known anything but the Marines in the twenty-four years since.

It was a convincing argument. At least it sounded so to Caid.

To Mia, he simply sounded like a person trying desperately to convince himself that he didn't have a choice.

"If you've been in your Marines since you were seventeen," she said quietly, "then perhaps the reason you're having trouble deciding what you want to do is because you don't want to be on your own.''

The look he sent her would have made his best men flinch. ''I've always been on my own,'' he said, in a tone as flat as the horizon. ''Here.'' Not looking at all pleased with her conclusion, he motioned for her to take his seat. ''Keep the wheel straight while I check the anchor.''

''It was just a thought,'' she said defensively, wondering what he'd meant about always having been on his own. Doubting he'd be amenable to a question about that at the moment, she turned her frown from his back to the wheel. ''How do I drive this?''

''Steer. On a boat, you don't drive. You steer.''

''Fine. How do I steer it, then?''

He'd been wasting his breath talking to her. What did she know of his life, anyway? Or of him?

Wondering if she'd intended to imply that he might actually be *afraid* to leave the military, he took her hands and placed them on the wheel.

All he wanted was for her to keep the boat from turning. She didn't have to steer it much at all. Just hold the wheel in place. So he told her exactly that, refusing to think about what the scent of her hair did to his body, and turned back to drop the anchor.

''Thank you,'' he heard her mutter, being far more good-natured than he was at the moment.

Amazed at how easily she could push his buttons, he muttered, ''You're welcome,'' in return.

''Caid?''

''What?''

''How are we going to find Jack from here?''

The inexplicable irritation he'd felt at her suggestion—along with the faint hint of consternation at her having just hit on something he might do well to consider—subsided as quickly as it had arisen. In its place came a nagging sense of disquiet. He found it interesting that he could hide his doubts about her situation with her father from her so much more easily than he could the things she made him feel.

The waterfall rose ahead of them, cascading through the tree-lined rocks to the side of the sheer rock face. When they were close enough, he took the wheel to ease the boat's bow onto the sandy beach and dropped the anchor over the back end, since he hadn't yet replaced the mechanism that lowered and raised it through the side.

"I asked Tom to see what he can find out about your father," Caid told her as he cut the engine.

Without the dull roar, only the cries of birds could be heard over the lap of the waves. "When we were talking this morning, I mentioned the articles I'd seen in the paper. Tom had seen them, too, so I asked if he could do a little digging to see if the police have any information they haven't released."

"Does this man know Jack?"

Caid told her that he didn't. Tom knew of the history Jack shared with Caid, though. Because of that, and because he was a man who'd fought elbow-to-elbow in the trenches himself, he'd agreed to see what he could do. Having been involved in a few cooperative efforts between the military police and the local law-enforcement agencies over the years, Tom had made some valuable contacts.

"He'll call as soon as he learns anything," he told her, and with the boat secured and bobbing gently in the protected cove, he headed into the cabin.

Still sitting in the captain's chair, Mia leaned forward. Caid had the sack of groceries they'd bought, and was putting them away. "He can reach you here?"

"He'll call at the Millers'."

"But they know I'm with you."

"They know there's a woman with me. That's all. I didn't mention you to Tom." Not with the police still looking for her. No one other than last night's intruder and the Millers knew she was with him. The Millers were safe. And the intruder had been left in their wake. "But my commander had to know where to reach me, Mia. An officer is always accountable for his whereabouts. Even on leave."

A cupboard door slammed. Then another. A moment later, Caid stepped back out into the sunlight.

His whereabouts weren't all an officer was accountable for. He was also accountable for his actions at any given time. At the moment, Caid wasn't so sure that what he was doing with Mia wouldn't be considered obstructing justice at some level. Were she wanted for more than just questioning, there'd be no doubt in his mind that would be exactly what he was doing.

But, just as it was his duty as an officer to uphold the code of the Corps, it was also his duty to exercise sound individual judgment. A man did what he had to do.

At the moment, what Caid had to do was work off some of the restlessness he felt.

"Can I help?" he heard her ask as he tossed aside one of the blue cushions from the side bench and lifted the lid to reveal a large storage area.

"I'm just going to set up camp."

"Camp?"

"You know. The tent. Make a fire ring. Get wood."

She did not know. Nor, at the moment, did she care.

"I thought we were going fishing."

One hand on the raised lid, the other on a large piece of canvas, Caid paused. "What?"

"That's why you told Marta we couldn't stay and have dinner with them. Remember?"

Of course he remembered. He just hadn't been serious, was all.

"You *want* to go fishing?"

"Sure."

Caid's glance grew skeptical.

"Have you ever been deep-sea fishing before?"

She had to admit that she hadn't. She'd never been any kind of fishing before, though she'd certainly cleaned and cooked her fair share of the scaly creatures at the orphanage.

"I'd like to try it. If you wouldn't mind."

Caid wasn't sure exactly what was responsible for the phenomenon. But as the anticipation in her eyes lit her face, he felt the tension leave his body by those same slow degrees. Two minutes ago he'd thought that what he needed was physical exertion. What he really needed, he realized, seeing her smile, was to see Mia going toe-to-fin with a striped marlin.

It wasn't a marlin Mia had on her line a little over an hour later. In fact, the little yellowtail she wound up throwing back because she said it was too pretty to keep hardly required the heavy line and reel she struggled with. But Caid had to admit that watching the sheer determination in her expression as she'd managed the heavy pole and tackle, and the excitement in her smile when she'd finally hauled the flopping fish onto the deck, was almost worth the frustration she caused him.

Since she'd never handled a pole and reel before, he'd stood behind her, his torso at her back and his arms parallel to hers as he showed her how to reel the fish in. He hadn't spent but two minutes with her sweet little backside pressed to his thighs and his chin brushing the top of her head, but every time they'd straightened to pull back on the line, then bent forward together to reel in the slack, he'd sworn the process was taking forever.

Mia had seemed almost as relieved as he when she finally got the rhythm and he stepped away. But she'd grown quieter after that. Almost cautious.

That sense of caution seemed to grow as the afternoon lengthened. There wasn't anything specific that she did or said that made him notice it, but an enervating tension began to surround even their simplest, most innocent exchanges. He could see that Mia enjoyed being outside, that she truly relished the first freedom she'd felt in days, for her smiles came often. But every time Caid would hold her glance for more than a moment, her smile would fade and her breathing would seem to quicken. Other times, when she didn't know he was watching her, he would see her muscles tense and her expression shadow over.

It wasn't until they were on the way back in and she was sitting at the stern, huddled into herself as she watched the wake churning behind the boat, that he realized what was wrong.

She was remembering last night. Thoughts of it would come to her in bits and pieces, and she'd gamely attempt to push away whatever part of those hours she was remembering. But just as he felt certain that she was experiencing flashes of the same awareness he felt, Caid was sure she was dealing with the more frightening aspects of what had happened. With all that she'd been through in the past few days—coupled with whatever she'd been through before—he wasn't so sure that, despite her own statement to the contrary, she now wasn't just a little bit frightened of him, too. Or, at least, of how she'd reacted to him when he held her.

He hated to think that she would think of him and be afraid. He hated even more that she might shy away from his touch.

That was why he tried to keep her busy when they returned to the cove, hoping the activity of pitching the tent and preparing dinner over the fire would take her mind off whatever occupied it and ease the odd strain growing between them. He didn't know what to say to ease the anxiety she clearly didn't want him to see, so while they ate their stew and cleaned up the dishes he tried distracting her with remarks about the island.

As it turned out, she was far more adept at distracting him. He'd mentioned the pool at the waterfall, and the buffalo that roamed the interior of the island. She wanted to see them both, but it was too late to hike into the interior now. So they went to the waterfall instead, and for a while she seemed to escape what was troubling her and take pleasure in the peace and seclusion he'd always found in this place.

But it was she who found beauty in places Caid would never have thought to look as he led her through the trees and into the cool, damp woods. Her smile would all but steal his breath when she found yet another delight in his cove, and he could only wonder at how he'd missed so much before he brought her here. He'd thought he'd been over every inch of this cove and the land surrounding it, but she could find the tiniest treasures, seemingly insignificant things Caid never would have noticed on his own. A tiny pink flower struggling through a crack in a moss-covered rock; pebbles as white as opals in a tiny stream beyond the pool of the waterfall. Even the way she viewed what she saw gave him a different perspective on the place. To her, the sound of the waterfall was like the music of a thousand reeds played all at once, and the spray misting the ferns surrounding the pool looked like powdered diamonds as it caught the last rays of the sun.

"What does it look like to you?" he heard her ask, her face tipped up toward the top of the falls cascading over the rim above them.

Caid couldn't reply. The best he could do was shrug, because he really hadn't been thinking about the waterfall or the ferns as he watched the play of light and shadow on her face. And because his response was so seemingly indifferent, the delight she'd taken in what he'd wanted to share with her turned to self-consciousness.

"You must think me quite foolish," she said with a self-deprecating smile, and turned away. Earlier, she'd mentioned wanting to go out to the boulders to see if there were any signs of the seals she'd spotted that morning. Now, looking as if she could use some time to herself, she headed toward the spill of huge rocks that had tumbled from cliff to surf.

Caid thought he should stop her. If for no reason other than to tell her he didn't think her foolish at all. He thought her dangerous, though. Definitely dangerous. And that was why he let her go. She made him feel things he didn't understand, much less trust. But he didn't feel relieved as he watched her head for the boulders at the edge of the sea. What he felt was concern. And after she'd been gone for nearly an hour, he found himself going after her. He didn't think she should be alone in the dark, anyway.

The gray clouds rolling in from the horizon had blended into the twilight gray of the sky when Mia saw Caid's shadowy form coming down the beach. He'd added more wood to the fire a while ago, and she'd already started up toward the orange glow. As much as she needed to be away from him, she needed the safety of the light more.

All afternoon, ever since those few moments on the boat when he'd had his arms around her as he showed her how to reel in the fish, she'd been thinking of how he'd kissed her last night. Remembering the strength and security she'd felt in his arms had helped ease the sudden surges of panic she would feel when her mind suddenly flashed a picture of a knife slicing past her face, or when the sore spots on her leg and head reminded her of being banged around in the dark. That security wasn't all she'd felt, though, and recalling the heat that had filled her when his mouth covered hers made her restless, edgy and more than a little apprehensive. Especially when she remembered how big and swollen that...that part of his body...had been. Whenever she thought of that, her stomach would feel all liquid and strange, and the restless feeling would compound itself.

It was that edginess that had overshadowed the afternoon. But it was that sense of security that threatened her the most. As appealing as it was, as badly as she wanted it, she couldn't trust it. It was false security, born of her own need for it to be there. That was the most dangerous kind, for right when she needed it most it would vanish like the illusion it was. It simply wouldn't be there anymore.

Like her mother.

Like Father Marquette.

Like Jack.

Caid had stopped a few yards up the beach.

"I was just coming back," she said when she reached him. "I saw the fire."

"We're going to need it tonight."

We? she thought, wondering if he meant for her to sleep in the tent with him. She thought she'd sleep on the boat. The idea of sleeping on hard ground obviously held some appeal for Caid, since he apparently did it with some regularity here, but she'd done enough of that to last her a lifetime. Her idea of comfort was a soft bed, a sturdy roof and walls. Not a sleeping bag inside the flimsy canvas tent they approached. She didn't know how American women felt about what Caid called camping, but she had the feeling most of them were no crazier about the idea than she was.

Since he'd said nothing specific about sleeping arrangements, Mia decided to wait before mentioning them herself. It wasn't exactly something she wanted to think about with his eyes following her every move. She probably wouldn't sleep anyway no matter where she lay down.

"Forget it, Mia," she heard him say.

Her glance flew to Caid. He wasn't looking at her now, though. He'd sat down on the ground beside her, his elbows on his bent knees and a cup of coffee in his hand as he stared at the sparks rising in the smoke. "There are two sleeping bags in there. But there's only one bed on the boat."

"So I'll take the bed." She could leave the light on in the cabin, too. Here she'd have to keep stoking the fire. "You can have the tent."

"I don't think so."

"Why not?"

"Because I'm not leaving you alone."

It was only about fifty feet out to the boat. Granted, she'd have to wade out to it, but she could put her shorts on again and carry her sweatpants and tennis shoes, as she had before.

She didn't get a chance to mention that. Caid reached up, snagged her wrist and gave it a gentle tug.

The moment she was on the ground beside him, he released her.

"I want you within reach, Mia." He probably shouldn't have put it quite like that. Still, it was the truth. "I'll rest better if I don't have to lie awake listening for you."

He probably wouldn't rest at all with her so close. But he wasn't going to argue this with her. They'd already decided they were evenly matched for stubbornness, but he had one distinct advantage. He was bigger.

"Maybe we should have stayed at the Millers' this afternoon," he said, changing the subject to something else he'd decided while she was gone. If they had stayed, she wouldn't have had to spend so much time avoiding him now. Aside from that, when he'd declined the invitation from the Millers, he'd been thinking only of himself. It hadn't occurred to him at the time that she might want to accept their offer. "If you want to go there tomorrow, we will."

Night had settled around them completely now. The only evidence of the ocean was in the sound of its waves crashing against the boulders. No one would even have known the woods were there had it not been for the rustle of the wind through the tops of the trees. There were no stars, and there was no moon. Just the inky darkness, and the pool of golden light from the fire.

In the glow of the crackling blaze, Mia studied Caid's implacable profile. The change of subject had been glaringly obvious. But it was what he'd changed the subject to that kept her from considering just how little room there would be in that tent.

"What made you change your mind?"

"I just thought you might want to go back," he said, when what he really thought was that the distraction of other people might do them both some good.

She turned to watch the fire herself, hugging her knees to her chest. "It would be fun," she admitted. "The cake Marta made for Lisa is really pretty, and I've never been to a birthday party before. I don't want to go if you'll be uncomfortable, though."

With a twinge of chagrin, Caid took a sip of his coffee. He didn't want to know how she knew he'd be uncomfortable. Nor did he want to consider that he cared more about her feelings at the moment than he did his own. "We'll go."

"Really?"

"Yeah," he muttered, thinking she looked impossibly young when her face lit up like that. "Really."

"Are we to do anything? Bring food or presents?"

"Some people give gifts on birthdays. But you don't have to bring food. I'm sure they don't expect anything at all."

"A gift," she repeated, hugging her knees tighter. "Any particular kind? We don't usually celebrate birthdays where I come from," she told him, feeling she needed to explain both her ignorance and her excitement. "Only a child's first birthday is noted. Here, I understand, you celebrate every one."

Caid sat back, watching the play of the firelight on Mia's hair as he told her again that he was sure the Millers didn't expect anything, but that a gift could be anything appropriate for the person. For some reason, that made her smile, and because he was curious to know what had brought that light to her eyes again, he asked why she was grinning.

"It is like that with a child's first birthday, too," she told him. "But until the celebration, it isn't known what will be appropriate."

The custom in Vietnam was called *thoi noi,* she told him, and it signified the child's leaving its cradle. While its family gathered around, the toddler was placed in the middle of a large circle of items intended to signify occupations. The first thing the child crawled to and touched was supposed to determine what he or she would grow up to be. Scissors for a tailor. A clump of dirt for a farmer. A pen for a scholar.

"Did you do this?"

Mia nodded.

"What did you touch?"

"My mother said I touched a ruler."

"And that meant?"

"That I would be a teacher." A philosophical shrug accompanied her smile. "Since that is what I became, it seemed to be my destiny."

Caid didn't buy that at all. "You became a teacher because that's what you're good at. Destiny doesn't have anything to do with it."

It was the certainty in his voice that threw her. "If you don't believe in it, why is that the name of your boat?"

"That's the name it came with."

The fire was warm, but her shoulders were cold, so Mia angled her back more toward the fire. In the process, she found herself facing this man who seemed to become more of a puzzle with every new piece she discovered.

"You don't believe there's anything you're destined to do?"

There was no accusation in her tone, no censure in her voice, at his cynicism. All Caid could see in Mia's expression was the quiet interest he'd heard in the gentle inquiry.

It seemed inevitable that he should touch her. So in that respect, he supposed, he did believe in some sort of fate. As he lifted his hand to her cheek, cautiously, because he didn't want her to be afraid of him or what he might do, his eyes locked on hers.

"Yeah," he whispered, slowly moving his thumb over her lower lip as he held her eyes. "I rather think there is. I'm just not sure how you feel about it."

Chapter 9

Caid was not a selfless man. It didn't matter that Mia had labeled him honorable or kind or whatever it was she'd called him the other day. He was just a man. With a man's needs. With her sitting in the firelight, the fine grain of her skin feeling like satin beneath his hand and her heart pounding at his touch, it was all he could do to keep from leaning forward to taste the sweetness of her mouth. But he wasn't a masochist, either. And he knew that if he kissed her the way he wanted to right now, he'd only be setting himself up for a long and miserable night.

He felt her breath flutter against his hand, warm and tremulous.

"How I feel about what?" she asked, her voice strained.

His glance followed the motion of his thumb against her lip. She hadn't shied away from him, as he'd feared she might. The knowledge did something strangely freeing to his heart.

"This," he told her, in a voice as low as the drone of the

sea. Gently, with more restraint than he'd realized he possessed, he brushed his mouth over hers. "Good night, Mia."

He raised his head, his eyes never leaving her face. She was supposed to pull back now, to look away from him. And he was supposed to pull his hand away and tell her to go to bed so that he could stare at the fire while he contemplated the benefits of standing under the waterfall for a while. She made him think about things he'd never felt any need to consider before. Things like a home and children and belonging to a family that celebrated things like birthdays. More and more he saw his own future simply as a continuation of his past. But he could easily see Mia in a house with a picket fence, with kids hanging on her apron strings.

He saw her raise her fingertips to her lips, her eyes locked with his. It was insanity not to move away himself, to leave well enough alone and stop thinking about her. More than anything, he needed to stop wanting her.

And that was about as easy as denying himself his next breath.

She didn't pull back. Neither did he. Instead, his hand moved around to cup the back of her neck.

Mia didn't know why Caid seemed to hesitate as his head came down. Or what thought brought the low curse he murmured just before his mouth lowered over hers. It was almost as if she'd done something he didn't like. But she'd barely moved. She'd scarcely even breathed since the moment she felt the warmth of his fingers on her cheek.

Those thoughts fled under the tender assault of his lips and the feel of his hands pulling her closer. So did any thought of the apprehension she'd felt earlier, for it wasn't nearly so strong as her need for the gentleness she felt in his kiss. She knew how to kiss him back now, too, and, at the first touch of his tongue, she opened to him.

With a kittenish sound of longing, she leaned into him, seeking as he sought.

The gentleness was there. In the beginning. Tantalizing. Provocative. Deceptive. He drew her into the kiss slowly, changing its course and texture and depth so gradually that she scarcely noticed when his tenderness turned to hunger—a raw, aching hunger filled with an urgency that would have frightened her had she not felt that same yearning herself. She didn't need to be frightened with Caid. He wouldn't hurt her. She knew that with a certainty she didn't even think to question. Even when his hand slipped under her shirt, she felt only anticipation. And when his palm covered her bare breast and she heard the almost animal-like groan wrenched from deep in his throat, it was only her own response that startled her. She seemed to have no control over the sensations he caused her to feel. Her breast seemed to swell, her nipple tingling where it poked his palm, and when he moved his hand to brush her tight bud with his thumb, she felt the tingling deep in her womb.

Would it feel like that if he were to put his mouth to her breast? she wondered, and her heart jerked at the thought.

She gripped the back of his shirt, needing him to be closer. There was something else over which she seemed to have little control. She was coming to believe in Caid. Whether it was wise or not, she was beginning to trust him. And because she trusted him, she wanted the security, however fleeting, that she felt in his arms. She wanted it desperately, as desperately as he seemed to want her.

Caid didn't want to want her, though. Not only was she under his protection, the woman was dangerous to his mental health. Realizing that he was about to pull her shirt over her head and push her back to the ground, his last thought finally made him ease her away.

He didn't look at her as he set her back.

Breathing hard, he faced the fire, his expression as black as the night beyond. "Go to bed, Mia."

"Caid?"

"I said, go to bed. Take either sleeping bag. Just be asleep by the time I get in there."

He stood then, frustration with her and anger at himself tensing every muscle in his body as he shoved his fingers through his hair. He'd known better than to reach for her that second time. He'd known better than to touch her at all. The woman was like some kind of weird narcotic that totally anesthetized his common sense.

Mia said nothing else. Not sure what she'd done, and too hurt by his abruptness to confront him about it, she whipped aside the flap on the tent, pulled off her shoes and crawled into one of the flannel-lined sleeping bags.

She'd done what he'd said, not because he'd ordered her to, but because there was nowhere else for her to go that wouldn't put her out in the night alone. She hated that she was again fearful of the dark, hated it almost as much as she abhorred the idea that Caid was now under the impression that she'd instantly obeyed him.

Her insides in knots, she punched the pillow and pulled her knees to her chest. Let him think what he wanted. She might have gone to bed, but no way was she going to be able to sleep.

It was a long time before Mia heard Caid come into the cramped little tent. She'd lain awake for what seemed like hours, listening to the crackling of the fire and watching its light glow through the canvas walls, while she tried to keep her personal demons at bay. When she finally heard him come in, he was deliberately quiet—determined, no doubt, to keep from waking her.

The other sleeping bag rustled as he slowly unzipped it and crawled in.

"Caid?"

The rustling stopped.

"What did I do?" she asked.

For a moment, she didn't think he was going to answer. In the darkness, all she could hear were the sounds of the night, and his long, low expulsion of breath.

"You didn't do anything, Mia. It was my fault."

She wasn't buying that. She must have done something for him to have pushed her away as he had. "I'm not sure what you want me to do. When you touch me like that, I just want to be close to you. It . . . it feels good to be close."

Lying on her side, with her back to him, she had no idea how her honesty affected him. Or if it affected him at all. Even were she to turn over, she wouldn't be able to see his face. So she stayed where she was, curled into herself.

His voice came toward her, husky and low. "There are different kinds of 'closeness,' Mia. What was happening out there was getting out of hand."

"In your opinion," she said to the dark wall of the tent.

"In my opinion," he said, his voice scarcely above the whisper the darkness seemed to demand, "we were leading straight to something we might have both regretted."

"By 'something,' I assume you mean making love. Believe it or not, just because I haven't had the experience, doesn't mean I don't understand the principle."

Because her tone was as subdued as his, it failed to betray the hurt Caid's words had brought. Until he'd said what he had, she'd doubted very much that she would have regretted making love with him—even though she knew it wasn't terribly wise to want him quite so badly. He'd said himself that he didn't think in terms of the future, or make the kinds of plans most other people made for themselves. But Mia could no longer think in terms of the future herself, for her own seemed so precarious. With her, with Caid, there was only the present.

And at present he didn't want her.

"I'll make my own decisions about what I'll regret doing," she told him, with a defiance she didn't feel at all. "But if you would regret making love with me, then I'm glad you made us stop."

Caid said nothing. As Mia all but held her breath, not a single word came from behind her to ease the awful quiet filling the space they shared.

She had no idea what Caid's silence meant. She had plenty of time to think about it, however, as she lay there listening to her heart pounding in her ears. It seemed a full minute passed before she heard the rustle of his sleeping bag again as he settled down into it. After that, she heard nothing from him at all.

Blinking into the darkness, she pushed her hand under her cheek and drew her knees closer to her chest.

She wished he'd left the fire burning.

She had the fire going herself when Caid awoke the next morning. He heard the snap and sizzle of flame burning pitch patches on the logs even before he left the tent. When he did step outside, pulling on his sweatshirt as he did, he caught the smell of wood smoke in the cool morning air. He loved mornings in this cove.

It was last night he wished he could do over again.

Mia sat by the fire, her back to him. She had the pad she'd bought yesterday propped on her knees—and looked as natural against the backdrop of ocean and sky as the dawn itself as she sketched something only she could see off in the distance.

The morning suited her.

The thought struck him as he moved from beneath the protective overhang of rock where the tent sat and toward the inviting blaze several yards beyond. But other thoughts overtook that one as he walked across the dew-dampened and sandy earth. As intent as she seemed to be, his presence might not be particularly welcome.

She wouldn't have stopped him last night. Knowing that had made keeping his mouth shut and his hands off her one of the most difficult things he'd ever done.

A shell crunched beneath his foot. Hearing it, Mia snapped her head around.

Immediately she closed the cover on the pad. All Caid cared about was that she didn't turn away.

"Hi," she said, before indicating the aluminum pot on the grill. "I don't know how good it will be, but it'll be coffee soon. You seem to need it when you first get up."

That she was becoming so attuned to his habits gave him pause. That she wasn't freezing him out, however, was more important at the moment. He'd half expected the strain between them this morning to be as thick as the clouds obscuring the sun.

Not sure that strain wasn't there anyway, he ran his hand over the stubble on his face. "I didn't hear you get up."

"I didn't want to wake you."

She'd been up for at least an hour. Long enough, she told him, to get a decent start on the picture she wanted to give Lisa this afternoon for her birthday. "I know you said we didn't have to take anything," she added as the coffee began to boil over with a splutter and a splash. "But we can't go without some sort of gift."

As she snatched the heavy green pot holder from atop the duffel holding their supplies, Caid's glance fell on the pad she'd laid beside the flat rock where she'd been sitting. "What are you drawing?"

She wouldn't tell him. She wouldn't let him see, either. Eyeing him a little uneasily, as if she hadn't yet figured out his mood, she set the pot away from the flame and reached into the duffel for mugs. "You take it black, right?"

"I take it stronger," he said, the instant he saw the pale brew. "That looks like tea."

Her nose wrinkling, she started to say, "That's what Jack..." only to have her voice fade out.

"That's what Jack...what?"

"Always says," she concluded, and poured a cup of the weak stuff for herself before she set the pot back on the fire.

Looking very much as if she wished the memory hadn't asserted itself, she tossed the pot holder back and picked up her pad again. Now that she'd mentioned Jack, it was clear that whatever escape she'd managed with her drawing had been circumvented. Her father was now very much on her mind.

"Do you think it will be very long before we hear from your commander?"

Seeking the warmth of the fire, Caid hunched down beside her and spread his palms toward the heat. It bothered him when the animation drained out of her as it just had.

"I don't think it'll be too long. Tom said he'd call, one way or the other. Since it's the weekend, he probably won't make any calls himself until tomorrow." Tomorrow was Monday. "I'm sure we'll know whether or not he was able to come up with anything by Tuesday."

Tiny white sparks drifted up from the orange-and-yellow flames. Watching them blink out when they got too far from the fire, Mia sipped her coffee. "Two days isn't that long, I suppose." It actually felt like a lifetime to her just now. Yet, compared to the time she'd spent waiting to find her father, two days was as fleeting as the life of the sparks she continued to follow. "And there are definitely worse places to spend the time waiting. It's nice here."

She tried to smile. She even managed a hint of one, until she looked back up at the sky. The clouds were thicker than they had been when she awakened. She was sure of it.

Not wanting it to matter, telling herself it didn't, she casually glanced over at Caid. "Do you think it will rain?"

The hard line of his jaw came into sharp relief as he looked up, his chiseled profile stark against the background of beige rock wall looming beyond him. "Probably," came his less-than-reassuring reply. "No big deal if it does. The tent stays pretty dry under that ledge."

Staying dry wasn't Mia's concern. Not, she reminded herself, that she was really all that worried. Soft mists and gentle drizzles could be rather nice sometimes. It was storms she hated, the kind when the rain came in torrents and the sky split with lightning. The pearly clouds riding the breeze looked harmless enough, at the moment. It was the darker clouds on the horizon that she fervently hoped would stay right where they were.

"It shouldn't be too bad, though. Right?"

The weather. Hearing Mia's question, Caid mentally shook his head at the digression. Had he looked at her then, he might have seen the faint strain tensing her features. But all he noticed was the calm sound of her voice.

He couldn't believe they were actually talking about the weather. Especially with the more pertinent matters they could be discussing. He had to admit, though, that he really didn't want to ask the questions he'd lain awake pondering about the guard at the museum until he'd had his coffee. And since they were both avoiding the subject of what had happened on this very spot last night, he might as well take his cue from her.

"I didn't catch a weather report, so I really don't know. It should be okay if the wind doesn't come up," he added, thinking her approach was probably best. Keep it surface. Keep it safe.

The tension he'd missed in her expression had faded by the time she'd lifted the pot from the grill again. The coffee was now the color of mud.

Caid pronounced it perfect, thinking she looked kind of cute when she did that wrinkle-thing with her nose while she poured the thick brew. More relieved than he wanted to admit that things seemed to be okay between them for the moment, he sat back while she asked if he still planned to take the anchor motor apart, as he'd mentioned yesterday. He told her he might, after he saw how the opal eye were biting out by the rocks.

Since she'd never heard of opal eye—and being naturally curious—she asked what they were. So Caid described the flat fish with eyes that looked like opals, and as they talked he was struck again by the thought he'd had when he first saw her sitting by the fire. The thought about how well the morning suited her.

There was something about the beginning of a new day that held a certain promise—like Mia herself. A new day was a clean slate, a chance to start over. Mistakes made yesterday belonged to the past, and all that lay ahead was the moment, and whatever a person chose to make of it. Mia, he was coming to know, seemed to handle everything that way, choosing to make the best of everything in the process.

Caid had never regarded himself as a particularly insightful man; certainly he didn't think himself a philosophical one. It was only through knowing Mia, by thinking of her optimism and her unfailing sense of hope, that such thoughts had even occurred to him. She believed in new beginnings, in giving herself a chance. In giving others a chance, too, even though she'd probably been let down more times than she could count. Yet, as hard as it must be for her to make herself vulnerable to someone, to truly trust, she was at least willing to try.

That was more than he could say for himself.

The wind picked up around noon. Since it didn't carry deep into the trees by the waterfall, that was where Mia finished the small drawing of two little girls watching an earthworm inch between them. It wasn't much, but it was all she could offer, and she had it finished by the time Caid returned from fishing out on the rocks.

There had been no discussion about it earlier, but he'd gone his way for the morning, and she'd gone hers. Until she saw him come up the beach to their camp, though, Mia hadn't realized how she missed his solid presence. Even when they were at odds, she felt better when he was around. Now, as he showed her what he'd caught and they prepared his catch over the fire, she felt better simply because his attitude toward her was much as it had always been. Especially when he started asking about the guard she'd run into at the museum.

Since Caid's intention to pay a visit to the museum had been circumvented by his and Mia's departure to the island, he had given more thought to her supposition about the guard's possible involvement with the theft. It didn't make any sense to Caid, though, that the man could have simply walked out with the crown in his lunch bag, as Mia had suggested. There had to be some sort of check on the guard himself. Without one, he—or any of the other security personnel—could walk out with something of value at any time.

The argument was logical. And, as Mia explained to him while trying to keep the ants out of her lunch, there was a check system of sorts in place. The guard service the museum used was licensed and bonded, and presumably hired people of integrity. In addition, anything small enough to be hidden in clothing or a lunch bag was displayed in individually secured cases—as the crown had been. Those were the checks the museum used for night employees—but they would work only if the people hired by the service were honest and the security systems for the cases fully activated. As badly as she wanted to believe that the stocky little man had taken the crown, however, she couldn't understand why the police would be looking to arrest Jack if they had anything on the guard.

Caid apparently couldn't understand that, either. He didn't say anything about the guard after that, though Mia would have welcomed any theory he might have come up with. Even an implausible one. She needed the distraction.

It had started to rain.

When Mia mentioned the increasingly ominous clouds to Caid this time, he didn't think she was just making conversation. He caught the concern he'd missed earlier. But he thought it was because bad weather might make them miss the birthday party at the Millers'. Since he had no real desire to go to a child's birthday party himself, the weather didn't much matter to him. He felt bad that she'd worked so hard on a gift she might not be able to give, though. So, for her sake, he hoped the sky would clear.

The hope proved futile. Within the hour the clouds grew heavier, the wind blew stronger, and, between the sporadic fits and starts of showers that occasionally sent Mia under the ledge over the tent, the sea became choppier. High waves meant deep troughs, and since Caid had no desire to navigate an antagonized ocean, he finally had to tell her, about the time they would have departed for the Millers', that they couldn't make the party.

"It's all right," she said with a forgiving smile—but he knew by now that she never let the full extent of her disappointment show.

The rain fell steadily all afternoon, a light rain that was just heavy enough to keep them inside the tent with the flap open so that they could look out over the shades of gray melding sky into sea. Having the flap open helped let in the light, too, which Caid needed to see the parts of the small motor he'd decided to take apart, since there wasn't much else he could do without getting drenched.

The motor lay in pieces on an old towel he'd spread between the two sleeping bags. He sat Indian-style on one of the bags, elbows on his knees, as he cleaned the pieces of black and silver metal. Mia, mirroring his position, sat on the bag across from him, more interested in the intensity of his concentration than in what he was doing.

Mia didn't know an armature from a contact ring. She knew nothing about electricity, either. Not the AC and DC kinds Caid understood. She was beginning to understand another type, though. The kind she felt when Caid's hand would touch hers while she held the motor upright for him, or when his eyes would hold hers for longer than two seconds. Since Caid didn't appear at all affected by their enforced closeness, she used her energy to pretend she wasn't, either. The task was actually quite beneficial. Thinking about him kept thoughts of her other, equally disquieting circumstances at bay.

Talking helped, too.

As Caid worked, he mentioned that he'd known the motor was going out when he first bought the boat. There had been so much else that needed to be done to the craft, though, that he'd just let it go until it finally broke. He liked working on boats, she discovered. *Destiny* was his third since he'd been transferred to California from Virginia six years ago. Once he got a boat fixed up, he sold it and bought another that needed work.

It seemed to Mia as she listened—asking, too, about the place called Virginia, and what the country was like there—that he didn't let himself get attached to much of anything. Much less anyone. Unable to identify with such a need to remain separate, she wished she understood how he could feel that way. It wasn't until he had the motor back together and they were starting to clean up, though, that she thought she might have caught a glimpse of just how long he'd held that conviction.

On the way back from the Millers' yesterday, he'd about taken her head off when she suggested he might not want to leave his Marines because he didn't want to be on his own. He'd also implied that he'd always had to fend for himself.

Encouraged by the unusually companionable atmosphere that had settled over the long afternoon, Mia decided she'd ask how long "always" had been—just as soon as he got back.

Caid wasn't gone but a minute. Shivering as a gust of wet wind came back in with him, Mia snagged the flapping tent door while he set down the pan of steaming water he'd gone to retrieve. He'd kept the fire stoked, but since evening had set in, the rain had gotten heavier and finally put the fire out. This was the only warm water they would have.

"How is it that you're alone, Caid?" she asked as he reclaimed his space and pulled off his wet shoes. Outside the wind whipped the rain around them and rattled the canvas walls of their shelter. By focusing on Caid, Mia was almost able to pretend that the increasing intensity of the storm didn't bother her. Almost. "You said you always have been. Don't you have a family, either?"

A frown touched Caid's forehead. Not sure how the conversation had gotten from his boat to his lack of ties in the minute he'd been outside, he rolled the oil-spotted towel around the motor and set it in the corner with his shoes. He then reached for a bar of soap and a clean towel.

He handed them to her first. He'd make the water a lot dirtier than she would.

"I did have one," he said, not looking terribly pleased with the question. "I haven't talked to my mother in years." He picked up a wet leaf and tossed it aside. "My father died in the Korean War."

"He was a soldier, too?"

"Yeah," Caid muttered, watching warm water drip from her slender hands as she absently caressed the bar of soap. "He was a soldier. I don't remember him, though. I was two when he was killed."

"I'm sorry."

At the quiet expression of sympathy, Caid met her eyes. There was an empathy there that he didn't quite know how to acknowledge. No one had ever expressed sympathy to him about his father before. Possibly because he rarely mentioned the man. It felt strange. And a little uncomfortable.

"It was difficult for you and your mother, then," he heard her say.

"Not the way you're thinking, Mia." It hadn't been difficult in the way it had for her and her mother. Even from what little Mia had described of her own life, Caid knew that to be absolutely true. "My mother wasn't ostracized by her family. Or by anyone else, for that matter. I don't know how old I was when she remarried the first time, but I'd been through two stepfathers and a few 'uncles' by the time I graduated from high school."

The edge of bitterness in his voice brought her eyes to his face. "By the way you say 'uncles,' I assume you do not mean either of your parents' brothers."

She assumed correctly. "She always had somebody in the house." And in her bed. "Everybody liked it better when I wasn't around, so I tended to make myself scarce. It was easier."

Easier than listening to his mother tell him to be good so that the current beau would like him—which, in turn, meant the guy might actually stick around for a while. Caid hadn't given a damn if anyone liked him or not. Those guys had all been more important to his mother than he, and not one of them had cared a whit about "the kid."

By the time he was seventeen, the only image of a man that Caid had trusted at all was the image he held of his father. The soldier.

"So you became a soldier, too," she said, with a simplicity that was utterly remarkable given the impact of her words. "He was your hero."

With an arch of her eyebrow, Mia handed him the washcloth she'd just wrung out. Caid took it from her, wondering as he did how she could shake him so easily with her quiet observations.

"Maybe," he heard himself say, though he'd never thought of his father as a hero before. But possibly that was the image he'd held of him—an image his father hadn't had a chance to tarnish. Much as Mia had held an image of Jack before she found him.

Caid reached for the soap and lathered the grease from his hands. Their circumstances were very different, but their insecurities sounded suspiciously similar.

Some of them, anyway.

When he heard the thunder rumble off in the distance, he didn't give it much more than a passing thought. Mia, on the other hand, sucked in her breath and went absolutely still. What Caid noticed, though, when he looked up to see

er uneasily eyeing the zippered flap, was the dark streak on
er jaw.

"You've got grease on your face."

Seeming surprised by the sound of his voice, she jerked
er head toward him. "Wha—?" she began, only to have
vhat he'd said register.

She lifted her hand to her face. "Grease? Where?"

"By your ear. You must have gotten it on you one of the
imes you pushed your hair back. Here."

Since she couldn't see it, he leaned forward to take her
hin in his hand. Turning her head to one side, angling it
oward the glow of the lantern, he rubbed the wet wash-
loth over the inch long streak.

Rain, driven by wind, pelted the sides of the tent. *So
nuch for the overhang of the ledge keeping us dry*, he
hought, just as a deep, rolling rumble sounded again.

Beneath his hand, he felt Mia jump, the tension in her
ody so real he swore he could feel it himself. "Hey," he
nuttered, letting her go. "Are you all right?"

"I'm sorry." Her breath shuddered out. "Thunder just
nakes me nervous."

"It's not going to hurt anything."

She swallowed. "I know. Silly, isn't it?"

She didn't sound convinced. Despite her tremulous smile,
he didn't look convinced, either.

"Is the grease gone?" she asked

"Not quite." Her skin had a definite redness to it where
e'd rubbed. It also still had a streak of gray. Not knowing
: he was rubbing too hard or if a woman's skin was just that
nuch more sensitive than a man's, he started to hand the
loth to her. "Maybe you'd better do it."

Before she could think about what she was doing, her
ingers gripped his wrist. "You do it. Please," she added,
hen he hesitated. "I can't see where it is."

Mia didn't know if Caid thought her reasoning logical or
ame. The truth of it was, she didn't care. She just didn't
ant him to move back over to the other side of the invisi-

ble line that seemed to have been drawn down the the middle of the floor. As it was, only his arms were stretched over
it now. But if all she could have was the touch of his hand
on her face, she would take it.

"Then move over so I can see it better," she heard him
say, and, a moment later he'd crossed the line completely.

He knelt beside her now, taking her chin as he had before. All too soon, he pronounced the spot gone, pitched the
cloth into the pot of darkened water and leaned back. As he
did, a flash of light illuminated the inside of the tent, then
vanished to plunge it back into the dim glow of the lantern.

Mia had started to thank him, but the words froze in her
throat.

The walls suddenly seemed so close, the rain so much
louder than before. An awful feeling of suffocation pressed
down on her, the sensation forcing her to draw a deliberately deep breath. *This isn't the same,* she told herself, hating that the memories kept wanting to surface. *This night
won't be like that one.*

Slowly she drew her knees up, hugging her arms around
them.

"Tell me more about your boats. Or the Marines," she
added hurriedly.

"The Marines?" he repeated, his puzzlement at her reaction and her request making it seem as if he'd never heard
of the outfit.

"About what it's like to be one. Or tell me about the sea.
I know you like the sea." She didn't care what he talked
about. So long as he kept her distracted. And so long as he
stayed close. "Just talk to me. Okay?"

For a moment she feared he was going to move back over
the line. He said nothing as his glance swept her face, his
brow furrowing.

"Instead of me talking to you, maybe it would be a better idea if you talked to me." He cocked his head, his scrutiny becoming more intense. "It's more than just the
thunder. Isn't it?"

After several seconds of silence, he tried again. "Does the thunder remind you of something?"

Even as he posed the question, Caid felt certain of the answer. He should have seen it before. But he'd been so intent on keeping emotional distance between them that he hadn't allowed himself to acknowledge the strain she'd been under all day. He'd dismissed her questions about the weather with handy excuses, and ignored the fact that her concern hadn't lessened after the decision was made to pass on the party. But trying to keep her at arm's length hadn't helped at all. All it had done was cause Mia to keep whatever was troubling her to herself.

"My mother." She rested her chin on her knees, her focus on the wet leaf he had tossed aside a while ago. "It was on a night like this that she died. I haven't had the nightmares for years. But the past few days..."

The sentence was completed with a shrug. The motion wasn't as dismissive as she'd intended, though. Not for an instant did Caid believe she felt anywhere near as calm as she sounded.

"The past few days have brought it all back," he concluded for her. "Because of the stress."

With the tip of his finger, he nudged her chin upward. She didn't seem to want to look at him. When she did, he could have sworn the heaviness he felt in his chest was his own heart aching for her. She bore her fears alone. Just as she'd borne her memories alone. He didn't know what she'd been through, but he'd seen more than enough himself while he was in Vietnam for his imagination to run rampant. All Mia had had was her mother, and after the woman had died, she'd been left alone.

"It was the monsoon," she said, grateful that he understood. "Do you know the monsoon?"

"Yeah." His fingers drifted from her chin. "I do."

"It sounds just like this. Doesn't it?"

He had to agree that it did. In fact, with the rain hammering the earth, thunder rolling ever closer and lightning filling their cozy space with its brief light, they could easily have been in the middle of the seasonal monsoon that fed and flooded the rivers and deltas of Southeast Asia. When the thunder came this time, though, Mia didn't jump. She only hugged her knees tighter.

In direct contrast, Caid sat beside her, his legs drawn up his knees apart and his arms wrapped loosely around them.

"Maybe it would help if you told me what happened. Talking it out can help, Mia." At least it could help some people. He knew of some guys, though, whose flashbacks were so severe they'd never recovered. "Why don't you tell me about that night?"

She started to say she didn't think that was such a good idea. If she started thinking about it any more than she already had, it might all come back. Already she was trying desperately not to think about the little bits and pieces of the nightmare that had kept her from sleep. She didn't know if she could bear to recall any more than she had, for each memory brought the awful panic that already felt so real it nearly suffocated her at times.

Yet, as she'd noticed before, Caid's rock-solid steadiness seemed to provide a buffer against those memories. Or maybe it was simply that now, in his own way, he was asking her to share what troubled her so. If she split the burden, she wouldn't have quite so much to carry.

Whether he realized it or not, he was reaching out. And in doing so, he was finally letting her in.

"I don't know that there's that much to tell." She wasn't even sure what her mother had died of, though pneumonia was a good possibility.

"Just start with whatever you remember." His tone was steady, encouraging.

That was easy. "What I remember most is the storm, and being frightened because she wouldn't wake up."

She remembered being cold, too. And she remembered the man who had taken her mother's body away. But that hadn't been at night. Daylight had come by the time the

arled old man lifted the cardboard roof that had col-
)sed during the deluge and made Mia let her go. What she
)uld recall most when she would awaken from the night-
are, though, was the memory of the darkness, and of
mething lying over her, pressing down.

"Maybe what I remember is the cardboard roof," she
id. "But when I wake up, it always seems like it was
mething so much heavier than such a covering must have
en."

"You were only a child."

She supposed Caid meant the observation to explain her
rception of the roof's size or weight. Mia couldn't tell
)m his subdued voice. She knew only that it wasn't so hard
talk when he was so close, and that the boom of thunder
d the flash of lightning weren't nearly as startling as they
d been a while ago.

Because of that, she was able to tell him what she re-
led of living on the streets after he asked what she'd done
en the man took away her mother. She told him how
e'd learned to sleep during the day, because it was too
ngerous to remain unguarded at night, when there were
many other people living on the streets, people who were
lling to relieve a person of what little she possessed. She
d him, too, about having to hide from the people who
)loited children like her by having them work as prosti-
es and drug runners, and about the police and soldiers
asing her through the markets when she would steal rice,
fruit, or something to cover herself with. Most of the time
:y couldn't catch her, because she was so fast, but when
:y did it sometimes took weeks for the bruises to heal.
at sometimes happened when she'd pick pockets, too.

It was about the time Mia mentioned what the police and
diers had done that Caid noticed how much quieter her
ice had become. As she'd spoken, she'd remained hud-
d into herself, just as she had when she sat on the sofa in
apartment that first night and told him about Jack. And
t as she had after she was attacked. As he had those other

nights, he saw the brightness in her eyes that spoke of tea
wanting to be shed.

She wouldn't cry, though.

He knew that now.

"I wish I wasn't so afraid," he heard her say.

She was speaking of the police. Those after her now.

When Caid realized that, a dull heaviness filled his che
There was nothing he could say that would change h
present circumstances; neither was there anything he cou
say that would change a single thing that had happened
her past. But when she looked over at him and he saw t
naked need in her eyes, he knew there was one small thi
he could do that might make her feel a little less alone.

"How about a pair of arms?" he asked.

Incredibly, she managed a soft little smile.

She needed him. With him, she felt safe.

Wishing she'd never experienced what she had, wond
ing how her gentleness had survived, Caid unlocked h
arms from around her knees and drew her to him. Before
could guide her head to his shoulder, though, she touch
her slender fingers to his face.

"That was all a long time ago," she reminded him, b
cause he seemed to care. Voicing what she'd kept inside
so long had been more cathartic than she could have ima
ined. It was as if taking the dark memories and exposi
them to light had somehow reduced their power over h
"It might not seem like it right now, but I don't usua
think about all of that so much anymore. After Fath
Marquette took me in, things got better. Honest. It's ju
that the last few days have been a little...extraordinar
Slowly she withdrew her hand. "Rather like you."

Her skin was luminous in the pale light, and her eyes w
shining. But it was the warmth of her mouth beneath
that Caid noticed most.

Chapter 10

Caid didn't know who leaned forward first. Mia was the first to draw back, though, long before he would have let her go.

As she did, stilling when his hands on her shoulders allowed her to go no farther, she apologized. "I shouldn't have done that." The tips of her fingers trembled slightly as she touched her mouth, the motion seeming to hold his kiss in place. "I'm sorry."

"Why?" he wanted to know, puzzled as much by her apology as her withdrawal.

"I don't want you to do anything you'll regret."

At the sound of his own words coming back to him, Caid closed his eyes. She'd been hurt last night when he pushed her away. Even now he could sense the rejection she must have felt. He'd bet anything she'd drawn back now to avoid having the same thing happen again.

Swearing at himself, Caid scarcely noticed the gust of wind battering the tent, or the beat of the driving rain closing in around them. There was something he had to tell her, something she needed to know that might help explain his behavior—just in case she was operating under the assumption that he didn't find her desirable.

"Last night was my fault. I tried to tell you that." His voice was low, rumbling like the thunder itself. "What I didn't tell you is how badly I want you. How badly I've wanted you since the night you walked in my door. Or how hard it is being this close to you and not doing everything I've lain awake at night imagining." Hell, he thought, she had no idea how hard he *was* from one lousy kiss. "I'm just trying to do what's right," he finally muttered.

"You think wanting me is wrong?"

The blue of his eyes turned as stormy as the night, the clench of his jaw as tight as his grip on her arms. "That's not what I mean at all."

He wasn't sure what he meant anymore. Wanting her didn't feel wrong. In fact, it had somehow come to feel very right. The problem was that wanting her was also beginning to feel necessary.

What felt necessary, too, was the need to chase away the demons shadowing her lovely eyes.

For some reason unknown to him, she seemed to take comfort in his touch. She'd said last night that she liked being close to him, too. So, because he couldn't bear to see the shadows, because he ached to hold her against him, he did what he'd been wanting to do all day.

Putting his hands on her waist, he pulled her between his spread legs and lifted her to her knees. "Put your arms around my neck."

He took her mouth even before her hands reached their destination. She tasted as sweet as the rain, and she smelled like the wildflowers she found near the waterfall yesterday. There was something wildly erotic about such innocence. It was almost as tantalizing as the way she leaned into him, fitting herself to his chest. With her arms around his neck, his hands were free to roam over her back and along her sides. He moved slowly, letting her become accustomed to the feel of his hands on her. Every once in a while she would tense, as she did when he molded the sides of her hips and the backs of her supple thighs. But within moments she instinctively relaxed against him again.

She felt so good. No matter how he held her, she fitted him perfectly. Splaying his hands on her hips, he drew her more firmly against his stomach. He could only imagine how he would fit between her legs.

"I've never thought wanting you was wrong," he heard her whisper.

The words, coming on the heels of his thoughts, nearly stole his breath.

"Don't say things like that."

"Why not? It's true."

She was testing him. She had to be. There wasn't a female over the age of fourteen who didn't know that telling a man she wanted him had to make him even hotter than he already was.

He shook his head. *I don't know what to do with you,* he thought. Or, maybe he said the words aloud.

He must have.

Still on her knees, she leaned back to see his face, leaving her arms looped around his neck. "You could show me what you've imagined."

"What?"

"You said you'd lain awake at night imagining what you'd do to me." The delicate cords of her neck moved as she swallowed. Her voice grew softer. "You could show me."

At the suggestion, a primitive light flared in his eyes. The hard line of his jaw went absolutely rigid. "If I do that, you won't be a virgin anymore."

Mia held his eyes, her heart beating wildly in her throat. He wasn't going to push her away this time. She wasn't sure exactly how she knew that, but some innate feminine wisdom told her that, if he was going to, he would have done so by now.

Emboldened by that knowledge, and by the way his nostrils flared when his glance fell to her mouth, she moved a scant inch nearer.

"So, how does what you've imagined begin?"

"Mia."

He fairly growled her name, making it sound very much like a warning. Yet, even as he warned her away, his hands drew her closer.

She managed another inch. "Do I kiss you first? Or do you kiss me?"

Lightning flashed, and her heart bumped against her ribs. Not because of the lightning, though. With his hands touching her, with his eyes boring into hers, the lightning no longer felt threatening. For that brief instant, the white light threw his beautifully tortured features into stark relief, etching their noble lines in her mind's eye. It was that memory she would recall the next time it stormed, along with all the others he was giving her to replace the fears that had returned to haunt her.

"Don't you want to tell me?" she asked, anticipation coursing through her as his hand worked up her side.

"You kiss me."

That she knew how to do. So she did, aware that he held himself absolutely still as she leaned toward him. His mouth was warm, full and soft beneath hers—and her insides turned liquid when he parted his lips at the touch of her tongue. She kissed him as he had taught her, though she wasn't quite so bold in her exploration as he might have been. Still, she felt his body tense against hers.

"Then what?" she whispered when, breathless, she lifted her head long moments later.

The muscle in his jaw jerked. "Then I do this."

His hands moved down her back and over her bottom, rubbing with long, slow strokes as his lips caressed her neck, her jaw, her ear.

"And this," he breathed, his hands pushing under her sweatshirt to trace her ribs and tease the soft skin below the fullness of her breasts.

Mia thought she heard thunder. It could just as easily have been the sound of her heart pounding in her ears when he pushed her shirt up and began trailing a path of moist heat up her stomach. She felt his tongue tease the curve of her breast, the heat making goose bumps spring up all over her skin. But when she felt his tongue touch her nipple, and his mouth closed over the tight bud, exquisite sensation coursed through her. She slipped her fingers into his hair, urging him closer, holding him to her. The sensual pull was heady. Almost as heady as the knowledge that this man wanted her.

She'd waited all her life for him.

His hands left her sides, moving up to slip the sweatshirt over her head. The cool air she'd ignored before now hit full-force. As Caid leaned back, though, pulling her with him, the cold scarcely registered. One moment she was lying on top of him; the next, he'd rolled them over, his hard body covering hers as if to protect her from the chill.

She would have thought his weight would crush her, as big as he was. But, with his hands in her hair, he seemed to bear his weight on his elbows as he kissed her. So it was the heaviness of his hips she noticed most, and their slow movement as he pressed down on the heat between her legs.

Mia no longer thought about what came next in Caid's imaginings. She thought only of how powerful his sculpted body looked when he reared back and pulled off his shirt. His silver dog tags caught the light of the lantern as he tossed his shirt aside, the glint of the chain contrasting with his tanned skin and the soft mat of dark hair arching over his broad chest. Unwittingly her glance strayed to the arrow of hair disappearing into the waistband of his jeans, then moved up to see Caid watching her.

Her unknowingly provocative glance caused him to pause. His eyes never leaving hers, he slowly unbuckled his belt. Moments later, with the rasp of his zipper, his jeans joined his shirt.

"You have too many clothes on," she heard him whisper as he pulled the rest of her clothing from her.

The heat of his body as he settled next to her and pulled the other sleeping bag over them brought her an entirely new set of sensations—the feel of the coarse hair of his legs against her smooth ones, the tantalizing friction of skin against skin.

"I don't want to hurt you."

She felt the faint vibration of his words against her mouth.

"I know," she murmured, and threaded her fingers through his hair.

The kiss was slow and deep, dragging her under by slow degrees. The feel of his hand as it worked from her breast to the soft skin of her inner thighs brought a low moan to her throat. Caid drank in that small sound, his fingers creating little lines of shimmering heat when he eased her legs apart.

"That's it," he coaxed as she relaxed and allowed him to touch her more intimately.

Her unspoken trust inflamed his senses, causing a shudder to ripple through him. He wanted nothing more than to bury himself in her softness, to lose himself in the gentle innocence of this woman who had touched his weary soul. Knowing he had to hold back, that this first time would be far from perfect, he lifted himself over her.

"It's okay," she whispered, as if she read his concern.

He eased forward, murmuring to her as he slipped his hand beneath her hips. He tried to be gentle. She felt certain of that. The effort was in the taut lines of his face and in the tension quivering through his body when he finally began to enter her. But she didn't want him to be gentle anymore. She wanted him with a desperation that astounded her, wanted to discover all the sweet sensations he could make her feel, and make him feel them in return.

He breathed her name, the beckoning sound of his voice causing her to arch toward him. Her tiny gasp of pain was lost as his mouth covered hers, and he went as still as she. But in those precious moments as they held each other, waiting for her to become accustomed to him, he began slowly stroking the inside of her mouth with his tongue. When he felt her body become fluid, he began mimicking the provocative motions with his hips. Slowly at first. He was replacing the pain with pleasure, just as he had replaced her fears with his strength.

Her body flowed toward him, with him, as she instinctively matched the rhythm he was teaching her. Yes, she wanted him. But, more than anything, she wanted the sense of belonging she felt in his arms. She'd never felt that in all her life. Caid made the fears go away. And for now, the security he offered was real.

Just as real as the storm raging outside. Just as real as the storm exploding within them.

Caid awoke before Mia did. He lay on his back, with her curled up in the crook of his arm, her soft hair fanning over his shoulder and her hand on his chest. She'd actually fallen asleep with the rain still pounding away outside last night. Either she hadn't felt quite so frightened after they made love, or he'd exhausted her. Whichever, Caid felt good to know she slept.

He also felt guilty as hell.

He didn't understand how it had happened, how he'd let her affect him so. But she had, far more deeply than he would have imagined possible. Even after the lust had been sated, the sense of wanting had stayed with him. Or maybe it was need, which was all the more frightening. It didn't matter whether it was want or need at the moment. What did matter was that she was Jack's daughter.

That thought had been nagging at him ever since he awakened with the first light of dawn. Only now he wasn't sure if he felt he'd betrayed the trust Jack must have had in him when he told his daughter she could count on him, or if what he felt was an enormous sense of irritation with himself for feeling guilty in the first place. Mia was an adult and, as she'd pointed out, quite capable of making her own decisions. He'd hardly coerced her into making love with him.

His last thought would have assuaged his conscience, had she been any other woman. It didn't work with Mia. He knew why, too. He was coming to care for her far more than he wanted to consider. Because he cared, he knew why the guilt was there. Mia deserved stability, permanence. A home. It was what she wanted, after all, and after all she'd been through, she deserved no less. He couldn't offer her any of that. He didn't even know what he was going to be doing six months from now.

For that matter, if the situation with Jack wasn't cleared up soon, he didn't know what *she'd* be doing six months from now.

With one arm keeping her secure at his side, the forearm of the other resting on his forehead, he stared at the stitching in the top of the tent.

"It stopped raining."

At the sound of her voice, his arm came down.

"Sounds like it," he said, tucking her closer. The wind had died down, too. "You okay?"

She nodded against his chest, her hair tickling his chin. "But you aren't, are you?"

Caid went still. He knew nothing in his expression had given him away. She hadn't known he was troubled by his thoughts from looking at his face. Except to nod a moment ago and move her hand a little higher on his chest, she hadn't even moved. Yet, somehow, she'd known.

"I don't regret what we did, if that's what you're thinking."

With the tip of her index finger, she traced through the swirl of hair centered over his breastbone. "I'm glad."

"I just don't want to hurt you, Mia."

Her finger stopped.

"I'm not in a position to promise you anything," he told her. "Except that I'll help you find your father. And that I'll keep my hands off you. If that's what you want."

The tension in his body seemed to increase in the moments before she tipped back her head. But it was only a matter of seconds before the quality of that tension changed.

Her smile was soft as she brought her hand to his cheek. "I don't expect promises from you, Caid. But I very much want your hands on me."

A groan centered deep in his chest. He wouldn't have thought it possible to want her as badly as he did just then. Lying with her as she slept, wrestling with his conscience, he'd told himself to ignore how hard he was simply from holding her. He couldn't ignore it now. Not with the gentle light in her eyes turning impish, and the feel of her body when she moved conjuring images of how willingly she'd given herself to him last night.

He'd tried to go easy with her, but she'd become as impatient as he, and his good intentions had taken a hike. So, when he rolled her onto her back a moment later, no matter how impatient she became, he made sure he took his dear sweet time.

It was midmorning when Mia awoke to the sound of a boat entering the cove. The deep roar of the engine grew closer, drowning out the screech of the gulls, before fading to a sputtering idle.

Caid must have heard it, too. He lay curled around her back, one arm draped over her waist and the other beneath her head. She was pushing her hair out of her eyes when she heard him say, "That's Hank."

Sitting up, she grabbed for her sweatshirt. "How can you tell?"

"His engine misses when it idles." Planting a kiss by her ear, he whispered, "Hand me my pants."

Having no idea what Hank's engined missed, and far more concerned with the idea that they now had company, she handed Caid his clothes and pulled on her sweatpants under the sleeping bag. It wasn't shyness that made her dress under the covers. Between last night and this morning, Caid had seen and touched every inch of her body, so it was a little late for that. It was just cold. When his hands had been on her, she'd scarcely noticed the chill at all.

Caid had his jeans and shoes on and was pulling on his shirt when he left the tent. Mia was a little slower. There was a definite soreness in her muscles as she dressed, the bruised feeling owing as much to sleeping on the hard ground as to Caid's lovemaking. Not that she would even have contemplated complaining. She wouldn't have traded the past twelve hours for anything.

She'd found her mirror in her knapsack and was digging for the brush when Caid flipped back the flap of the tent.

"Tom called," he said as he lowered himself to his knees beside her. "I've got to go to the Millers' and call him back."

"Did he find out anything?"

"I don't know. Hank just came to tell me he'd called. We need to go."

We. "I'll stay here."

"Mia."

"I'll be fine. You're just going to call him, right?"

"Aren't you anxious to know if he's learned anything?"

Of course she was. She already had a knot in her stomach just from thinking Jack might have turned up.

"I'd just rather not visit with Mrs. Miller until I've had a chance to clean up. I couldn't very well stay on the boat if I went over with you. It would be rude. It's only a few minutes over there and back. You won't be gone that long."

She could clean up in the boat's cabin. But what she was really after was some time to herself. Fortunately, Caid seemed to realize that as his glance moved possessively to her kiss-swollen mouth. Or maybe he just realized that it truly wasn't necessary to drag her along when she was so obviously safe here. Other than the Millers, they hadn't seen another person since they arrived two days ago.

Taking her face between his hands, Caid kissed her. Hard. "Anyone pulls into the cove other than Hank, you head into the trees. I'll be half an hour at the most. Be careful."

The trip over and back took less than ten minutes each way. Caid's conversation with Tom took less than five. The problem facing Caid as he cruised back into the cove and anchored his boat by the fallen tree that served as a gangplank of sorts was how to convey what he'd learned in those five minutes of conversation to Mia.

He'd rather cut out his tongue than hurt her. Yet what he had to tell her was going to break her heart.

"I hope you brought some dry wood," he heard her call as she approached over the wet sand. "There's nothing here that isn't soaked through."

He'd seen her start down from the tent to meet him when he entered the cove, a pastel spot of pink against the backdrop of another gray day. Though it hadn't rained this morning, the sky still held the threat.

"Did your commander have any luck?"

She posed the question from ten feet away, trying not to look anxious, but not doing a very good job of it. Or possibly she was masking her concerns as well as she always did, but Caid was just becoming so attuned to her that she couldn't fool him as easily as she once had.

"I didn't get any wood." He hadn't even thought about it. "Come aboard. It'll be warmer here."

Forced to unwrap her arms for balance, Mia traversed the log to within two feet of the boat. The log disappeared into the water there. But before she could grab the side of the boat and haul herself over, Caid reached out to grasp her by the waist. A moment later, he'd lifted her over the side and her tennis shoes were on the deck.

"Thanks," she would have said, but then she saw his eyes, and the word stilled in her throat. It seemed he couldn't fool her as easily as he once could, either.

With one hand holding back a fluttering strand of her hair, she searched his brooding face.

The panic began to fill her. "You found out something," she said. "Caid? What's happened?"

"Come inside."

Taking her by the hand, he ducked his head and stepped into the cabin. A moment later, he reached for the coffee-pot. Hank had already given him a cup from the ever-present pot in his little office, but the activity bought him some time.

He took the filter Mia handed him, more aware than he wanted to be of how worriedly she was watching him. "Tom never got around to calling his contacts this morning. He didn't have to," he began, deciding to start with the part his commander had mentioned first. "Some detective showed up at the base looking for me this morning. It seems they were requestioning everyone they've talked to about Jack, and someone told him I'd been to Jack's office looking for football tickets."

"Football tickets?"

"That was the excuse I used to get a look at Jack's calendar. What I can't figure out is how whoever it was knew who *I* was. I didn't give anyone in that office my name. In fact, I was very careful not to."

He hadn't mentioned that to Tom. All Caid had said to him was that the police must be talking to everybody Jack had any contact with, a conclusion with which Tom had easily agreed. Tom had also mentioned that there hadn't seemed to be any particular urgency on the part of the detective, that the questioning was simply routine. The detective would appreciate a call from Caid in the next day or two, though.

The trepidation knotting Caid's gut had absolutely nothing to do with talking to the police. That was a problem he'd deal with if and when the time came. The unfamiliar feeling was solely due to the woman whose sense of hope he was about to shatter.

"The other thing he found out was in this morning's paper." Putting the pot on to perk, he quietly added, "You'd better sit down."

There was something about that phrase that automatically made a person's knees a little weaker. He watched her slowly sink to the blue-cushioned bench, then sat down beside her, wishing as he did that he could make this easier for her.

There wasn't a way, though. This kind of news could never be easy to deliver, or to hear.

"They found Jack." Before the relief could register in her eyes, Caid's hand closed over hers. "He's dead, Mia."

He knew it would happen. The quick spark of light his first words brought to her face flickered out in the space of a heartbeat, leaving her face suddenly devoid of expression.

She didn't blink. Not a muscle in her face moved. But even as she held his glance, she slowly pulled her clasped hands from beneath his.

"No," she whispered, utterly disbelieving. "It can't be. He'll come back."

"Honey, I'm sorry." Caid touched her hand again. She didn't seem to notice. "A jogger found him in Balboa Park."

Actually, according to the article in the paper Tom had read, it was the jogger's dog that had found him—stuffed under the concert stage.

"They'd found him last Wednesday, the morning after the crown turned up missing. But the coroner just identified his body." He paused. "They're still looking for you."

His last words didn't even register. "His heart," she said, her tone carrying the same numbness as her expression. "He didn't have his medicine."

Caid drew a deep breath and slowly let it out. What he had to tell her wasn't getting any easier.

"It wasn't his heart, Mia. His neck was broken."

The sound that escaped Mia's throat was barely audible, but the pain behind it, the sheer anguish of that muffled sob, tore straight through to his heart. Her hand covered her mouth, and her eyes stared blankly at the narrow window opposite where they sat.

Not knowing what else to do, he slipped his arm over her shoulder and pulled her to him.

"I'm so sorry," he repeated, never having realized before how inadequate those words could be. She needed more. Having been Jack's friend, he needed to give more. "We'll find out what happened. I promise you. And I'll see you're taken care of," he added, because he knew her father had been all she had. "I owe Jack that."

Beneath his hands, he felt her go still. She hadn't relaxed against him, but Caid thought he felt her stiffen even more.

She drew back, looking completely lost, and slowly pulled out of his arms.

"Mia?" he said, not sure what to do now. Before, he'd been able to offer her his arms. Now that didn't even seem to help. "Talk to me, honey. Tell me what you want me to do."

"Just let me go," she said, her voice little more than a choked whisper.

He did as she requested. Not because he wanted to, but because, at that moment, he would have done anything she asked to take the anguish from her beautiful eyes.

Caid had thought Mia intended to go out to the deck. Thinking to give her a moment before he followed, he felt the boat dip to port and hurried out of the cabin himself.

Mia was already over the side and scrambling over the log to the shore.

"Mia! Don't!" he called, only to see her race along the scallops of foam left by the waves before she darted up the beach and disappeared into the tent.

Chasing after her was the last thing she wanted him to do. It was him she was running from, after all, him and the news he had brought. It had been hard for Caid to hear what had happened to Jack, and he knew that the news had to be devastating to her. Finding her father had been her lifelong dream, the one thing that had kept her going when she had nothing else. Jack had been her father. The family she so desperately wanted. And she'd clung to the dream as if it were a talisman.

She had believed in Jack, too—or at least in the image she'd had of him—to the point where she'd refused to consider that her father would compromise or abandon her.

A strange sense of ambivalence swept through Caid at that thought. It would seem that her belief in Jack had been justified. To a point. He hadn't abandoned her. Not willingly, anyway. Yet, according to the article Tom had read, the crown was still missing, and the police were still looking for Mia in connection with its disappearance—and, possibly, Jack's death.

Caid left her alone for nearly three hours after she went into the tent. When she came out, she didn't come toward the boat, though. Without so much as a glance in its direction, she headed for some boulders on the opposite side of the cove from where they were anchored.

Obviously she still wanted to be alone.

Caid didn't care. He needed to be sure she was all right.

There wasn't much on the island that had dried out since last night's rainstorm. The sky was still heavy with clouds, only an occasional break allowing a hint of sun to shine through. A shaft of that sunlight was pouring over the rocks where Mia sat when she saw him approach. Wishing he'd stayed away, she turned back to the foaming surf.

Sea spray, caught by the wind as it shot up from the rocks the waves battered, caught the prisms of light, making rainbows. Staring at those shimmering colors, she settled back into the numbness.

I'll see you're taken care of. I owe Jack that.

Caid had no doubt meant his statement to ease her mind.
He was the pragmatic sort, after all, his mind automatically turning to the practical and the necessary. No doubt
such a trait was commendable. For Mia, though, his words
had only added to the pain of losing the father she'd only
just found. But it was a different pain—more of an ache that
left her with a hollowness she'd never felt before. Because,
before Caid, that place in her heart hadn't existed.

What she wanted from him had nothing to do with being
taken care of. What she wanted from him had nothing to do
with her father, either. She'd meant it when she told Caid
she didn't expect promises from him. She expected nothing
from anyone. It was just that, for a few fleeting hours, she'd
actually let herself believe that he truly cared about her. *Her.*
Not some obligation he felt to Jack.

And that was no one's fault but her own.

She didn't look at Caid when he sat down beside her.

That didn't stop him from openly watching her, though.
Feet planted two feet apart, he drew his knees up, resting his
wrists on them, and quietly studied her profile. "How are
you doing?"

"I'm doing fine," she told him, because she had to be.
The panic was there, as it inevitably was, just below the
surface of her composure. She'd be lost if she ever gave in
to it. "I'm just trying to figure out what I should do now. I
kept thinking that all I had to do was find Jack and everything would be all right."

"I told you—"

"I know what you told me," she said, interrupting him,
because she didn't want to hear him say it again. "And I
appreciate the thought. I really do. But I don't need to be
taken care of. I've done that one way or another for as long
as I can remember. All I need is some way to clear myself."

And to see that my father is properly buried, she thought.
But at the moment, she was hardly free to make such arrangements.

Several moments passed before Caid spoke. When he did, he made no comment whatsoever about her refusal of his generosity.

"I also told you we'd find out what happened. When we do, that should clear you."

"I'm not your obligation."

"No," he returned, his voice deceptively mild. "I don't suppose you are. But once I start something, I like to see it through."

Mia had no idea what Caid's thoughts were as silence fell between them. She was still focused on the rainbow, desperately needing to concentrate on its beauty, rather than on the sense of desolation that wanted to be felt.

It was that struggle that kept Caid silent. As his glance skimmed her profile, he realized that he'd been wrong about her. Mia had never really been dependent on him. Not the way his male ego had made him think. There was a strength within her that had withstood far greater tragedies than this one. And while she certainly grieved for her father, her sorrow was for the loss of the dream, as much as for the loss of the man. The man she'd known less than a year; the dream she'd been born with.

She would survive those losses with or without him.

The knowledge wasn't quite as freeing as it might once have been. Even as part of him felt relieved that she'd absolved him of responsibility for her, another part wished she'd lean on him again.

"I'm going to find out what happened," he assured her. "I'd owe Jack that, whether you were involved or not. Since you are, you might as well come along for the ride."

He could have told her, too, that he didn't believe for a minute that she wanted him simply to disappear. Whether he wanted to admit it or not, she needed him right now. He also could have told her that she might be pretending to be all right, but he knew she wasn't. Not the way she was sitting there hugging her knees.

Caid didn't get a chance to say any of that, though—no
that he really wanted to. The *Marta II,* her white and gray
paint all but blending into the waves, came screaming into
the cove, her engine wound as high as it would go.

The craft arced sharply, its wide wake increasing the size
of the waves heading for shore. With a frown, Caid left Mia
staring at the tiny crab wandering over a rock next to her
and headed to the shore. It wasn't like Hank to enter the
cove so fast.

When Hank was about thirty yards out—as close as he
could come in without beaching his boat—he cupped his
hands to his mouth and yelled to Caid.

"That colonel called again! He said you're to call him on
the double!"

Giving Hank a thumbs-up to indicate he'd understood,
Caid swiveled in the sand as Hank hit the throttle again
then headed back to Mia. He didn't climb up the boulder
this time, though. He just stood at the base of the bottom
one and hollered.

"Come on. I've got to make a call."

"I heard. I'll stay here."

"I'm not leaving you."

Finally she faced him, shoving back the hair the breeze
blew in her face as she did. "You did this morning."

"This morning was different." It was one thing to give her
some space. It was quite another to leave her alone with her
eyes so suspiciously bright.

"I really don't want to visit with anyone now."

"Mrs. Miller's not there. Hank told me this morning that
she flew back with her grandkids yesterday to spend some
time at her daughter's. You can stay on the boat."

He would carry her if she refused. She could tell by the
absolute determination in his stance. The man was as stub
born as the barnacles clinging to the rocks below.

Lacking the strength to argue, and seeing no point in it
she climbed down from her boulder and headed for Caid'
boat. Going to the marina might not be a bad idea. Mr

Miller might have some information about the island there. If it truly was as sparsely populated as Caid had indicated, maybe she could live by the little waterfall.

"They found it where?"

"In your bedroom," Tom repeated over the line. "Stripped of its jewels. I want you in here, Colonel. Now."

Caid gripped the telephone in disbelief. There was a warrant out for his arrest. The police had just left Tom's office.

"I'm being set up, Tom. You've got to believe that."

"I don't know what's going on with you, Caid. All I do know is that the civilian authorities want you in jail. After that Detective Webster left, I called a captain I know in Burglary at SDPD. He told me they'd received an anonymous tip that the female accomplice in that museum theft had been staying at your apartment.

"The woman who'd been living with Jack," Tom went on, as if to make sure Caid understood who he was talking about. "Since Jack is currently cooling in the morgue, they got a warrant and went through your place. The crown was there, minus the glitter.

"You don't have to say a thing right now," he went on. "Just get yourself in here as fast as that little boat of yours will carry you. You can explain it to me then."

"Give me twenty-four hours—" Caid began, only to have his superior cut him off.

"You've got three."

"But—"

"That's an order, Colonel."

The line went dead long before Caid was ready to hang up. As he did, he turned to face the man whose office he was using.

"You have a problem, son?" Hank Miller asked.

Not sure how much Hank had heard, thinking it couldn't have been much, since Tom had done all the talking, he muttered, "Sure looks like it."

"I'd be obliged to help, if I'm able." The elderly gentle-man pulled his pipe from his shirt pocket, and his glance strayed to the photo of the young soldier on his desk as he reached for his can of tobacco. "You never have let the missus and me do anything to repay what you did for us. Can't imagine what we could do that could ever come close, but you need something, I'd surely like to help you out."

"Thanks, Hank," Caid said, truly appreciating the of-fer. "But I really don't know what you could do about this."

"That was your commander, right?"

"Right."

Caid shoved his fingers through his hair. Tom hadn't *had* to call. Certainly he hadn't had to warn him. He could sim-ply have complied with the civilian authorities' request for his whereabouts and left the matter up to them. The fact that the stripped crown had been found in his apartment was a civilian matter, not a military one. But Caid was nonethe-less accountable for the civilian charge. Conduct unbecom-ing an officer was only one of many charges the military could file against him if the civil matter bore out. Or even if it didn't. Tom was just giving Caid the benefit of the doubt.

"There is something you can do for me, Hank."

The Millers knew nothing about Mia's circumstances. Because Hank and Marta lived in their own little world, it was also highly unlikely they would hear about what was going on, either. The Millers had basically left civilization when civilization had taken their son. That meant they'd left behind newspapers and televisions, too.

"My commander wants me back at the base in three hours," Caid went on when Hank's thick eyebrows raised expectantly. "I won't be able to get the lady with me back to her place. Can she stay with you until I can send for her?"

"Won't be a problem at all. She can go on up to the house and just make herself at home. You got enough gas to get you Overtown?"

"I'd better top off the tank."

Both men turned to the open doorway—which was precisely where Mia stood.

"Excuse me," she said, smiling politely at the kindly older gentleman. Then the smile faded. "May I see you for a moment, Caid? Outside?"

Chapter 11

While Caid used the telephone in Hank's office, Mia had hurriedly read through the tourist brochures near the cash register. She hadn't meant to eavesdrop. But as Marta had mentioned the other day, as small as the market was, it was impossible not to overhear what was being said from the other room. Not that there had been much to hear—until Caid and Hank started talking.

It was their conversation that had drawn Mia toward the office—and put a knot the size of a small fist in her stomach.

Now, standing in the doorway, Mia boldly held Caid's impenetrable gaze. His expression was as closed as she'd ever seen it, yet she refused to look away. She also refused to budge until he agreed to tell her what was going on.

Hank, clearly uncomfortable with the sudden silence, cleared his throat. "I've got a battery on a charger out back," he said, sounding most grateful to have recalled that particular matter. "I'd better go check it. You two...take your time."

Hitching up his red suspenders, he clamped his unlit pipe in the corner of his mouth and started toward the door. A step later, he stopped, removing the pipe as he did.

"You're welcome here, Mia," he told her, then glanced back over at Caid. "Whatever you decide is fine with me."

A moment later, he was gone, the bell over the outer door sounding obscenely cheerful as the friendly gentleman removed himself from his own premises. What he left behind was a stony silence Mia had no intention of prolonging.

"Would you mind telling me what's going on?" Arms crossed protectively, she stepped inside the small office, with its cluttered bulletin board and equally cluttered desk. The room smelled of dampness, pipe tobacco, and the coffee in the pot atop the tall metal file cabinet. All Mia really noticed, though, was how Caid dominated the room. "Whatever it is, it isn't necessary for you to make arrangements for my care and feeding. I told you, I can take care of myself."

Caid ignored her conclusion. With his hand clamped over the back of his neck, he turned to the small four-paned window beside him. Rain-stained and cloudy with age, the glass gave a surreal effect to the view beyond.

"The police found the crown." His voice was low and harsh. "Someone planted it in my apartment."

Her disbelieving "What?" was little more than a whisper.

He turned back, the suppressed fury in his voice tensing every muscle in his powerful body. That rage darkened his face, too. But his anger was under control, a cold, calculated control that sharply focused that volatile energy and made it all the more dangerous. All the more revealing.

Unlike the fear encompassing Mia at being unjustly suspected, Caid's reaction was to be totally affronted by the gall of whoever had impugned his integrity by attempting to palm the crime off on him. He was not a man to be intimidated, pushed or crossed. Nor was he a man to act rashly. It was the latter trait that gave him his edge.

"You need to stay here," he told her, his voice clipped. "You'll be safer."

"Why?"

"There's a warrant out for my arrest. If they find me, they'll find you."

The knot of anxiety in her stomach doubled itself. "Will your commander help you?"

It was then that he saw the concern in her eyes. Not for herself. For him. Obviously she'd overheard most of his and Hank's conversation. "I don't know what Tom's going to do," Caid replied in all honesty. "All I know is that you're staying here and I'm going to San Diego."

"But the base is in Oceanside. You told your commander you were going back there."

Caid knew full well where the base was. He also knew what he'd implied to Tom. And to Hank, for that matter. He didn't find it necessary to mention that to Mia. He simply held her worried gaze for several very long seconds, the muscle in his jaw working as he silently dared her to challenge his decision.

Despite what he'd indicated to his commander, Caid had no intention of going to the base. He knew exactly how the system worked. To keep him out of the hands of the civil authorities for a while, Tom could have the military police take him into custody on a charge of "conduct unbecoming." Once that happened, Caid would be at the mercy of some newly commissioned lieutenant from the JAG Corps who would do battle with the local police over who had first crack at him. In the meantime, he'd be completely powerless to get any answers on his own. He also wouldn't be able to protect Mia.

It was that unquestioned need that was forcing him to do something he'd never done in his entire military career: disobey a direct order.

The thought only fueled his increasing agitation.

Suddenly feeling like a caged animal in the cramped and cluttered room, he grabbed Mia by the hand and led her into the relatively open space of the market. He had to leave. He also needed to let Mia know that, for now, he was going to take care of her. Whether she liked the idea or not.

"I'll try to be back tonight," he said on the way down the canned-goods aisle. "I'll tell Hank you're staying."

"Where are you going?"

"To see Jack's girlfriend. I know I didn't give my name to anyone in Jack's office." Nor had he left his name at any of the places he'd looked for Jack that first night in San Diego and Tijuana. "But I introduced myself to Roselyn. She's the only other person who knew I'd been asking about him."

Letting go of her hand, Caid came to a halt near the door.

He stood in front of her now, as immovable as any mountain. This was the man she'd first met. The dispassionate, pragmatic man whose inscrutable expression made it impossible for her to know what was going on behind his steely blue eyes.

Thinking it had all been so much easier before she'd come to need his touch, Mia hugged her arms around her middle.

"You said whoever mentioned your name told the police you'd been in the office looking for football tickets. How would Roselyn know that?"

"She said herself that just about everyone in that office eats at her diner. Roselyn's the friendly type. She was also Jack's girlfriend. As hot a topic as he was, someone from there could have told her about a guy asking about tickets and described me to her."

Mia's concern turned to doubt. "You don't think she's responsible for... What did you call it? Setting you up?"

"That's what I called it," he confirmed, eyeing her as if he now realized she'd overheard every word he'd said. "As to whether or not she's responsible, anything's possible. It's not like she wouldn't have a motive. Taking that crown would be a good way to get even with a boyfriend she thought was two-timing her and cause a lot of grief for the 'other woman.' Setting me up could just be punishment for helping you.

"On the other hand," he added smoothly, thinking the possibility was more likely, "maybe she just has a big mouth. That's why I want to talk to her. To find out who she's given my name to."

When she first heard it, Mia thought the scenario Caid had drawn around Roselyn seemed a little too realistic to be dismissed quite so easily. Especially since she knew that the woman couldn't stand her. But she also supposed that plausible motives could be contrived for herself or for Caid, too—and the police might well have already done that. Yet, as chilling as that thought was, it wasn't what made Mia fall silent. What did was the implication, grounded or otherwise, that it might somehow have been her presence that had brought her father to harm.

Just as her presence now harmed Caid. He'd never have been involved at all if she hadn't come to him.

Mia's heart pounded heavily in her chest as she watched him glance toward the back of the store. Hank could be seen through the long row of paned windows there, tinkering with a huge wrench.

"Hank doesn't know anything, other than I've got a problem at the base. That's best, for his sake."

"I understand," Mia said quietly, and glanced up just as Caid looked back at her.

She could have told him to be careful. She probably should have. But as they stood there trying to figure out who should make the first move, neither willing to risk the other's rejection, the words wouldn't come. The seconds just ticked by, stretching the silence until finally he muttered, "See you later," turned on his heel and strode out the door.

As focused as he was on his mission, as determined as he'd been as to what she was to do, he hadn't noticed how easily she'd acquiesced. He'd simply issued orders and expected them to be followed.

Mia never had followed orders very well.

She also had no intention of remaining behind. That was why she hadn't argued with Caid about staying. In fact, as soon as she saw him reach Hank, she slipped out the door, standing on tiptoe as she did to silence the little bell in case the breeze decided to carry the sound in their direction, and backed down the dock to Caid's boat. As quietly as she moved, the boat scarcely even rocked when she slipped into the cabin and crawled beneath the rumpled blanket on the bed beneath the bow.

They were five miles out before she emerged from the cabin to face Caid's wrath.

She didn't startle him when she stepped onto the deck. Though he couldn't possibly have expected to see her just then, he didn't so much as flinch when her head popped out the cabin door. All he did was increase the intensity of his brooding scowl.

"Damn it, Mia, what in the hell do you think you're doing?"

"Stop swearing," she said, pulling the jacket he'd lent her around herself as she climbed into the first mate's chair and slipped on her sunglasses. The sun wasn't out, but she rather liked being able to hide behind the dark lenses. Especially right now. She wasn't feeling anywhere near as brave as she needed to be. The camouflage helped.

"I'll swear if I damn well want to. What are you doing here? I told you to stay—"

"At the Millers'," she said, casually flicking a piece of fuzz from her sweatpants into the wind. "I know. That was your decision. Not mine. I'm going to Roselyn's with you. If she knows anything about this, I want to hear it."

"And if she doesn't?"

He meant to jar her, to rattle her with the reminder that there was someone out there who did know exactly what was going on—the someone who had no doubt stolen the crown, killed her father, and tried to do the same to her the other night. The only question seemed to be whether that person had stolen the crown himself, or stolen it from Jack.

"I need to know that, too," came her too-calm reply.

Caid swore. "I thought you were safe," he muttered darkly.

Mia saw his mouth move, but the wind rushing past her ears made it hard to hear. The two-hundred-and-fifty horse engine was going at full gallop. With the bow lifted off the water, the boat fairly flew over the calm swells of the open sea. The sea, however, was the only calm thing in sight at the moment. Caid had one hand on the wheel, his grip turning his knuckles white. Watching him, wondering if his back teeth weren't about to shatter from the way he was grinding them together, she asked him to repeat himself. Minus the curse. That much, she'd caught.

"I said, I thought you'd be okay where you were for a while. It'd be easier for me to get around without having to worry about you. The police are looking for me, Mia. For all I know, Tom might even have a 'friendly escort' out looking for me when I don't show up at the base on time. You're not safe with me right now. Don't you understand that?"

There wasn't a thing wrong with her cognitive abilities. And while she was sure he thought his argument would dissuade her, all it did was strengthen her purpose. He was about to jeopardize his career—a career that seemed to be all he'd ever really had—because of a situation she'd gotten him into. She couldn't let him do that.

Just as she hadn't been able to stay at the Millers' and possibly involve them.

"I understand. Completely," she assured him. "But I'm not sure you do. You know how you don't like being obligated to anyone? Well, I don't much care for it, either. You don't need to worry about me anymore. I'm indebted enough to you as it is."

Caid heard what she said. Every subtly accented word. He couldn't blame her for feeling as she did. The problem was the hint of vulnerability in her expression, which even her ridiculously large glasses couldn't hide. It was as if she were pushing him away not because she wanted to, but because she had no other choice.

Not sure if his exasperation was with the situation, with himself or with her, he slapped his other hand on the wheel. With both hands clutching it in a stranglehold, it was a wonder the thing didn't snap in two.

"You don't owe me anything," he said, then decided to let the whole matter go when she didn't say anything else. He didn't trust her silence. Under any other circumstances, he'd probably even have worried about it. Right now, however, he had half a dozen other things on his mind.

The expression "Tensions are high" popped into his head. The military phrase meant a potential strike situation existed. It also meant that it would take only the slightest provocation from the other side for a weapon to be fired. It was that kind of tautness that filled the air as they sped toward the coast of California. The feeling really didn't make any sense to him, either. He and Mia were on the same side.

By the time they entered San Diego Bay and the huge marina nearest the downtown, the sun had set and the silence aboard the *Destiny* had become as thick as a fog bank. The anxiety Mia had tried to fight had returned with a vengeance. It was hard enough coming back to the danger and fear Caid had taken her away from only days ago. But facing the moment when she and Caid would part was almost more than she could bear.

She hadn't let herself think in terms of what might happen between them tomorrow or next week or next year. Yet, as the land came within sight and they came closer to the lights of the darkening skyline, she'd known she wanted a future with him so badly it made her ache to think of it. There was no future, though. There was only the next hour—and thinking about what she was about to do nearly made it impossible for her to breathe.

"We'll have to walk."

Nodding numbly as Caid tied off the stern and stepped onto the dock, she reached up for the hand he offered. Except to get her to move from one place to another, he hadn't touched her since those awful moments in the boat's cabin this morning. That was why she expected him to release her hand the moment she was beside him.

He didn't let her go, though. Muttering a tight "This way," he laced her fingers through his and led her away from the crowds milling about the shops and restaurants farther down the wharf. "It'll be a little longer this way, but there won't be so many people."

They didn't want to be recognized. Not that Mia was likely to be, with her floppy pink hat covering the top half of her face. But Caid didn't know if the police had obtained or released a photo of him, and he wasn't taking any chances. He was pretty good at blending into dark alleys, anyway. After all, he'd been down plenty in his military career.

It didn't take them long to find the street they were looking for. Caid remembered the diner being right around the corner from Jack's office on Union. How far down Union, he wasn't sure, since he'd never come from this direction before. But Mia spotted an art gallery she'd peeked in the day she met Jack to go to the races and remembered it was two blocks up from there.

There were few people on the street, the business section being all but deserted this time of evening. They hurried along, Caid's strides purposeful but not rushed, as much in deference to her shorter legs as to any desire not to call attention to them. Not once as they walked did he try to talk Mia out of accompanying him. Not that she would have let him. He did ask if she was sure she knew what she was doing, though, when he pulled her to a stop just short of the arching *Nickelodeon* painted on the diner's window.

Still holding her hand, he pulled her around to face him. "Are you sure you want to do this?"

Her insides felt like mush, which was about how stable her knees felt, too. But that didn't matter. She couldn't let it matter.

Her grip on his hand tightened. "He was my father. If she's done anything to involve you in what happened to him, I want to hear it myself." She also needed to repay Caid for helping her. Once inside the diner, maybe she could do both.

"You're not worried about me, are you?"

Dear heaven, yes, she was. So worried she was near sick with it. But that wasn't what he wanted to hear. Not when he was looking at her with his eyebrow arched and what she could have sworn was a hint of disbelief in his eyes. "Somebody should," she muttered.

Caid's expression softened. Or maybe it was just the red neon lights around the doorway that removed the sharper edges. Whichever, Mia knew that if she stood there looking into those deep blue eyes a moment longer she'd do or say something embarrassing or stupid or both.

So, before she could reach for him, she reached for the door.

The diner was all but empty, the patrons at the green Formica counter and in the booths pretty much a repeat of those Caid had seen a week ago when he'd come in about this time—which meant a total of two. A waitress was on duty tonight, though, a tall redhead who snapped her gum and wore a button on her pink uniform that read Eat at Joe's.

Maybe Roselyn wasn't even here.

"I'll see" was the woman's gum-cracking response when Caid asked anyway.

Pushing on both of the double doors leading into the kitchen, the waitress with the attitude disappeared into the brightly lit interior. Her muffled "You've got company" drifted out over the clank of pots and pans.

A few moments later, the waitress was back, carrying a plate of french fries and a grilled-cheese sandwich. "She's in her office," she said, dipping her head toward the still-swinging doors and setting the food in front of the cabbie at the end of the counter.

The announcement was apparently their cue to go on back.

Not quite sure where this office was, but certain they'd find it, Caid led Mia along the side of a gleaming kitchen, past a storeroom and on to an open door at the back of a narrow hallway.

Roselyn was already on her feet when they stopped in the doorway of the small, surprisingly neat room where she tended her books. Silver-rimmed reading glasses in hand, she crossed her arms defensively over her denim jumpsuit. Her eyes looked a little red.

"Sorry." She spoke to Caid, since she recognized him as Jack's friend but was clueless as to the identity of the woman under the pink hat behind him. "If you're here to commiserate, I'm not in the mood."

"You've heard about Jack," came his obvious conclusion.

"Yeah. Now, if you'll excuse me, I was just going home. I really don't feel like talking about him right now."

That was too bad. Intent on getting answers, Caid wasn't in any mood to offer sympathies himself. He also didn't feel like putting up with her querulousness.

Taking her by the arm, he backed her into her office.

"Mia," he called over his shoulder. "Come in here and close the door." The moment he had Roselyn where he wanted her, which was in front of the chair by her desk, he let her go. "We need to talk."

Startled by Caid's brusque manner, and equally offended by it, Roselyn immediately rounded on him. But just as she opened her mouth to ask the disturbingly attractive colonel just what in the devil he thought he was doing, her glance swung to the woman quietly closing the door.

In an instant, her glare was trained on Caid again. "That's her? That's that—? How dare you bring her here!"

"I dare to bring her here," Caid replied, his tone tight with irritation, "because we need to talk to you."

"I have nothing to say to her."

The woman wouldn't speak to Mia directly. She wouldn't even look at her—until Mia slowly pulled off her hat and pushed her fingers through her hair.

"Please," Mia began, doing an admirable job of hiding the hurt the woman's animosity must have caused her. "We've got to—"

Roselyn held up a silencing hand, her fingers trembling despite the implacable expression on her face. "When I heard about Jack this morning, I didn't think today could possibly get any worse. I was obviously wrong. Get out. I have nothing to say to you, and there isn't anything you can say to me that I want to hear."

"Then you'll listen to me," Caid cut in, refusing to put up with her bullheadedness. "Mia's not Jack's girl-friend—"

"I don't care who she is," the woman shot back at him, clearly not interested in listening.

Caid's voice overrode hers. "She's his daughter. Now will you please sit—"

"And I'm his great-aunt Hattie," the clearly distressed woman all but shouted over him—only to have her sarcasm lose its strength as what he'd said finally registered.

Her carefully penciled eyebrows lowered, and her glance turned doubtful. "His daughter?" she repeated, clearly not willing to trust the information.

Refusing to let the woman treat the quietly poised lady by the door as if she weren't there, Caid looked to Mia. Because he did, Roselyn did, too.

"It's a long story," Mia said, very much appreciating Caid's silent but pointed support. "But Jack is—was—my father. I swear."

Slowly, as if air were gradually being let out of her legs, Roselyn sank into her chair. Where a moment ago she could scarcely bring herself to glance at the slender young woman with the gamine features and the tousled hair, she now couldn't take her eyes from her.

For several seconds, as the atmosphere in the room quieted, she studied Mia's features: the exotic and intelligent eyes, the full mouth, the lovely—and stubborn—line of her jaw. The intelligence and the stubbornness were definitely Jack. So was the gray of her eyes. "He never told me."

The shrug Mia managed was protective at best. "He never told anyone."

Roselyn reached behind her, absently setting the glasses she held on the strip of tape spiraling from an adding machine. With the tips of her fingers, she pinched the bridge of her nose. "I don't believe this," she said, shaking her head. She let her hand fall to her lap, then glanced around the room, as if searching for answers on the bare walls. "I mean, I don't believe how this...how any of this...could have happened."

She wasn't speaking only of the misconstrued relationship. It was everything that had gone on for the past week that she couldn't comprehend. Sharing the feeling, Caid sent a glance in Mia's direction to make sure she was okay, and moved to the end of the desk.

He was also feeling a little more sympathetic than he had only moments ago. Though, in truth, a goodly portion of that sympathy leaned in Mia's direction. She wasn't exactly having the best day of her life, either.

"That's what we're trying to find out, Roselyn. I'm hoping you can help us. How much of the news have you heard today?"

Sucking in a deep breath, the distraught woman glanced up. "All of it." She motioned to the small television near the chair behind Mia. "There wasn't anything on the noon news that wasn't in the morning paper. But on the evening news a while ago, they said they had a suspect. They didn't release a name." She looked to Mia, not in suspicion so much as in puzzlement. "The newscaster said they still hadn't found you."

From the corner of his eye, Caid saw Mia take a step back. A moment later, she sank into the chair. Watching her fold her hands in a knot on her lap, wondering if she didn't look just a little paler than she had a moment ago, he tried to concentrate on the one positive in this mess.

His name wasn't out yet.

He leaned against the end of the desk, casually crossing his arms and stretching his long legs out in front of him. The position allowed him a clear view of both women. Roselyn he wanted to watch for reactions. Mia he wanted to watch simply because he was concerned about her.

"Mia's as much in the dark about what's going on as anybody else," Caid told the woman in front of him. "She had nothing to do with the disappearance of that crown. We don't know what Jack's involvement was, either. What we do know is that the suspect they're looking for now...is me.

"I've been set up," he added before Roselyn could jump to any conclusions. Watching her carefully, he kept his voice mild. "Do you have any idea who might have done something like that?"

Her gaze never faltered. Not by so much as the twitch of an eyelash did it appear that she had the faintest idea what he was talking about.

"How would I know that?" she asked, truly at a loss.

Caid trusted his instincts. On more than one occasion, his life had depended on them. Those carefully honed instincts told him now that if Roselyn had any involvement at all, it was purely unwitting.

Unwitting or not, he had to know who she'd talked to. "I understand the police made a second round of calls on Jack's acquaintances and co-workers a few days ago. Did you tell the police I was in here asking about Jack?"

She hadn't. She swore it. All the police had asked was if any of the patrons who usually frequented the place had stopped coming in after Jack disappeared.

"What about anyone in Jack's office? Did you mention me to anyone from there?"

Again, she was sure she hadn't. "I didn't even mention you to Keith when he was in here complaining about how hard it was to get any work done with all the people coming through asking about Jack. Besides the police, I guess they've had newspaper and television reporters to contend with. They even had some nut in there who insisted he was a sixteenth-century Austrian duke. He wanted to hold something of Jack's to get vibes from so he could go get his crown back."

"Keith," he repeated, reserving comment on the weirdo. "He's the mouthy one married to the owner's daughter, right?"

Roselyn's mouth thinned. "'Mouthy' is certainly one way to describe him. He's the one who couldn't wait to tell me about Mia living with Jack.

"I'll never forget it," she said, though she'd certainly attempted to. "I was right in the middle of the lunch rush, and he's eating at the counter—which is packed with customers, mind you—when he decides to describe this 'sweet young thing' that came into the office to meet Jack the day before. He then proceeds to tell me that Jack said she was living with him. That she had been for weeks," she added, looking at Mia with something of the pain she must have felt that day showing in her eyes. The animosity was no longer there. Only the hurt remained.

"Jack hadn't said a word about you. Not a word," she repeated, her voice quieter than it had been only moments before. "And all that time we'd been, well . . . intimate, you know?"

Mia knew. Unaware of how her expression softened, she glanced toward Caid. There was something about that kind of intimacy that made a woman all the more vulnerable. Maybe it was because so much of her heart was involved.

Not knowing what to say to relieve the sense of betrayal the woman must have felt—or what to make of the quiet way Caid was watching her—she could only turn back to Roselyn with a quiet "I'm sorry."

"It wasn't your fault," the woman was now quick to say. "If it was anyone's, it was probably mine. I was so angry when I confronted Jack with what Keith had said that I didn't give him a chance to explain. Once he confirmed that you were living with him, I went off the deep end. I don't remember what all I said, but I do recall telling him he had to get rid of you if he wanted to keep seeing me. He said he wouldn't talk to me until I calmed down, then walked out." She grew quiet for a moment, her expression bereft. "You might have noticed, I'm not real good at backing down.

"Anyway," she went on, looking to Caid when she realized she'd digressed, "Keith is married to the owner's daughter. I take it you know him."

"I met him. Once." He'd thought the guy was a jerk. He just hadn't realized quite how big a jerk. "When he was in here, did he say anything to you about football tickets?"

The overhead lights caught the shades of blond and silver in her frosted brown hair as she shook her head. "The only ticket he mentioned was the one that won him a bundle in the lottery. That was Friday." Her eyes frosted over. "He didn't say anything to me, but I was standing right behind Angie out there while he was going on about not having to lick his father-in-law's boots anymore. He said as soon as he got the money, he'd be out of that office for good."

"What lottery?"

"I don't know that he said. We've the state ones, you know. And there are lots of others. Somebody in that office was always playing the Irish Sweepstakes, and that thing down in Florida. Al, especially."

If Caid remembered correctly, Al was the one in charge of the pool on when Jack would turn up. He was also the person who'd gone to the races with Jack and Mia. It was the timing of Keith-the-Clod's newfound wealth that had his attention, though.

"Do you know where Keith lives?"

"Sure. Top of Carmella Circle in La Jolla. He's always bragging about it."

It took big bucks to live in La Jolla. Even bigger bucks to live at the top of any of its circles, lanes or streets. Remembering the crack the guy named Al had made about Keith having married for money, Caid was almost willing to bet that the place had been bought with Keith's wife's funds, too. Living off his wife's wealth—while apparently also having to work for her father —could be pretty hard on a guy's ego. When a guy had an ego the size of Keith's, such circumstances could be pretty emasculating.

Winning a lottery would be an easy way to explain suddenly having come into money. Money obtained by cashing in hot jewels, perhaps. And what better way for Keith to restore his self-esteem than to suddenly be as wealthy as his wife?

With a surge of lean muscle, Caid pushed himself away from the desk. "Do you have a car here, Roselyn? And a map?"

She did. Roselyn had no problem with Caid borrowing her car, either, provided he would give her a couple of minutes to turn the closing of the restaurant over to her waitress, then drop her off at her place. She also had no problem with Mia staying with her while Caid paid a visit to Keith. In fact, to Caid's surprise, it was Mia who asked the remarkably subdued woman if she would mind her coming in for a while when, half an hour later, he pulled the conservative beige sedan into the driveway of the neat little duplex Roselyn indicated.

Sitting next to him on the bench seat, surreptitiously glancing at his profile in the green glow of the dashboard lights, Mia knew full well that Caid was puzzled by her request to stay. After all, she'd insisted on coming with him to see Roselyn, so he had no doubt anticipated that she'd want to go with him to Keith's, too. She also knew he wasn't about to take her. There was a hardness about him now that she'd only glimpsed before. A kind of deadly calm that frightened her a little, especially since she knew how angry he was at being set up.

The frown furrowing his brow at the moment, however, was one of puzzlement. Thinking it rather interesting that he actually seemed disappointed at not having to argue with her, she told Roselyn she'd be right there as the woman dug through her purse for her extra keys and opened the passenger door. Mia wanted very much to know this woman who had cared about her father. To know her, and perhaps to learn something of her father through her. But first—and it felt far more necessary—she needed to know how much time she had.

Roselyn was headed up the short walk and into the welcoming light on the porch when Mia turned to Caid. He'd left the engine running.

Knowing he wanted to leave, that his thoughts were far from her, she decided to keep her goodbye brief.

"You said it's about half an hour to Keith's place from here. What will you do after you talk to him?"

The muscle in his jaw jerked. "Depends on what he says. I'll either call you or come back here."

She could only count on an hour for sure. "You won't do anything to get into trouble, will you?"

"No, Mia. I won't."

That he wouldn't say what he was going to do worried her a little. "Please be careful. I mean that, Caid."

It was then that he saw it, the luminous light in her eyes that told him there was more she wanted to say. More she might have said, had he encouraged her.

There was a lot he needed to say to her, too. But for now, because he didn't trust the way his physical desire for her had somehow gotten all knotted up with his need to protect her, all he managed was a quiet "You, too."

A trembling smile touched her mouth. Lifting his hand from the wheel, he cupped her face, the lovely face that had now been etched indelibly in his memory. Like the feel of her. The taste of her.

He brushed his lips over hers, the kiss soft and bitter-sweet. She leaned into him, slowly flowing toward him as she'd done every other time he'd kissed her, every other time he'd held her. Except that last time. But that last time didn't matter now. Nor did it matter that he wished they were back at their cove so that he could carry her into the tent and make love with her until they were too weak to move. All that was of any consequence now was that the entire situation seemed to be getting more complicated by the second.

He couldn't deny the bond that had grown between them. But even as his mouth moved over hers and he breathed in her breath as if her essence were all that sustained him, he knew how tenuous that bond was. It had been forged by his need to protect her and by her need to depend on him until she could somehow be cleared. He knew Mia realized that, too. And that had made their being together much less complicated. At least it had until the lines he'd drawn for himself with her had somehow become so obscured. That was why, when he finally lifted his head and drew his knuckles down her cheek, silence seemed preferable to the words he couldn't find.

Mia found them, though. Slipping from his arms as he put the car into gear, she slid across the seat. But just as her feet hit the pavement, she looked back over her shoulder. "I love you," she said, her voice hushed.

An instant later, she slid on out and closed the door.

She didn't look back. Not even to wave after Roselyn opened the screen and motioned her inside. She simply walked up the steps with her easy, graceful stride, clutching her pink hat in her hand, and disappeared behind the door.

For several seconds, Caid sat unmoving as he stared at the little white duplex with its yellow shutters and glowing yellow porch lights.

Mia's words had definitely unsettled him. But as he finally sucked in a deep breath and backed out of the drive, he realized that the way she'd said them bothered him even more. She hadn't expected a response from him. Or wanted one, for that matter. It was almost as if she'd wanted him to know how she felt—in case something happened to separate them.

As he headed down the quiet residential street, his grip tightened on the wheel. She needed to have a little more faith in him than that. He wasn't going to let himself get picked up. The way he figured it, he had about twelve hours to get the answers he needed, and then he'd go to the police himself. Mia and Roselyn were getting along fine now that the air had been cleared, so Mia would be okay with her until he got back.

Reminding himself that it was this very type of distraction that could cause a man to make mistakes, he forced himself to stop thinking of Mia and concentrate only on the obnoxious guy with the big mouth and the chip on his shoulder—and possibly money from the crown jewels in his pocket.

Mia would be fine with Roselyn, he had to assure himself just one more time. After all, she had nowhere else to go.

Neither did Caid.

He realized that two hours later, when he pulled into the parking lot of the Laundromat across the street from his apartment. Depending on what Tom had done when he hadn't shown up, the police could well be all over Catalina by now. They didn't seem to be expecting him here, though. Caid had watched for the past fifteen minutes and there didn't appear to be a surveillance team in sight.

Driving to La Jolla had been a waste of time. Keith hadn't been home. In fact, no one had. After waiting for half an hour, and mindful of a neighbor who kept poking his head between his drapes, Caid had figured it was best to leave. He'd go back after he'd checked out his apartment.

Leaving Roselyn's car in the Laundromat's parking lot, Caid headed into the dark alley that ran behind the building, then crossed the street. Rather than go through the courtyard and risk detection by a neighbor, he went to the side of the complex, unscrewed the bulb in the front security lamp and, satisfied that it was dark enough, climbed the trellis—swearing all the way—to his balcony. The bougainvillea thorns were long and sharp as needles. Even with the sleeves of his navy sweatshirt pulled down, the annoying barbs stuck right through the fabric. The blasted things got him a couple of times through his jeans, too.

Lights from a car coming along the highway swept past, seeming like searchlight beams. Waiting in the thick foliage until the car was gone, he finally scrambled up and over the railing. Once on the slatted deck, and crouched low, he was completely hidden by the solid waist-high balcony walls. Within a matter of moments, he was in his bedroom.

Pocketing the key he'd used on the sliding glass door, he slowly scanned his room. As dark as it was, and with only the light filtering in from outside, he couldn't see much. But he was familiar enough with his space to know where he needed to go to get what he wanted.

At least he had been, until the place had been searched.

The flashlight he was looking for wasn't on the right-hand side of his nightstand drawer. When he found it, it was in the back, on the left, the contents of the drawer having been completely rearranged. The idea of having his things pawed through was enough to cause the veins in his temples to throb. But Caid wouldn't give in to the fury now. Right now, he just wanted to see if the police had taken the knife Mia had knocked from her attacker's hands.

That knife could work for or against him and Mia. Its presence would corroborate her story about someone trying to attack her, and, if its owner could be identified, it might very well let him off the hook. On the other hand, she'd said the attacker had worn gloves. Caid, too, had been careful not to touch it. But the knife had been in his apartment, and if it had been used for any other crime, there was no telling what charges he might face, besides theft and murder.

A knot tightening his gut, Caid followed the flashlight beam down the stairs.

The knife was gone. But what he found barely protruding from near the leg of the sofa seemed to let Keith off the hook.

The little red pencil had a chewed-up tip, and several more teeth marks along its stubby length. Caid didn't own any red pencils. Especially not red pencils with the Independent Insurance Adjustments' logo on them. He also didn't mangle the pencils he did have.

But he knew someone who did.

Chapter 12

It had been a long time since Caid had felt the strange un
certainty that settled over him as he headed down the free
way. It was the kind of uncertainty he'd felt when heading
into a potential ambush situation, or when he'd entered an
enemy area and not known what little surprise might lurk
around the next corner or building or bush. The feeling
didn't make any sense to him, either. Especially since there
was now no doubt in his mind who he was looking for.

The day Caid had gone to Jack's office, it had been Al
who asked who he was. Not just once, but several times,
using the excuse of having the football tickets delivered to
get him to leave his name and address. He'd thought the guy
seemed a little nervous. But, he'd chalked the behavior up
to the man just being the high-strung type—especially since
he'd had that pocketful of gnawed-up pencils. Red pencils.

It wasn't just the stub in Caid's pocket that convinced him
that Al wasn't quite the friend of Jack's that he'd professed
to be. Al gambled. On just about anything, it seemed. From
office pools to the horses to the sweeps. A habit like that

took money. More than the average insurance adjuster would make. Al's office was right next to Jack's, too, which meant he could overhear any conversation Jack had—including any conversation he would have had with Mia about what time they would go to the museum. The man was also about the right height and physical build to have been Mia's attacker.

How Al had learned who Caid was and where he lived was something Caid hadn't yet figured out. Nor did he know how Al and the crown and Jack all fitted together. He was just certain they did. Yet, as convinced as he was of all that, the terrible sense that something was wrong persisted. Not with his conclusions. With Mia.

Telling himself it was only fatigue catching up with him, that he was just getting twitchy because he was so close to nailing the little creep, he nonetheless slipped Roselyn's nondescript sedan into a lane of faster-moving traffic. He wanted to ask Mia if she'd seen Al around anywhere the night of the museum job, and to find out where the guy lived. Mostly he just wanted to make sure she was all right.

The closer he got to San Diego, the more convinced he became that she wasn't. Never having been that attuned to another person before, he didn't know what to make of the feeling. By the time he'd left the freeway, forcing himself to stay at the speed limit on the surface streets to avoid getting stopped, he was certain only that he shouldn't have left her. At least not without making her promise not to leave Roselyn's.

It was a little past nine o'clock when Caid bolted from the car and knocked on Roselyn's front door. Only moments after that, the reason for the foreboding dogging him made itself apparent. He couldn't believe what he heard Roselyn tell him, though.

"She went where?"

He stood in the pool of light on Roselyn's front porch, his disbelieving eyes sweeping the poor woman's tired face.

She'd asked him to come in. What she'd said, though—what she repeated now—kept him rooted in place.

"To the police. They left with her not twenty minutes ago."

Impossible. "She wouldn't have done that. She's terrified of the authorities."

"I know. She got sick just before they got here."

Caid shoved his fingers through his hair. He had no trouble at all believing that. "This doesn't make any sense. Why would she go now? Just when everything's gotten so much worse?"

The woman in the doorway cocked her head as she tightened her coral chenille robe against the night's chill. For a moment, something like sympathy—or maybe it was pity for his lack of insight—passed through her narrowed brown eyes. "You really don't know, do you?"

"If I knew, I wouldn't be asking."

"She did it to clear you."

Caid opened his mouth. Then promptly shut it as the enormity of what Mia had done sank in. For several seconds, he simply stood there, stunned into silence—until Roselyn stepped aside and pushed the screen door open.

"The officer who picked her up left the address of the station she took her to. Come on in and I'll get it for you."

Caid followed her inside, the impression of warmth and coziness settling around him as he entered her small but comfortable living room. An afghan lay bunched up in an easy chair near a softly glowing lamp. It was to the table holding the lamp that Roselyn headed.

"She asked me to give you a message."

"The officer?"

"Mia," Roselyn returned patiently, a little curious at how shaken the big marine appeared to be. She held out a piece of paper with an address on it, and a folded note. "You know, I think her mother was the only woman Jack ever loved.

"He told me," she went on, seeing Caid's uncomprehending glance swing from the papers he'd taken from her. "He didn't come right out and say it in those words. But we were having one of those conversations right after we first met. You know, the kind where you've been drinking together and it's okay to be honest because you're not that involved yet? Anyway, I asked him if he'd ever been in love. He said he had. Once. With a woman he couldn't marry 'because of all the red tape.' He never said any more about her than that." She shoved her hands into the pockets of her robe. "It wasn't easy for men to marry women they met over there, was it?"

Since her question had actually been more of a statement, Caid just shook his head. It had been next to impossible for a soldier to marry a Vietnamese woman during the war. Usually, if he couldn't be talked out of it, permission was simply denied. If the guy went ahead and did it anyway, aside from being in all kinds of hot water with his C.O., he'd be up to his dog tags in red tape trying to get his family out of the country.

"Did you tell Mia that?"

"I thought she'd want to know."

The knowledge would be important to her. Caid knew that. It made him feel better about Jack, too.

It also raised his opinion of Roselyn another notch. Despite the conjecture as to the conclusion, relaying the story to Mia had been a very generous thing for the woman to do.

But not nearly as generous as what Mia had done for him.

He flipped open the folded piece of paper, his glance settling on her delicate script.

I meant what I said. But that's my problem, not yours.
Please call your colonel.

Folding the note, Caid pushed it into his pocket. He couldn't stand the thought of Mia sitting in an interrogation room. Or, worse, in a cell. She was an amazingly strong woman, far stronger than she probably even realized, but he knew how truly frightened she must be.

If he could, he'd be with her this very second. But he couldn't go near the police with them looking for him. At least not without the guy who'd set him up.

"Do you know a guy named Al from Jack's office?"

After the past week—not to mention the past day—Roselyn wasn't too surprised by anything. Not even the totally incongruous change of subject.

"Sure. Al Baker. Tall, thin guy. Nice. Drinks gallons of coffee. Why?"

"Do you know where he lives?"

She shook her head. "Sorry. There's a phone book right here, if you want to look him up." She reached to the shelf under the table, turning the light up another notch as she rose with book in hand. "You think he might know something about Keith? I assume Mr. Mouth didn't tell you what you wanted to hear."

"I didn't talk to him." Bending over the table, Caid flipped through the *B*s in the thick volume of white pages. "Al's the guy we're looking for."

"You're kidding."

He wasn't. He also wasn't finding Al Baker in the listings. "There must be twenty Albert Bakers in here."

"It's E. Alphonse."

At Caid's sideways and somewhat baffled glance, Roselyn shrugged. "He used to write checks at the diner. Until they started bouncing. He's strictly cash now. You think Al killed Jack?"

"I think he tried to kill Mia, anyway." Pulling out Mia's note, he wrote Baker's address on the back and stuffed it into the front pocket of his jeans. "That much I think we can prove. Hang on a minute."

With the phone book still open, he snatched up the telephone from beside the lamp and dialed Al's number. A young girl answered. After asking for Al by name, Caid learned that her daddy was in the garage fixing her brother's bicycle, but she'd go get him. Caid told her not to bother him right now. That he'd call back later. Hanging up, he looked to the woman, whose only energy now seemed to come from her curiosity.

"I need you to do something for me."

As concisely as he could, Caid told Roselyn what he'd pieced together of E. Alphonse Baker's involvement, including mention of the pencil with the IIA logo and what would probably prove to be his teeth marks on it. Roselyn needed to know what he knew, because he wanted her to pass everything he told her on to the officer who had picked up Mia. He also wanted her to relay that information to whoever in Homicide was working on the case, and to be sure to tell both of those people that he was at Al's house and to give them the address.

"Don't call them until ten minutes after I leave," he told her on his way out the door. "And ask them to bring Mia. I don't know if they'll go for that or not, but I'm hoping whoever's got this case will understand I'm not trying to jerk them around. They can bring as much backup as they want. Just tell them that between the two of us, Mia and I can show them that they're looking for the wrong guy."

Caid wanted to get there first. But he didn't want the police to be too far behind. He needed enough time to leave Al with no doubt in his mind that there was no way he was palming his dirty work off on him, and to get the whole story out of the little weasel before the cops showed up. Once the police were there, they'd take over, and Caid knew he wouldn't be able to get near the guy then. On the other hand, he didn't want to sit on the guy, twiddling his thumbs waiting for the authorities, either. Or to have so much time on his hands that Al had a chance to make him do something he might regret later.

The lights were out in the garage when Caid pulled up across from the tidy little Tudor on the dark street. So were the lights in the front of the house, while those glowing through the upstairs windows seemed to indicate that the occupants were preparing for bed. In a way, it was best that it was late. The last thing Caid wanted was a confrontation in front of the man's family. Especially in front of his kids.

The doorbell seemed to be broken, so Caid rapped his knuckles against the frame of the aluminum screen door and waited.

When a full minute passed, he knocked again.

A few seconds later, the porch light came on and the door cracked a few inches.

"Hi, Al," Caid said, as casually as if the guy were a jogging buddy. "Got a minute?"

E. Alphonse Baker was remarkable. For a split second, his pale eyes seemed to widen. Then he actually had the nerve to look annoyed. "What do you want?"

"Answers."

"I don't know what you're talking about."

"I'll explain it to you. Am I coming in, or are you coming out? I'll break the door down if I have to, Al."

Caid spoke mildly, but there was no doubting the sincerity of his intent. The guy with the sandy hair and the patches of psoriasis at his temples seemed to realize that, too.

Uneasily eyeing Caid's calm facade, his lean features taking on an edge of desperation in the process, Al muttered, "I'll meet you by the garage."

The door closed with a faint click, and the porch light went out. A moment later, hearing only the crickets in the bushes and the leaves crunching beneath his feet, Caid crossed the lawn and stopped in the shadows along the edge of the driveway. With the moon hidden by clouds and the light from the street lamps filtered by overgrown trees, it was a little darker than Caid would have liked. He could see well enough, though, to catch the door opening at the side of the house, and he could easily make out Al's tall, wiry frame as he soundlessly pulled the door closed.

Al hadn't yet been ready for bed himself. He still had on his long-sleeved white dress shirt, complete with pocket protector and pencils, and the slacks he'd worn to the office. But it was his hands Caid focused on. They hung at his sides, the fingers of both fists twitching against his thumbs.

Al dipped his head to the building opposite the house. "Let's go in the garage."

Caid didn't like that idea. There were things like screwdrivers and saws and hammers in garages. Items a desperate man might be tempted to use as weapons. "Right here's fine."

"If you want to talk, we'll go in there. Otherwise . . ."

"Otherwise what? You'll do to me what you did to Jack? What you tried to do to Mia? Come on," Caid quietly taunted. "What will you do?"

Caid was pushing on purpose. But Al didn't say a single word to indicate surprise or puzzlement or anger over the accusations. In the shadows, it was too dark to really see what expression might betray him, though. Not that Caid was about to move closer for a better look. Not until he knew whether or not Al had a weapon, and where that weapon might be. Caid had a good fifty pounds on the man, as well as a couple inches in height, and training that would allow him to snap the man in half if that was what he needed to do. But he didn't want to hurt him—not too badly, anyway—and he certainly wasn't going to underestimate him. He already knew how lethal those hands could be.

"You don't have anything on me, Matlock." Tense as a spring, Al took a single step sideways. "Your coming here was a mistake."

"You made the mistakes, Al. You left your calling card in my apartment. A little red pencil," Caid went on, wishing he could see the look on the man's face. "I'd never have known if it hadn't been for that."

The man was fast. One moment Al stood like a specter in the shadows. The next he was tearing across the driveway and out onto the sidewalk, leaves scattering in the pool of light beneath a street lamp. The neighbor's dog barked, setting off another one the next house over, and already he was nearing the end of the block.

Caid was right behind him, his feet pounding on the pavement, the sound echoing off the houses they raced past. Cars were parked all along the curb. Al darted between two of them, charging into the street as a pickup rounded the corner. The squeal of brakes overrode Caid's curse as the truck missed him by a breath and Al shot ahead, leaving Caid to bear the brunt of the driver's curses as he darted over to the next block.

As dark as it was, Caid couldn't tell where he was headed. He just kept his eyes on the white shirt, following it like a beacon toward a huge dark area devoid of cars or houses or street lamps.

Al got no farther than the corner of what appeared to be a neighborhood park when Caid, arms and heart pumping furiously, caught up with him. He took a flying leap toward the thinner man, his arms catching him at the knees. Al went down with a sickening thud, but as heavily as he landed, within seconds he flipped around swinging.

Adrenaline surging, his reflexes lightning-quick, Caid caught his arm in midair and, with a powerful jerk, flipped him right back around, shoving his bent arm up between his shoulder blades and his face into the dirt. With his knee in Al's back, he leaned back on the man's hips, panting.

Al bucked upward, muttering a string of obscenities as he tried to free his trapped hand from beneath him. Busy gulping a lungful of air, Caid simply increased the pressure of his knee and hitched the guy's arm higher.

"Lay still or I break it. I'm too old for this crap."

It had always been a point of pride with Caid that he had no trouble keeping up on five-mile runs with the younger guys. At the moment, his heart beating like a trip-hammer and his lungs about to explode, he wasn't sure how he'd ever managed that particular feat. He wasn't feeling particularly appreciative toward Al—who was probably a good ten years his junior—for making him consider that right now, either.

"I said I wanted answers," he reminded the man struggling like a worm under him. "You can start by explaining how you figured out who I was."

"I'm not telling you a damn thing." He coughed, a little short on air himself. "Get the hell off me."

"I said," Caid repeated, using his free hand to shove the guy's head back down, "how did you know who I was?"

Having his face rubbed in the dirt apparently did the trick. The threat of having his backbone snapped by the knee wedged between his kidneys probably helped, too. "I followed you to your car and ran your plates. You're hurting my arm."

"I'm going to do worse than hurt your arm, Baker. Why did you follow me?"

"I got suspicious," he muttered, his words muffled by the way Caid had his face pushed down. "You said you were looking for football tickets. I knew you were lying when I started to open the side drawer in Jack's desk. You said you'd already checked there. You couldn't have. That drawer squeaks when it's opened, and I can always hear it."

"What about Mia?"

"What about her?"

"How did you know she was with me?"

"I saw her through the window when I went by your place that night. Come on, man, I can't breathe."

With a wheeze, Al sucked in a deep breath. As deep as he could, anyway. Caid's weight on his back made filling his lungs a bit difficult.

Knowing it would be easier for the guy to talk if he had air, Caid eased up just enough to keep from suffocating him. But not enough to let him think he might be going anywhere. It was that manaclelike hold—and the realization that Caid could very well break his arm—that prompted Al to admit he'd come after Mia because he thought she knew he'd been at the museum the night she and Jack were there.

It seemed that his betting had increased while his luck had taken a dive. His wife knew nothing of his habit, and after his latest bets hadn't come through, Al had waited for weeks to follow Jack on one of his jobs. Al's "banker" had started putting real pressure on him about the time Al started over-hearing Jack on the phone working out the details on a se-curity check at Pacific Museum. Al had known the exhibition of jewels was there, so he'd followed Jack and Mia in, lifting the crown while the security systems were down and slipping out before they had time to reactivate them. He'd almost gotten caught when Jack came back to make sure the crown wouldn't fall from the statue he'd put it on, but Jack hadn't noticed him hiding behind another sculpture. Jack had seen Al get into his car outside the mu-seum, though, and, suspicious of his presence, he'd fol-lowed him on a chase that ended in the heavily wooded Balboa Park.

Jack had just wanted whatever it was Al had taken. He'd even said he'd overlook what had happened and try to get him help. But Al couldn't give it to him. He'd needed the money from the jewels too badly. Badly enough to kill Jack to keep him from taking the crown away. And badly enough to make sure the woman with him was silenced, too, in case Jack had told her he was going after him, or she'd seen him herself.

"It doesn't matter what I tell you," the man in the dirt said, in a voice that was rather too confident for his current position. "You repeat any of this, and I'll just tell 'em you're trying to set me up. Nobody's going to believe a thing you say. When I couldn't get to the girl, I made it look like you two were responsible for everything. The crown was found in your apartment, and the girl's been with you all this time. Anything she says against me is only going to look like she's conspiring with you. You've got nothing on me."

"I've got your pencil."

"Right." He snorted the word. "And if anyone wants to know how you got it, all I have to do is say you took it from my desk when you were in the office last week. Or you took it when it fell out of my pocket."

Caid was breathing normally now, but it suddenly felt as if the air were slowly being sucked from his lungs. The guy was right. At that very moment, lying not two feet from the guy's head were two little pencils, complete with chewed-up tips. They'd been knocked out of his pocket when Caid tackled him.

The breeze carried the sounds of sirens from off in the distance. "The knife you attacked Mia with," Caid said, refusing to let the guy know he had him on that one. "The police already have it."

"Nice try." The guy actually chuckled. "That knife is right back in my wife's knife rack, where it belongs. I picked it up when I dropped off the crown at your place. By the way, Jack's wallet was there, too. Thought you should know that so you don't look too surprised when the cops mention it. I tell you, man, I'm covered. Got a little careless leaving the pencil, but like they say, no big deal."

An ominous knot settled in Caid's stomach. The sirens were getting closer, and when he glanced up, still holding Al down, he saw the flash of red and blue lights as two cars swung onto the street. The house they were headed for was two blocks up. They'd sail right past, and then . . .

Then what?

He wasn't guilty. Neither was Mia. But it didn't seem they had a snowball's chance in hell of proving it at the moment.

The patrol cars didn't speed right on by. Not exactly. They whizzed past, lights on but sirens now off, and slammed on their brakes halfway down the block. Caid was just letting go of Al's arm when, the nearest car having backed up, a spotlight hit them both dead on.

"Stay where you are," boomed the command from behind the blinding light.

Al started talking first. Lifting himself to his feet, rubbing his arm as he did, he began yelling to the approaching uniformed officer that he'd been attacked by this guy who'd been harassing him for the past week over an insurance claim. "He was in my office last week accusing me of being bought off because I wouldn't give him what he wanted for the car he'd wrecked. Now he's trying to beat me up and keeps saying 'You'll pay.' It's hard telling what he'll do next."

Caid had to admit the man was quick. Already he'd laid the groundwork for why Caid would try to set him up. But then, he'd probably always had to paddle pretty fast to keep his head above water. He was going on a mile a minute, piling up more lies that sounded all too plausible, when the second car pulled up.

Caid felt his heart jerk against his ribs.

Mia was in the back seat. He saw her lean forward to speak through the security panel separating front seat from back, then glance toward him. More relieved than he'd been in his life to see anyone, he started across the grass toward her.

Al was still rattling on to the young officer, who'd now been joined by his partner. It was his partner, a raw-boned veteran of the streets, who stepped forward to stop Caid.

"I just want to talk to the lady over there," Caid explained when the blue uniform blocked his progress.

"Can't let you do that, sir. Can I see some ID, please?"

Handing the unsmiling bulldog his military identification, and mentioning, too, that it was he who'd had the call placed that brought them here, Caid watched as a female officer with bright blond hair opened the back door of the second vehicle.

With the lights still sweeping arcs of blue and red, Mia stepped out, holding her hair back in her familiar way as the late-evening breeze lifted the strands around her face. He remembered seeing her do that the very first time he'd laid eyes on her.

She went still when she saw him. With the lights from the cars illuminating the tiny park, he saw a smile, faint and terribly uncertain, touch her mouth. She started toward him, only to have the lady at her side touch her arm and shake her head.

"You'll stay right here," Caid was told.

Caid merely nodded, aware of how quiet Al had become now that he, too, had seen her.

As Caid had known would happen, once the authorities took over, no one could do much of anything without permission. He and Mia and Al were all kept apart, each with an officer at his or her elbow, while a budding Dick Tracy type in a double-breasted blazer, who'd emerged from the car Mia had been in, wandered between them asking questions that would all be repeated down at the station anyway. Just because there were fifteen feet separating them, though, that didn't mean he and Mia couldn't communicate.

Are you all right? his eyes seemed to say as they hungrily searched her face.

What are we doing? she seemed to ask in return.

He didn't have an answer. Mia knew that from Caid's shuttered expression as everything he said to the short, stocky guy who'd identified himself as Detective Bowman was systematically refuted by the man she recognized as Al from Jack's office. And every time Al opened his mouth, Mia felt her blood pressure surge.

Growing more angry than nervous as she heard Al's lies spew forth, she ignored the warning look in Caid's eyes and turned to the woman at her side. It had all been so very terrifying when the officers had first come to take her away. But all the time she'd sat in the cold white room with the mirror and the scarred table, she'd made herself think of how Caid had questioned her and tried to pretend it was him making her go over her story again and again and again. By focusing on him, she'd been able to get through it. Just as, by focusing on him, she'd made it through the storm.

Caid had obviously thought he had something to have brought them all here. There was just one little thing he seemed to have forgotten.

The female officer with Mia nodded and motioned to the detective. "Have him push up his sleeve."

"Okay, Baker," the young officer with Al said. "You heard her."

Looking exasperated, Al reached for his left sleeve.

"The other one," Mia called out.

Suddenly, his eyes darting quickly from Mia to the officer, Al didn't seem quite so anxious to cooperate.

"My kid did that," he muttered when the officer pushed the sleeve up for him and his flashlight caught the odd oval bruise on his forearm.

Mia took a step back, her glance narrowing on the man's face before she looked away. "That's where I bit him."

"Right where she told us earlier," the woman beside her confirmed.

It was two in the morning before the lady officer who had been with Mia bought her a cola from a machine in the hall as she went off duty, and pointed to an orange plastic chair in the precinct's main corridor where she could wait for word about her "friend." Mia was free to go, but there were likely to be more questions later, so she was to stay close to home. Al, the officer had told her just a short while ago, had finally confessed to everything.

Sinking into the chair, Mia focused on the caged-in clock above a closed window marked Information, and concentrated on ignoring the garishly garbed woman staring at her from half a dozen chairs away.

Half an hour went by—along with a steady stream of officers, other staff, and less-than-upstanding citizens.

Twenty minutes more passed, the parade growing more bizarre as the hour grew later.

It was taking forever for them to take Caid's statement. So much longer, it seemed, than it had hers. Not sure whether she should be alarmed by that circumstance, she'd just followed the second hand on the clock around for the umpteenth time when she glanced to the side and saw Caid at the end of the long hallway.

He headed straight toward her, his powerful strides eating up the distance as she slowly rose from the cracked plastic chair.

Fatigue was etched in his face, and his eyes looked more tired than she'd ever seen them when he stopped in front of her. For the briefest instant, his glance swept her features. Then, his jaw jerking, he reached out and brushed the backs of his fingers down the smooth skin of her cheek.

The concern in his touch drew her, as did its gentleness. But before she could respond, he drew his hand away. It was almost if he hadn't thought his touch would be welcome. Or perhaps, she thought, he'd simply touched her without thinking.

"How are you doing?" he asked, sounding every bit as tired as he looked.

She wasn't really sure. Not after what he'd just done. "I'm doing okay. How about you?"

His response was to clamp his hand around the knots in the back of his neck. "I've got to get back to Oceanside." He looked at his watch, then back to her. "If I leave now, I can be in Tom's office when he gets there. Where do you want me to take you?"

A vague sinking sensation centered in Mia's stomach. He obviously didn't want her with him. Not that she'd thought he would. Not, she had to admit, that she'd thought about it at all. After the police had finished with her, she'd simply waited to go with him because it hadn't occurred to her to do anything else.

For a woman who had been completely independent all her life, the knowledge was a little disconcerting.

"To Roselyn's," she said, because she couldn't face her other option at the moment. According to Caid, Jack's house had been thoroughly ransacked when the police

searched it last week. She simply wasn't up to facing tha
tonight. "She said I could come back if I needed a place t(
stay."

"Can you drive?"

She nodded. "Jack taught me. Why?"

"Because you can drop me off at my boat and I won'
have to worry about getting Roselyn's car back to her." H(
paused. "Or maybe I should just drop you off so you don'
have to drive back alone. I could call a—"

"I'll drive you," she said, amazed that even now h(
seemed to think he needed to take care of her. Not that sh(
didn't like the feeling. His concern just wasn't necessar;
when he had so much else on his mind. "Are you takin;
your boat back to Oceanside?"

The protective mode wasn't easy for him to break. Bu
aware of all he had yet to do, he conceded to her capabili
ties and led her down the scuff-marked hall. Oceanside wa
exactly where he was headed. His truck was at the marin
there, and he needed it to get to his apartment so that b(
could change clothes and head on to the base.

That was about all he said as he drove them through th(
deserted streets of San Diego to the marina where the *Des*
tiny was docked. The events of the past sixteen hours ha
left them both with plenty to consider, and it wasn't all ove
for Caid, either. From the way he drove, with his elbov
propped by the window and his fist against his mouth, Mi
felt certain that facing his commander was about all Cai
had on his mind.

It was pretty much all she could think about, too.

She had no idea how much trouble he would be in fo
disobeying his commander's order. Or how what he ha
done would affect the decision he needed to make abou
staying in his Marines. She didn't know if they would kic
him out, lock him up, or forget the entire incident. Askin
wasn't an option. Judging by his brooding expression, sh(
didn't think Caid knew the answer, either.

That dark brooding remained as he pulled into the brightly lit parking lot by the huge marina and told her to wait while he got her things from the boat. It was still shadowing the lean angles of his face when he returned a few minutes later and handed her her knapsack through the driver's window. She sat behind the wheel, looking up at him and wishing with all her heart that he hadn't put his precious career in jeopardy. She wished, too, that she could somehow find a way into his heart.

He knew she loved him. She'd told him so. He could probably even see it in her eyes, because she was simply too tired to haul up her defenses right now. But he didn't feel that way about her. Oh, she knew he cared in his own way. That much was in his kiss when he leaned down to brush his lips over hers, and in his touch when he drew back to nudge a strand of hair from her cheek. But Caid was a solitary man, and though he'd let her in for a while, he was now quietly closing her out. He'd done what he needed to do, for her, for Jack.

"You won't leave town without telling me, will you?"

Surprisingly, she managed the smile that wouldn't come only moments before. "I haven't the faintest idea where I'd go if I did. My life is here." Somewhere. "Listen, Caid." Her glance fell to his chest, then jerked back up when memories of how he'd held her to him threatened to make saying goodbye so much harder.

"I'm sorry for all the trouble I've caused you. I really am. Especially with your commander." The words sounded painfully inadequate to her. Or maybe it was just the pain of leaving him that was making her heart feel so heavy. "You live by rules, and you've broken them because of me. I don't know how I can ever repay you for what you've done."

It was hard to tell what caused the swift flash of disquiet in Caid's eyes. Or why he looked at her as if he couldn't quite believe what he was hearing. She couldn't read him anymore. They had shared so much, become so close. And yet now he seemed more of a stranger to her than he had been the day she met him.

He shook his head, his narrowed eyes never leaving her face. "You already did, Mia."

There seemed to be something he wanted to add, something about what she'd done. She'd been willing to sacrifice her freedom for him. But, a moment later, when he couldn't find the words, he pushed his fingers through his hair and took a step back. "I've got to go," he told her. "When are you going back to Jack's?"

"Sometime tomorrow. Today," she corrected, since it would be daylight in a couple of hours.

He didn't say anything then. He just lifted his chin in acknowledgment as weariness swept over him—and waited for her to back out before he turned to walk back to his boat.

Mia felt as if the telephone were a permanent appendage. She had spent the past two days on the thing, making arrangements for Jack's funeral, taking care of what affairs of his she could, and tracking down two of her professors so that she could turn in overdue papers and make up a quiz she'd missed last week. She also had an appointment with the head of the language department to sign on as a tutor so that she could pick up a few extra dollars. Jack had put her name on his savings account, and he'd paid up the lease on the house for three months, so she would be all right for a while. But she needed to take some positive steps toward her future, and that seemed as good a step as any at the moment.

She also needed to stay busy, which was why she was on a chair, struggling with the curtain rod in the dining room, when she heard the doorbell ring in the middle of the afternoon. Thinking it was Roselyn coming to pick up the pictures she and Jack had taken on their trip to Carmel, Mia hollered for her to come around back and wedged the rod holding the freshly pressed white priscillas into the bracket.

"Come on in," she called when she heard feet hit the back step. Balancing on the chair, she turned to hook the other end of the pole.

"You shouldn't leave your door open."

At the sound of Caid's voice, Mia jerked around to see him standing in the doorway of the utility room at the end of the brightly lit kitchen. He had his hands on the hips of his indecently snug jeans, and the Marine logo on his black T-shirt stretched over his broad and very solid chest. A pair of aviator-type sunglasses dangled from his pocket.

Lowering her hand from the rod to cover the pulse hammering in her throat, she watched him move toward her. As he did, his eyes roamed from her sock-clad feet to the neck of her cropped, peach-colored shirt. When his glance slid back down, it seemed to settle on the strip of bare skin visible above the top of her jeans.

"I left it open to get some fresh air." A little unnerved by the bold and vaguely possessive perusal, and more than a little startled by his unexpected appearance, she added, "I've... been cleaning."

The statement was hardly necessary. It was easy enough to see what she'd been doing. Jack's place was spotless. Windows and floors gleamed. Fresh flowers filled a glass bowl on the cloth-covered dining room table, and not so much as a single magazine was out of place on the tables in the living room. The last time Caid had been here, the house had been trashed.

"What are you doing here?" she asked from her perch on the chair.

With her standing where she was, the top of his head came to the middle of her chest. It was just below that area that he seemed to be staring.

"I wanted to talk to you." Pausing, he pulled his glance up to meet her eyes. An instant later, his glance darted to the pattern on the back of the chair she stood on. "Are you doing all right? I mean, do you need help with anything around here?"

"I'm doing fine," she assured him, wondering if it was a trick of the light, or if he actually looked a little less than his usual confident self. Even when Al Baker had been busy punching holes in every bit of evidence Caid had come up with, she hadn't seen him look as hesitant as he did right now.

"What happened with your commander?" she asked, hoping that wasn't the problem.

"I got that all worked out. He wasn't too happy with me, but nothing's going on my record."

"Oh, Caid," she said, not caring that she looked so obviously relieved. "I can't begin to tell you how good that is to hear."

And he couldn't begin to tell her how good it made him feel to see her smile. The warmth of that smile seeped into him, seeming to heal wounds he hadn't even known he'd suffered. To see her like that, with her eyes lit up and her face free of concern and worry, was worth every minute of the agonizing trip over here.

Almost. He had no idea how she would react to what he had to say.

"Would you mind coming down here? It might be easier to talk."

Her smile still in place, she reached for his shoulder, thinking she'd just step down. She felt his hands at her waist, though, the faint roughness of his palms as they slid onto her bare skin seeming to sear her with their heat.

He lifted her down as easily as he might have a sack of flower petals, the only sign of his effort being the bulge of his biceps against the bands of his short sleeves. But instead of leaving his hands on her when her feet touched the floor, instead of pulling her closer when his eyes locked on hers, he reluctantly released his hold and turned away.

"We left the gear on Catalina," she heard him say, his voice oddly husky. "I went back to get it after I talked to Tom. I was there until this morning."

That explained why he hadn't answered when she tried to call him last night. She'd been worried sick about what had happened at his base.

He pushed his hands into his pockets. "I had some thinking to do."

"About your decision," she prompted, more unsettled than she wanted to be by whatever was bothering him.

"About a lot of things. I've spent the last two days telling myself I did all I could for you, Mia. That my first priority was the decision I'd promised Tom. But every time I started thinking about whether or not I should stay in the Corps, those thoughts kept getting all mixed up with you." There hadn't been much of anything he'd thought about lately that didn't include her somehow. "I think I was fine until I found that picture you drew of those two little girls."

His hand swept through his hair, his expression mirroring the confusion in Mia's face as she watched him turn. She knew she'd left the pad with that picture in it on his boat. But, try as she might, she couldn't figure out what it had to do with anything—until he all but glared over at her.

"I'd never even *thought* about kids before you came along," he muttered.

Frustrated because she was looking at him as if he weren't making sense, and fearing she might be right, he began to pace.

"You got me thinking about a lot of things after that remark you made about my never letting myself be on my own. At the time, I thought that was the most ridiculous statement I'd ever heard...until I let myself really think about it. The more I did, the more I began to realize that you were probably right."

In that uncanny way she had of tossing out bullets and hitting bull's-eyes, she'd hit the mark dead on with her comment about him living by rules, too. The Marines had provided him with a set of rules and regulations, a job and a purpose. The Corps had been his mother, father and family, and he'd never once questioned his direction. But he'd been questioning that direction ever since the retirement issue had come up, and he hadn't quite known why—until she'd shown him in a dozen little ways what was missing in his life.

He came to a stop in front of her after he told her that, the sunlight from the window picking out hints of silver in the dark hair at his temples. With the tips of his fingers he grazed the side of her neck.

"A lot of it is still missing, Mia." He felt the delicate cords of her neck shudder as she swallowed, her eyes holding his with the same uncertainty he was feeling at that very moment. "But I don't want it to be missing anymore."

"So what did you decide?" she asked, her throat unbelievably tight.

He watched her carefully. "I've decided I'm retiring. In two years. Maybe up to the Oregon coast. Have you ever seen it?"

Not sure that her heart didn't skip a beat, she shook her head.

"I think you'd like it. It's beautiful up there. I thought I could buy another boat. Something big enough to charter, and a house with a yard. Near a school, where you could teach. You should have your teaching certificate in a couple of years, shouldn't you?"

It was only when her eyes widened and her head tipped to one side, as if she couldn't quite believe what she was hearing, that Caid himself realized what he was saying.

He'd known all the way over here that he needed to be with her. He'd just never realized before how empty he'd felt, how dead he'd been inside. But when he was with her, the emptiness wasn't there. It wasn't there because he cared more about her than he'd ever have dreamed possible.

"You said you loved me, Mia. I hope to God you meant that, because I love you, too. And I think I'm asking you to marry me." He swallowed, drawing her closer because he couldn't stand the thought of letting her go. "So say something, will you?"

She grinned, her lovely eyes shining. "When will you know for sure?"

"What?"

Her arms looped around his neck, and her smile got closer to his mouth. "You said you *think* you're asking. I'm not answering until you know for sure."

His mouth came down on hers, and her smile faded as she melted against him in that way that made it impossible for her to tell where her body ended and his began. She had so often been afraid to hope, yet she'd been more afraid not to. Especially with Caid. He was the other half of her being— the part that made her belong. And he wanted her. Not out of obligation, but because he needed her the way she needed him. Together they were secure. And, together, they would have what they'd never found separately. A real home. A real family.

Finally.

* * * * *

HE'S AN

AMERICAN HERO

January 1994 rings in the New Year—and a new lineup of sensational American Heroes. You can't seem to get enough of these men, and we're proud to feature one each month, created by some of your favorite authors.

January: CUTS BOTH WAYS by Dee Holmes: Erin Kenyon hired old acquaintance Ashe Seager to investigate the crash that claimed her husband's life, only to learn old memories never die.

February: A WANTED MAN by Kathleen Creighton: Mike Lanagan's exposé on corruption earned him accolades...and the threat of death. Running for his life, he found sanctuary in the arms of Lucy Brown—but for how long?

March: COOPER by Linda Turner: Cooper Rawlings wanted nothing to do with the daughter of the man who'd shot his brother. But when someone threatened Susannah Patterson's life, he found himself riding to the rescue....

AMERICAN HEROES: Men who give all they've got for their country, their work—the women they love.

Only from

Take 4 bestselling love stories FREE

Plus get a FREE surprise gift!

ROMANTIC TRADITIONS

Paula Detmer Riggs kicks off
ROMANTIC TRADITIONS this month with
ONCE UPON A WEDDING (IM #524), which
features a fresh spin on the marriage-of-
convenience motif. Jesse Dante married
Hazel O'Connor to help an orphaned baby,
underestimating the powers of passion and
parenthood....

Coming to stores in January will be bestselling
author Marilyn Pappano's **FINALLY A FATHER**
(IM #542), spotlighting the time-honored secret-
baby story line. Quin Ellis had lied about her
daughter's real parentage for over nine years.
But Mac McEwen's return to town signaled an
end to her secret.

In April, expect an innovative look at the
amnesia plot line in Carla Cassidy's
TRY TO REMEMBER.

And **ROMANTIC TRADITIONS** doesn't stop there! In
months to come we'll be bringing you more
classic plot lines told the Intimate Moments way.
So, if you're the romantic type who appreciates
tradition with a twist, come experience
ROMANTIC TRADITIONS—only in

SIMRT2

INTIMATE MOMENTS®

Silhouette™

Southern Alberta—wide open ranching country
marked by rolling rangelands and roiling passions.
That's where the McCall family make their home.
You can meet Tanner, the first of the McCalls, in
BEYOND ALL REASON, (IM #536), the premiere book in

JUDITH DUNCAN's

WIDE OPEN SPACES

miniseries beginning in December 1993.

Scarred by a cruel childhood and narrow-minded
neighbors, Tanner McCall had resigned himself to a
lonely life on the Circle S Ranch. But when Kate Quinn,
a woman with two sons and a big secret, hired on,
Tanner discovered newfound needs and a woman
worthy of his trust.

In months to come, join more of the McCalls as
they search for love while working Alberta's
WIDE OPEN SPACES—only in
Silhouette Intimate Moments

SILHOUETTE.... Where Passion Lives

Don't miss these Silhouette favorites by some of our most popular authors!
And now, you can receive a discount by ordering two or more titles!

Silhouette Desire®

#05751	THE MAN WITH THE MIDNIGHT EYES BJ James	$2.89	☐
#05763	THE COWBOY Cait London	$2.89	☐
#05774	TENNESSEE WALTZ Jackie Merritt	$2.89	☐
#05779	THE RANCHER AND THE RUNAWAY BRIDE Joan Johnston	$2.89	☐

Silhouette Intimate Moments®

#07417	WOLF AND THE ANGEL Kathleen Creighton	$3.29	☐
#07480	DIAMOND WILLOW Kathleen Eagle	$3.39	☐
#07486	MEMORIES OF LAURA Marilyn Pappano	$3.39	☐
#07493	QUINN EISLEY'S WAR Patricia Gardner Evans	$3.39	☐

Silhouette Shadows®

#27003	STRANGER IN THE MIST Lee Karr	$3.50	☐
#27007	FLASHBACK Terri Herrington	$3.50	☐
#27009	BREAK THE NIGHT Anne Stuart	$3.50	☐
#27012	DARK ENCHANTMENT Jane Toombs	$3.50	☐

Silhouette Special Edition®

#09754	THERE AND NOW Linda Lael Miller	$3.39	☐
#09770	FATHER: UNKNOWN Andrea Edwards	$3.39	☐
#09791	THE CAT THAT LIVED ON PARK AVENUE Tracy Sinclair	$3.39	☐
#09811	HE'S THE RICH BOY Lisa Jackson	$3.39	☐

Silhouette Romance®

#08893	LETTERS FROM HOME Toni Collins	$2.69	☐
#08915	NEW YEAR'S BABY Stella Bagwell	$2.69	☐
#08927	THE PURSUIT OF HAPPINESS Anne Peters	$2.69	☐
#08952	INSTANT FATHER Lucy Gordon	$2.75	☐

AMOUNT	$	_____
DEDUCT: **10% DISCOUNT FOR 2+ BOOKS**	$	_____
POSTAGE & HANDLING	$	_____
($1.00 for one book, 50¢ for each additional)		
APPLICABLE TAXES*	$	_____
TOTAL PAYABLE	$	_____
(check or money order—please do not send cash)		

To order, complete this form and send it, along with a check or money order for the total above, payable to Silhouette Books, to: *In the U.S.*: 3010 Walden Avenue, P.O. Box 9077, Buffalo, NY 14269-9077; *In Canada*: P.O. Box 636, Fort Erie, Ontario, L2A 5X3.

Name: _____

Address: _____ City: _____

State/Prov.: _____ Zip/Postal Code: _____

*New York residents remit applicable sales taxes.
Canadian residents remit applicable GST and provincial taxes.

SBACK-OD